★

## WATCHED

In the days following the break-in, Kemp found himself affected, in a mild form, by the very kind of paranoia he'd noticed in others. Partly it was the result of the unwelcome intrusion into all that he had of private life but, without letting his imagination run too deeply, there was the more unwelcome idea that he might be under scrutiny. He just hoped that if someone was keeping an eye on him, they would also keep their distance....

★

"... a plot that delivers more than its share of irony, twists and surprises. The ending is wholly unpredictable and packs a real punch."

—Naperville, Illinois *Sun*

"... a real treat..."

—*Courier Publications*, Rockland, Maine

"... the ending is a nice surprise."

—*Mystery News*

"Plenty of plot twists and action keep things lively."

—*Mystery Lovers Bookshop News*

# TOUCH

# & GO

# M.R.D. MEEK

## WORLDWIDE®

TORONTO • NEW YORK • LONDON
AMSTERDAM • PARIS • SYDNEY • HAMBURG
STOCKHOLM • ATHENS • TOKYO • MILAN
MADRID • WARSAW • BUDAPEST • AUCKLAND

**TOUCH AND GO**

A Worldwide Mystery/June 1994

This edition is reprinted by arrangement with Charles Scribner's Sons, an imprint of Macmillan Publishing Company.

ISBN 0-373-26146-2

# TOUCH

# &GO

# PROLOGUE

THE WOMAN HAD been beautiful. Now she was dying. The nurse had never seen the beauty nor would she have been greatly impressed if she had. To her this was simply another case of the kind she was supposed to specialize in because, it was said, she had the expertise.

'I asked for someone trained in dealing with terminal cancers,' the doctor had said when she arrived from the agency. 'I understand you have that experience?'

'Yes,' she'd replied, adding no more.

They had been standing in the doorway of the bedroom, and he'd looked over to where the patient lay asleep.

'She insisted she would not be hospitalized...' He had sighed and shrugged his shoulders, but not casually. 'They'd done all they could, anyway. That last tumour's inoperable, and she wanted to die at home. She does know... if it's any help to you.'

The nurse had nodded, making no comment.

'You'll only be required to stay a few days. I doubt if she'll last the week.' He had raised sad eyes to take in the luxury of the room as if the white and gold furniture, the peach-coloured velvet drapes at the big windows high above the muted roar of Fifth Avenue might in some measure mitigate the other misfortune. 'Some of the staff have been kept on, and the housekeeper, Mrs Hermanos, has been with the lady for many years. I think you will find the place quite comfortable.'

Following his glance, the nurse had given a half-smile. 'I've seen worse... Now I must attend to my duties.'

When he left the doctor was pleased by her attitude. With that blank face, those meek downcast eyes, the drab uniform worn without concession either to feminism or figure, he had had his doubts. But he trusted St Theresa's Nursing Agency; there was nowhere else left to put your trust in with these cases.

I mustn't get too used to this, the nurse thought as she unpacked her few personal belongings in one of the spare bedrooms, itself bigger than the whole of her walk-up flat in downtown Brooklyn.

Her duties proved not to be onerous but from habit she performed them well. The doctor called each day, staying no longer than half an hour to chat with the patient if she was awake, less if she was sleeping.

'It's only at night she's restless,' the nurse reported to him. 'Seems it's then she likes to talk. Night duty doesn't bother me, I'm used to it. I get the hours off in the daytime when Mrs Hermanos sits with her but even then I prefer to think I'm still on call...' If there had been in the nurse's tone implicit criticism of a lay person by a professional, it was muted. The doctor was relieved; Mrs Hermanos seemed devoted to her mistress but the case needed someone with medical knowledge and expertise. The nurse had both.

'So long as the patient is never allowed to be in pain,' he said, anxiously.

The nurse shook her head. 'The dosage you've prescribed has worked well so far, Doctor, and you can rely on me to see she doesn't suffer unnecessarily. When she's awake at night I'm always there and if she wants to talk, then I just let her go ahead. Lots of patients in her condition will ramble on to a stranger if they don't have any family around. We learn not to listen overmuch.'

This was not strictly true. Although it was the nurse's habit to take a book or a magazine into the sickroom to while away the long hours by the bedside, they remained largely unread. Establishing rapport by a sympathetic squeeze of the hand, murmured words of encouragement, and a proper attendance to the most trivial but essential matters of the patient's comfort, these things came naturally to her and in this case had been very rewarding.

For the life that was too early drawing to a close—the patient being only in her forty-fifth year—had been an intriguing one, lived in many places, and as the memories came and went the thin voice would strengthen and take on vigour in their telling. To the nurse it was like trying to follow a film told in flashback, and much more fascinating than skimming the pages of any novel. She'd never been much of a reader, anyway, reality for her providing troubles enough without getting into fictional ones.

Some nights there were outbursts of vanity.

'My make-up box...over there. Bring it, please.'

And the nurse would softly cream and powder the waxy skin, deftly touch with rose the hollowed cheeks and flick the little eyebrow pencil over the bony arches. Poor soul, she thought, that chemotherapy sure takes away the glamour...

She adroitly moved the table-lamp before handing over the mirror.

'You look very nice, madam,' she said, brushing the pale strands of fine hair across the high forehead, 'your hair's soft as a baby's.'

'Nonsense, Nurse. I look like a whited sepulchre, and you know it.' The dying woman was no fool but she recognized a good effort when she saw it. 'I'm sorry. You did your best...'

On the last night they had a fashion show.

'In those wardrobes...' The voice from the bed was breathless. 'Open them up...'

The nurse did as she was told. 'What will madam wear this evening?' she asked, entering into the spirit, even as her eyes took in the tussore silk suits, the tweeds and worsteds, the riding habits with their satin stocks, the pretty day dresses and the avenue of formals, chiffons pale as streams of water, dark velvets starred with diamanté...

'My Mandarin jacket... the scarlet one with the embroidered dragons. Put it round my shoulders.'

She was sitting up high on the pillows as the nurse slipped the red and gold garment across the bones standing out at the top of her arms.

'I used to wear my rubies with this. They were specially set in gold for me... Get them for me. They're in the jewel box.'

The nurse hesitated. 'Madam will tire herself,' she said, at her most soothing. 'Perhaps another night...'

'Not too many other nights...' But the patient's voice was faint, and her brow had puckered as it did before the onset of pain. The nurse took away the jacket, prepared and administered the relieving drug, and settled the sick woman gently down into fresh cool sheets, pulling away the soiled linen with no fuss as she had been trained to do. Such tasks were of no consequence to her, the incontinence of her patients simply a part of their illness and accepted by her as nature's failure, not theirs.

She replaced the scarlet coat, and closed the wardrobe doors but not before letting her eyes wander once more across the richness stored inside.

She tidied the bedside table, washed up and replenished the water carafe in the adjoining bathroom, then settled herself in the big armchair near the bed with one of her magazines. She yawned. She had not had her usual sleep during the day because there had been some sort of crisis in the kitchen department.

Normally she never went downstairs, everything was found for her on this floor, even her meals being served to her in the room allocated for her stay. Sometimes they were brought to her by Leonie, the maid, a silent creature who the nurse had diagnosed as being subnormal, or by Mrs Hermanos herself. The nurse couldn't make head or tail of Mrs Hermanos. On the surface she was friendly enough, though distant as if the nurse's position was far inferior to her own in the household. As well it might be, for Mrs Hermanos was more than housekeeper to the dying lady, she was much too familiar with her for that, calling her by her first name and, in the nurse's view, taking liberties.

Lunch that day had not arrived at one o'clock as it usually did, nor was there any sign of it an hour later so the nurse had gone down to investigate. She had found the kitchen in a state of chaos, and some sort of row going on between Mrs Hermanos and her husband, José. There was a broken cup on the table, and the remains of a plate on the floor by the sink where it had obviously been thrown at someone's head. The nurse had heard it shatter as she came down the stairs, at the same time as she'd heard the yelling voices. Leonie was nowhere to be seen so the uproar was a private quarrel between the Hermanos but the nurse had witnessed all too many of such scenes in other houses to let it bother her, so she simply asked if she could please have her lunch, pronto, and left them to it. About half an hour later it had arrived at the hands of Mrs Hermanos who looked both chastened and defiant as if daring the nurse to comment. The nurse had heard enough to know what the row was about but saw no reason to pass any remark. It wasn't her business anyhow.

José Hermanos's position on the staff—if he had any at all—was uncertain. The doctor had said that Florence—Mrs Hermanos—had only married him recently and it was she who had introduced him into the household as an English butler. On this point the doctor was sceptical.

'About as English as Hoboken,' he growled, 'and as for being a butler—a Spanish waiter more like! Florence now, well, she's been around our lady for years . . . I don't take to her myself but she keeps the place going, and she seems fond of her mistress.'

The nurse would not have put it in such terms. In her view Florence Hermanos had gotten herself a good job and was hanging in there, with expectations. However, she could be relied upon to run things smoothly enough, the invalid meals she served were both sensible and tasty even for a fast-declining appetite, and sometimes it was only through Florence's coaxing that the patient could be persuaded to eat at all.

'Madam tells me that she and Florence go back a long way,' she remarked, 'so she must have been in her service many years.'

'I wouldn't know.' The doctor had only known his patient since she had arrived in New York for treatment, by which time the disease had manifested itself in a form both rapid and relentless.

'She got no family of her own, then?'

'Apparently not. Nor many friends either that I can see. A firm of lawyers manages her affairs... It's none of my business, of course,' he went on brusquely, for he was by nature averse to gossip, 'I'm only responsible for what physical wellbeing she has left...and to see that she dies with dignity.'

'That is my duty also, Doctor,' said the nurse quietly as she showed him to the door.

This conversation had taken place late that afternoon but the nurse had not found it necessary to mention the scene she had witnessed in the kitchen earlier in the day. She felt it was not her place to do so.

Now she relaxed and stretched out her legs to rest on a little tapestried stool. Despite all the running around she'd done in the course of her work her ankles were still slim and she was proud of them. She yawned again, and let the magazine slip to the floor.

She was roused by a restless movement by her patient. She glanced at her watch. She must have been asleep for about three hours. She got up and went over to the bed, adjusted the dim night light and took hold of the hand, stroking the fingers that twitched like captive mice.

'It's all right, madam. I'm here. Are you in pain?'

The pale blue eyes showed no sign of distress. 'No...I don't think so... No pain. I feel a bit light...floating, somehow...' The sweet voice articulated slowly but clearly. 'What were we talking about earlier? I can't quite remember...'

The nurse poured some water, held the glass to the dry lips.

'Don't you try,' she said, 'just take it easy... Are you quite comfortable?'

'Yes, but I don't want to sleep. We were playing a game, weren't we, Nurse?'

'We had a little fashion show with your lovely dresses. It was fun, wasn't it?' Placating, pleasing, the words came easily to her as she felt for the pulse. Reassured, she seated herself by the bed still holding the thin, transparent hand.

'I remember now...I was going to show you my rubies...'

'Yes. Yes. In the morning you can show me.'

'Not in the morning. Now. Bring me the case.' There was new vigour in the voice, and a peremptory tone, so the nurse rose and went over to the dressing-table. In a top drawer there was a box—my trinket box, the patient called it— containing a jumble of pieces of jewellery. Sometimes she liked to have it brought to her and she would spread them out around her on the counterpane, trying on necklaces and playing with the rings.

'Not that box. These are only trinkets. I mean my real jewels...'

'Madam? I'm sorry, I don't know what you mean.' The nurse had turned with the pretty little japanned box in her hands.

The other woman gave a gesture of irritation. 'Everybody knows what's in that box. Costume jewellery, cameo brooches, paste and pearls. I don't mean *them*,' she said scornfully. 'They're rubbish and I don't care who has them.'

The nurse replaced the box and closed the drawer quietly and without fuss as she did everything else. The whims of the dying were nothing new to her. Now she crossed to the bed and laid a cool hand on the patient's forehead. 'Don't upset yourself, madam. Rest now. Such things are of no importance.'

But the blue eyes were wide open and alert.

'My jewels are to me. I want you to listen . . .'

'I am listening.'

'In the bottom of the wardrobe, right at the end, there is a small suitcase. Will you get it for me, please.'

It is in the patient's best interests to accede to any request so long as it is feasible. The interior was large enough for her to walk into and this she did, brushing past the silks and velvets, feeling their softness against her face and hair as she passed. She saw the rows of shoes, neat in their wooden trees, strappy sandals and silver slippers, patent-leather pumps and high suede boots. In the furthest corner under a tartan travelling rug there was a small brown suitcase. She hauled it out, and put it down on the floor, for it was heavier than it looked.

She adjusted the starched cap knocked awry in her passage through the avenue of clothes, then took up the case and brought it over to the bed.

'How very careful you are, Nurse, about your appearance!' The woman had pulled herself up on the pillows and was watching with amused eyes.

'Must be the way I'm made, madam.' She smiled back. 'Shall I open it for you? It's too heavy to go on the bed.'

'No. Not in this house.' The words came sharply and the effort made the patient breathless. After taking a moment to recover, she went on: 'It must not be opened in this house . . . and you're not to tell anyone. Just do as I say.'

'Yes, madam.' She would only want to touch it, that was all she had done with the other possessions she was leaving. Touching was still important to a dying patient, perhaps a kind of reassurance. The nurse was not one to analyse such feelings, her job simply to obey within her limits, to soothe and make things easy. So now she held out the suitcase in her own strong hands so that the fluttering fingers could stray across the locks.

'My rubies,' the woman murmured. 'The keys are in my purse...'

'Yes, madam, but you say you don't want it opened?'

'Not here...' As suddenly as the strength had come, so it waned. The voice faded to a whisper and the nurse had to bend down to hear the words. At one point she straightened up...

'But that wouldn't be right, madam...'

'Right or wrong, who cares? Never mind the papers, they're not your concern... And nothing matters to me any more...'

The patient lay back, exhausted. The blue-veined eyelids flickered, then closed. She gave a deep sigh.

Startled, the nurse threw the case on a chair, leaned over the bed and picked up the hand now at rest on the coverlet. The pulse was slow but it still throbbed, the breathing was even, there were not, as yet, any of the signs of approaching death she knew to respect. Thank God, she said to herself, for a moment there I thought she'd gone. That sudden clarity of speech, the momentary return of vigour, she'd seen them before, often they heralded the end. As she adjusted the pillows and slid the frail body into a more comfortable position, the patient said: 'I'll sleep now, Nurse. I'll sleep easy in my mind...'

'Of course you will, madam.' She touched the white forehead gently, smoothed back the once-bright hair. Even though she stooped low the nurse could not quite catch the next words. Anyway, they seemed to be in a foreign language. All she heard was: 'He told me once...a long time ago...'

THE WOMAN WHO HAD BEEN beautiful died the next morning at nine o'clock. She died peacefully in her sleep with her
doctor by the bedside. Correct in all she did, the nurse had
called him at seven when she saw how things might be.

'Did she have a restless night?' he asked.

'Not more than usual. She talked with me for a time, then
she slept. Her pulse had weakened but she wasn't in any
pain. I'd given her an injection earlier in the evening when
she'd had some discomfort but when she woke in the night
she didn't complain. After she'd talked a little she went off
to sleep again and she was still sleeping this morning when
I called you. I thought she might just slip away, and that you
should be here...'

'Quite right, Nurse. An easier death than I'd feared. She
looks at rest. I thought she might have struggled against it
at the end... She wasn't old, and she must have been lovely
once.'

By midday the nurse was ready to leave. There was nothing to keep her. The doctor had been satisfied with her me-
ticulous medical reports, and pleased at the manner of her
attendance. He thanked her, said he would be commending
her to the agency which had sent her.

She was scarcely noticed in the household that morning.
The hushed bedroom with the drawn curtains was no longer
her rightful place. The arrival of the undertakers, the comings and goings on the stairs, the incessant ringing of telephones and doorbells, the procession of long-faced men in
business suits treading softly through the empty rooms, all
these passed her by.

She had packed her toiletries, her nightwear, her spare
caps and aprons, her nursing equipment, her books and
magazines, in the holdall she'd brought with her when she
came. It was a lot heavier now.

She stood in the bare room that had been her home for six
days, and was suddenly in a fever to be gone. But she must
not appear to hurry. Meeting the housekeeper in the hall,

she paused and was careful to express thanks to the staff and her condolences.

'A sad occasion for you all,' she said, carrying the bag in one hand as if it was a light weight though the handles were straining her wrist. 'But in these situations when there is little hope...'

Mrs Hermanos hardly looked at her. She had other things on her mind.

'Goodbye, Nurse.'

Then the door was closed behind her, and she walked over to the elevator at her normal pace.

She drew a deep breath. She would get a cab at the corner. It was a long way to Brooklyn but by now she was frantic to get there. The holdall bumped roughly against her knees as if to remind her of what she must do. She had to run... and run fast.

She seemed to have spent her life running. In hospital training, running with bedpans, running alongside stretchers holding IVs, running for doctors, running to the telephones... As a girl she'd run away from school, and run away from a home racked by quarrels, then run back to nurse her dying mother. She'd not run to her father when he lay at the last, fighting death with curses, though he no longer had the strength to hit her. She'd walked in stoically, and treated him as she would any other patient in her care. When he died he left her nothing, and she took nothing from the battered frame house she'd once called home.

She'd run back to Brooklyn, back to the crowded streets and the squalid apartment block outside which the cab had just halted. She paid off the driver. She'd have to get another one to take her away... How long had she got? They traced cabs all too easily...

She ran along the passage, the noise of crying children behind closed doors following her up the worn stairs. Once in her own apartment she didn't stop. She threw the holdall on the settee which also served as her bed, took out the caps

and aprons and chucked them into the cupboard. She
wouldn't be wanting them again, that was for sure. She
packed a suitcase with a few clothes she had, sweaters,
blouses and skirts, a couple of dowdy dresses, underwear
and shoes.

Frantic now, she stripped herself of her uniform and
bundled that too into the cupboard. She emptied out the
magazine and books, leaving them scattered on the floor. It
made the holdall lighter, but not by much. She saw the little case lying snug at the bottom but left it undisturbed. One
quick look had been enough...

Just after she'd called the doctor—it would be ten minutes before he got there—she'd locked her bedroom door,
put the case on a chair and sprung the old-fashioned
catches, one on either side. When she raised the lid she had
seen the little boxes and the names on them. With fumbling
fingers she'd opened the ones on the top. The rubies had
glowed at her, even in the pale early morning light, warm
against their gold settings, rings, bracelets, brooches...
There were larger boxes further down nestling on a bed of
thick envelopes. She looked no further. She closed the suitcase, and put it carefully along the bottom of her holdall.
Then she had straightened her cap, smoothed her apron and
returned to the sickroom in readiness for the doctor.

Now she stuffed her washbag and a towel on the top along
with clean nightclothes. Her other nightdresses she left on
a chair. She dressed herself in the one good woollen suit she
possessed, and stood still for a brief moment, quivering...
Had she forgotten anything. Did it matter?

By now she was almost out of breath. No time to sit and
take stock. She remembered to unpin the nurse's watch from
her discarded uniform. Nearly two hours gone already!
How soon would they find out and come after her? That
Mrs Hermanos, she would know... The quarrel in the
kitchen, José had been shouting something about the
'jools'... They knew they were there, it was only a matter

of time. The agency had her address, they'd soon be in touch with the precinct police... She must hurry, hurry. She should have called the cab first, then she could have been away quicker.

She dashed for the bathroom.

Keep your head, she told herself. Remember your training.

She began to feel calmer. She opened the door on to the landing, and stood for a moment listening. There was only the sound of squabbling infants. She went back inside, picked up the phone with a steady hand and made the call to a private cab service—not the one she normally used. She said it was urgent; they wouldn't be long coming. She'd be better to wait in the apartment till she saw it in the street below. Although her neighbours on the other floors were used to her sudden departures when she was called out on cases, there was no need to call attention to herself this time.

She grabbed her short waterproof coat from the old wardrobe with the broken swinging door, put her suitcase and the holdall on the settee, and pushed her hair up under a knitted cap. Only then did she sit down to wait.

The minutes ticked on. She'd put the watch in her pocket but she could still hear it. Had she thought of everything? No need to check her handbag; when on resident duty she always carried all her personal papers in it, and sufficient money for emergencies. She could ignore her bank account, there was never much in it anyway.

In a fever of impatience she got up and went to the window. Now surely was the time to stop and think, time even to go back. She'd made a mistake... She'd never meant to... She could explain...

She'd said that to her father once when he'd yelled at her: 'If I catch you stealing again, I'll belt you black and blue...' 'I wasn't stealing... she gave me the things...' she'd blubbered then, but he'd belted her just the same.

Not this time, she told herself savagely, this time I'm not running away with nothing. This is my one chance. She thought of the red and gold treasures, snug in their little boxes... She saw the taxi-cab, heard the driver hoot. She gathered up her luggage, threw her coat over her arm and walked out of the apartment without a backward glance. No regrets. It was just a place she had been holed up in. By now she should have been able to afford better with all that money from her private nursing... Money down the drain, she thought with a sudden flash of resentment, for all the good it had done... Well, she would be rid of them too. There would be no going back.

As she was driven away she saw that the tree on the scrubby patch at the corner was budding green. Spring was coming; it must be a good omen.

# ONE

IT WAS SPRING TOO, in another town, another country. Lennox Kemp looked out of his office window through the gold lettering that said Gillorns, Solicitors, and saw that the darling buds of May were having a hard time of it. He sympathized; he too had been shaken by a rough wind, presaging change.

'That's wonderful news,' he lied to his secretary.

Elvira beamed at him. She looked in splendid health. He should have noticed.

'Great, isn't it? After all these years.'

'I didn't even know you were trying...' That didn't seem the right thing to say. 'I mean, of course, I'm delighted for you and Bill.'

'He's over the moon... What do you mean, Mr Kemp, you didn't know we were trying? Just because I'm over thirty doesn't stop me having my first child.'

Kemp hastily put aside his own feelings. That was the worst of getting middle-aged, you got irritable at the mere thought of disruption to routine. He got up, walked round his desk and planted a kiss on her freckled forehead. The colour could still run fast up into her ginger hair the way it had done all the years he'd known her from the gauche girl with ladylike aspirations at McCready's Detective Agency down in Walthamstow to the self-assured person she had become now, working for him in Newtown.

'This calls for a drink, Elvira. It's something to celebrate.'

'Oh, Mr Kemp, it's only eleven o'clock in the morning...'

'Blow that. I need it for shock.' He opened the cabinet and took out the sherry and glasses normally reserved for late clients requiring help to unwind.

'Well, just a little one, then.' She seated herself primly on the edge of a chair and put her notebook down on the desk.

'Here's to you, and Bill. When's it due?'

'Not for ages yet. Christmastime. And I'll go on working right up to the last minute.'

'Indeed you won't. I'm not having you running around humping great files up and down the stairs.'

Elvira grinned.

'You're quite out of date, Mr Kemp. Everybody these days goes on working when they're pregnant. I'll be here at least till November so you don't have to worry.'

'Who's worried? Anyway, it's high time you had some assistance. I should have had someone in to help you ages ago now we've got so much work...' He ran his fingers through his thinning hair. 'It's just that I've got so used to having you around, Elvira.'

'I'll be around for a while yet,' she reassured him. 'But it wouldn't be a bad idea if we did get someone in, someone I could train. It's no good just making do with temps be-cause—' Elvira hesitated—'I'm afraid I won't be coming back afterwards. I know lots of women do but me and Bill, well, we don't think like that. We've waited so long to start a family...'

Kemp looked at her with affection. Even when he first knew her, Elvira had been an old-fashioned girl for all that she'd been a child of the swinging 'sixties.

'Of course I wouldn't expect you to come back. The baby's going to be the most important thing in your life from now on, and that's the way it ought to be.'

Elvira picked up their glasses. 'I'll just get these washed,' she said, 'before your eleven-thirty appointment arrives.' She was apt to get a little embarrassed when the relation-ship between herself and her boss verged on the personal.

'And perhaps next month we might start putting an ad in the dailies... They have special days now for legal secretaries. Unless you want to promote someone in the office?'

Kemp shook his head. 'It's not fair to pinch other people's secretaries. I'll leave it to you, Elvira, to pick your successor. But, please—not a dolly-bird!'

'I told you you were out of date, Mr Kemp. They're all career women nowadays.'

Left to himself, Kemp contemplated the idea of a career woman, and was not cheered. He would miss Elvira. She was a link with the past although she was never the one to speak of it. Well, he would just have to get used to the fact of her going.

It was not the only shock he was to receive in that month of May to jog him into remembrance of things past. The letter he received a few days later from New York told him baldly of the death of his former wife, Muriel. She had been Mrs Leo Probert when she died, and the solicitors who had been acting for her went on to say that it had been inoperable cancer from which she had suffered for over two years.

For a moment Lennox Kemp could read no further. He was shaken by a sense of unspeakable sadness. As if she was there in the room, he could see her face with its halo of golden hair brushed up in the fashion of twenty years ago, hear her high, sweet, schoolgirl voice, her tinkling laugh... He got up, pushed back his chair roughly, and went over to the window. The solid blocks of Newtown misted before his eyes, and he saw instead the green canopy of the Forest which had lain at their door, and he was walking with her down a glade between the hornbeams on a summer's evening in another world, another time.

She didn't deserve to end like that, he thought fiercely, not Muriel. She had been so beautiful, so much in love with life, reaching out for its highest peaks and the fast-running excitements that buoyed her up in hopes that would not wait...

For all she had made him suffer, the ruin of his early career, his forced penance on the wrong side of the law, the long years' endurance, he would never have wished her such ill-fortune as had now befallen her. She had been only a year younger than himself.

His hands were still shaking when he took up the letter again, and read on:

*'You may wonder why we have contacted you since there has been no communication, to our knowledge, between yourself and our late client for many years. Something has arisen, however, which we as executors of the deceased's estate find it necessary to bring to your notice. It is, in our judgement, too delicate a matter to be dealt with by correspondence. One of our partners is travelling to London early next month and we are suggesting that he call upon you at the first opportunity to discuss the situation. By that time it is hoped that our Mr Van Gryson will be in possession of all the available information, and he will be able to speak with you in the fullest confidence of your own discretion.'*

Kemp read the paragraph once more. He recognized the form of words lawyers tend to use when they want to convey something of importance without actually saying anything at all. He noted that Mr Van Gryson was fairly high up in the list of counsellors attached to the firm; if he was coming all the way to London it either spoke volumes for the 'delicacy' of the matter or, more probably, fat fees for the executorship. Perhaps both. Muriel appeared to have died rich.

Kemp lifted the phone and cancelled all interruptions for the next thirty minutes. Emotions could wait—there would be time enough for those—now he had to think.

No mention of Mr Probert. Leo Probert had been a well-heeled gentleman of sporting instincts when Muriel had married him, but he had not been young. He was a middle-aged American on vacation in London when she met him. He offered escape, and a dazzling future when he whisked her off to Las Vegas where he owned casinos, giving her the entrée to that greater gambling world she had just begun to taste the sweets of, the sugar already on her teeth.

Kemp sighed. One could moralize on that, and denounce sugar as poison to the system, medically and on principle, letting Muriel's addiction sink her without trace. But the facts were otherwise; she had flourished according to report, someone meeting the Proberts in later years having told Kemp she was still a lovely woman and living in style.

The letter ended with the usual expressions of condolence, in this case mere platitudes since neither the writer nor the recipient were acquainted.

Kemp dictated a reply, as carefully worded as Eikenberg & Lazard's communication had been to him, and saying no more than that he would look forward to receiving a call from their Mr Van Gryson whenever he was in London.

Speculation at this point as to the reason for such a visit would be unwise. Certainly at one time Muriel had owed her life to him, it might well be that across time and distance she had remembered him in her will. Then why couldn't her executors simply tell him so without this cloud of secrecy?

Later he would think about Muriel, the light-hearted girl who'd shared that house on the edge of Epping Forest. Now he reflected that to most individuals death was the end of their life's story; to lawyers it was often just the beginning.

# TWO

FLAMING JUNE HAD RUN nearly three weeks towards another hot summer when a hearty American voice on the telephone asked if that was Mr Kemp.

'Yes, Lennox Kemp speaking.'

'Dale Van Gryson here. I've just arrived from New York.'

'Kind of you to call so soon, Mr Van Gryson. Your firm told me you would be coming over this month.'

'Wa-al... Things took longer than we'd anticipated. I'd like to meet with you, Mr Kemp.'

'And I with you. As it appears to be personal, and doesn't involve my firm, I would not trouble you to come all the way out to Newtown. Where are you staying?'

'I'm at the Hilton. It would suit me just fine, Lennox, if we met here. It's a private matter, as you say, and better discussed in civilized surroundings, eh? Could you come in and have dinner with me tonight?'

'That would suit me, Mr Van Gryson.'

'Fine. Fine. And it's Dale. High time you and I got together on this... I'll have you paged in the downstairs bar around seven. I've gotten myself a pretty decent room in this place where we can talk business afterwards.'

And well he might, thought Kemp when the meeting arrangements had been completed; Eikenberg & Lazard would be paying—and presumably out of the estate of the late Mrs Muriel Probert.

Dale Van Gryson turned out to be as hearty as his voice. He was a large, loose-limbed man with the kind of shoulders that moved separately from the rest of his body as if he could as easily freewheel through a public house brawl as a crowded cocktail-party.

Kemp watched him lope across the carpet of the lounge, and knew him instantly, the wide, welcoming smile, the open palms; the type of outgoing American who would sell you anything from Christian Science to long-range missiles.

Kemp had risen from his seat anyway on hearing his name paged, and now found his hands grasped fervently in the manner of one white man finding another in a jungle. Indeed, Stanley and Livingstone were models of Victorian restraint by comparison, he reflected, as he allowed himself to be piloted to a secluded table.

While drinks were being ordered and brought, Dale Van Gryson continued to demonstrate his joy at meeting Kemp as though he had searched the earth for just such a one as he. There seemed little need to respond save for a muttered, 'Likewise . . .'

'You visit London often, Mr Van Gryson?' He eventually managed to interpose the question.

'Dale, please . . . Once or twice a year on business. I just love your city.' It was the bestowal of an accolade as well as a hint of part-ownership. The only bit of London Kemp might lay some claim to was the lower end of Walthamstow and he didn't think Van Gryson would care much for it, but he guessed the other man was being expansive to some purpose.

Over dinner they continued to discuss London, and the weather in the streets. They took a stroll through recent Anglo-American politics, probing at the undergrowth of their own political inclinations without either of them breaching the confidence of the ballot-box, like a couple of devils at an ecumenical conference. They talked of the courts and laws of their particular countries, and the rise in the crime figures, of education and the training of the young. Van Gryson made it known that he had a boy and

girl already well set up in careers, they having had the ines-
timable benefit of a good home and strict upbringing. Kemp
had nothing in this respect to offer in return, so confined
himself to opinions of a general nature, making sure he had
washed and rinsed them out first.

He was vastly amused by the whole charade, and well
aware of what was going on. Van Gryson was engaged in the
practice of a technique used by head-hunters the world over:
getting to know the essence of your man before you swallow him up. Whatever revelation was to come anent the estate of the late Mrs Probert, Van Gryson had been sent to
sound him out as to his lifestyle, his character and his likely
acceptance or rejection of some dubious proposition which
the American would get around to in due course—probably at the cheese-and-biscuits stage.

Kemp wasn't in the least worried. Many people, most of
them a good deal less brash than Van Gryson, had in the
past tried to discover the inner man of Lennox Kemp, what
fuelled his thinking, what made him tick. For all his innoc-
uous outward appearance—chubby verging on plain plump,
rather vacant grey eyes and receding hair—his was a secretive, even subversive nature, sceptical to the point of cyni-
cism about the motives and actions of others but reserved
in judgement of them. He had found life for the most part
to be unfair, and considered that perhaps that was what it
was meant to be, though he would not tell a client so, and
would do his utmost to achieve justice for them if it was deserved. He had his sentimental side too, vague romantic
notions of good and evil, which at times evaded his logic
and thrust him into situations where instinct had to come to
the rescue of intellect.

Trying to keep at distance his companion's egregious
bonhomie, Kemp began to wonder if this might not turn out
to be just such a situation.

Van Gryson had a well-used face across which the expressions chased themselves so freely they tended to catch

up with each other before the eyes had time to adjust. In fact his eyes were averted, scanning the contents of the sweets trolley, when he finally spoke of the matter he had come so far to discuss and his voice was suitably muted.

'Divorce is a sad time,' he observed sententiously, 'for all concerned . . . But of course it must be nearly twenty years since yours. And I understand that you and your ex-wife... May I call her Muriel?'

Call her what you like, thought Kemp, as he nodded. She's dead and can't hear you. In fact the friendly American habit of latching on to first names did seem vaguely obscene in the circumstances.

'I understand,' Dale went on as he acknowledged a plate of baked Alaska, 'that Muriel and you parted on amicable terms?'

'We did,' said Kemp shortly, giving all his attention to his fruit salad.

It had had to be amicable—a lawyer's word, covering many sins. Muriel had wanted that divorce. She was conventional at heart; she would not have run off with Leo Probert without marriage in view. Her gambling instinct confined itself to games of chance, not real issues.

'I only met her once,' Van Gryson said, 'the first time she came to Eikenbergs—that would be about two years ago. She was a real lady, Lennox, and still beautiful although she was already ill. She'd had a mastectomy out there in Vegas, but they reckoned there were secondaries...and they had to tell her.'

'I wish I'd known!' The words were out before he could stop himself but as he spoke Kemp knew they were true. Two years ago he'd been in Cornwall and contemplating marriage to Penelope Marsden. They had talked about Muriel then... He was suddenly struck by the poignancy of people who lose touch with each other, and the loneliness that comes of it.

Van Gryson was shaking his head vehemently. 'She wanted no one told. She'd come to New York for treatment. She'd rented an apartment on Fifth Avenue where she could be near the hospital where she had to undergo operations, none of which did any good. It sure was a bad time for her... Anyway, she came to us and asked us to handle all her financial affairs for her. Mr Eikenberg and myself she asked to be trustees. You get the picture?'

'She was putting her affairs in order,' said Kemp slowly, 'because she knew she was going to die...'

Dale was crumpling his napkin. He threw it down on the table, and got to his feet.

'We'll have the coffee and liqueurs in my room. And I'll have another bottle of that claret sent up. You're not going back to Newtown tonight, Lennox.'

Kemp demurred. 'I rather thought I was.'

'Nonsense. I've already booked you a room.'

My ex-wife must have left rich pickings, Kemp mused as he followed the American from the restaurant. The man wasn't a time-waster; he must have felt he had accomplished something during dinner. Perhaps he had found Kemp to be a fit and proper person to have a delicate matter laid before him?

If so, then Kemp was determined to get him to come to the point. The first question he asked when they were alone and comfortably settled was:

'Is there a will?'

'I'm glad you asked that,' said Dale in the eager manner of a Prime Minister about to hedge on a tricky question raised by the Opposition of which notice has been given. 'Mrs Probert made a will that same first day she came to us. It was properly drawn up, and executed in our presence.'

'And that was her only will?'

Van Gryson side-stepped the question. 'Don't you want to know what was in it?'

'Only if you want to tell me.'

Van Gryson took a small sip of coffee, and a larger one of Grand Marnier. 'When Muriel came to us she was in a very emotional state of mind. Don't get me wrong, Lennox... It was understandable. The thing was... You know Mr Probert had died?'

'No, I didn't. I'm sure you're very well aware of the fact that Muriel and I have been out of touch for nearly twenty years. I knew absolutely nothing of her life in America. I gather she had been living in Las Vegas?'

'When her husband died, you mean? Oh yes, they had a large house there. He owned several of the casinos as well as having franchises in all kinds of things.'

It was clear that the strict upbringing of the Van Gryson offspring, if the father's influence was anything to go by, would have protected them from the darker underside of American life. Leo Probert was spoken of with some disparagement despite the respect accorded his considerable wealth for all its dubious origins. In a hushed tone Van Gryson described the fortune left as substantial.

'And it all went to his wife,' he ended. 'She got the lot.'

'That must have been a right turn-up for the book,' observed Kemp sardonically. Meeting the query in the other man's eyes, he explained: 'It's an English expression. I only meant there must have been a lot of sour faces around. Leo would have had business partners?'

'He had, and they sure were mad as hell. There was trouble, and I suppose when your Muriel got ill she wasn't up to handling it.'

'What sort of trouble?' asked Kemp sharply.

'She wasn't specific. The estate had been settled in her favour by the time she came to us so we'd no part in it. Of course we checked things out with her law firm back in Vegas, and they confirmed everything was hunky-dory for her.' Dale looked at the expression and didn't like it much. 'Except as far as her health was concerned of course,' he finished, lamely.

Kemp felt it was time matters were brought to a head. 'So what was in this will she made with your office?'

Van Gryson had his briefcase open on the sofa beside him. He took out a fat folder, extracted a document and handed it to Kemp.

It was a will made in proper form by Muriel Probert, widow, dated March 1987 and running to several pages. Details of the assets in personalty and real estate consisted mainly of business concerns and properties in Las Vegas. Apart from some gifts to various charities, the principal beneficiaries were Preston John Madison and Clive Edwin Horth. At the end of a short list of legatees who appeared to be women friends or servants Kemp found his own name: 'To Lennox Kemp, my former husband, in fond remembrance and deep gratitude, my largest ruby necklace in the hope he has got himself a lady more worthy than me.'

Kemp grinned to hide a deeper feeling. 'At least she remembered me,' he said, 'but surely you haven't come all this way just to hand it over?'

Van Gryson put a hand to his forehead. 'God! If only it were that simple!'

Puzzled, Kemp gave the document back. 'I don't see any problems,' he said. 'Who are these lucky chaps, Madison and Horth? They're described as casino operators. I'd make a guess and say they're the late Mr Probert's partners.'

'And you'd be right, Lennox. Madison—he's called Prester John in gambling circles—he ran things for Leo Probert, and Horth's one of his henchmen.'

'So Muriel was just putting things right with them when she made this will. I don't see anything wrong with that. She'd no family of her own, and she couldn't have children. You knew that?'

'Naturally we inquired as to other possible heirs in view of the terms of the will.' Dale was huffed at the suggestion that Eikenberg & Lazard might not have been thorough. 'She told us she was childless.'

Kemp thought of the operation Muriel had undergone in the early years of their marriage. Just fibroids, the doctor had told them when she went into hospital, but afterwards the surgeon had been uneasy, and a hysterectomy was mentioned. Muriel would have none of it; she had been young then, and hopeful . . .

'Well,' said Kemp, 'all these assets were accumulated by Leo Probert. It seems perfectly fair to me that they should go back where they came from. Nice men, are they, Prester John and his pal, Clive?'

'The worst,' said Van Gryson morosely. 'Julius Eikenberg and myself, we both wondered if they'd put pressure on her. Make a will in our favour or take the consequences. We explained the undue influence thing to her pretty thoroughly, Lennox, just to be sure, but she was adamant that she was making the dispositions of her own free will so we had to take her word for it. Perhaps when she'd become ill she didn't have the strength to resist . . .'

Kemp nodded. 'That could well be. She'd been threatened by their like before. Poor Muriel.'

Van Gryson sat up. 'I'd sure like to know about that. She said something about it when your name came up. What did happen, Lennox?'

Kemp sighed as he dredged the old story up from where it had lain half-buried for years. 'She ran up gambling debts in London,' he said slowly. 'The kind not legally enforceable. She was told she'd get acid in her face. She tried to commit suicide. I paid them off.'

'She said you put your career on the line for her?'

'You could say that. I embezzled trust moneys. Well, it was an emergency . . . and I loved her.'

'You actually stole the money? You broke the law for her?' Van Gryson was staring at Kemp with undisguised astonishment. Eikenberg & Lazard might wheel and deal along the thin edge of legality for profit's sake but they knew their limits. 'Did you go to prison?'

Kemp laughed. 'It was a close-run thing. I sold all I possessed and reimbursed the trust fund just in time. But the Law Society got wind of it and I was struck off for six years... Don't worry, Dale, I've long since been reinstated on the right side of the law.'

Van Gryson was still shaking his head in bewilderment. 'You did all that for a woman!' he said solemnly. He was silent for some moments as if this revelation of Kemp's lapse had given him food for thought. 'Have another drink, Lennox,' he said at last. 'You're going to need it.'

He's decided to let me in on the secret, Kemp was thinking as he sat back and savoured the good wine. Muriel has probably given that necklace away to some woman friend who had been kind to her, or to a maid down on her luck. Muriel had often had these sudden generous impulses, and she would act upon them without further reflection in a way that had been both irritating and endearing. It really didn't matter. It was good to know she hadn't quite forgotten his sacrifice...

'This will—' Van Gryson was tapping it on the edge of the sofa—'would have been fine if Muriel Probert hadn't taken it into her head to make another one.'

It was Kemp's turn to sit up. 'She did?'

'It was all most unfortunate. We're a big firm, Lennox, and a busy one. It's not always easy to keep track of clients...I'm not making excuses for us...'

But that's just what you're about to do, thought Kemp, amused. And it's high time you got on with it.

'Julius and I were in Washington on Government contract business for most of April.' Van Gryson put on an air of importance which was not sustainable for long. 'The New York office was understaffed, and there'd been an unexpected late snowfall so that everyone was determined to get home...' Dale paused to drink, which he did thirstily. 'It was nearly closing time anyway when Mrs Probert came in and asked for either Mr Eikenberg or myself. Well, she was told we were not available by the only professional left in the office, a new recruit straight out of law school, our Miss Janvier. She saw before her a client in obvious distress who wanted help. Muriel apparently said that it was extremely urgent she make a will there and then—mark you, she never said change, she said, make a will—because she was soon going to die. Miss Janvier did what she saw to be her duty—more or less. She drew up the will, which was short, she got Muriel to sign it in the presence of one of the cleaners and a junior, neither of whom knew any more about the firm's business than Miss Janvier herself—and that wasn't much. Our little Miss Janvier had never drawn up a will for a client before, and her law school training doesn't seem to have included how to use a filing system ... '

Van Gryson stopped as his tone turned savage, and he wiped his brow with a large silk handkerchief as if trying to erase any memory of the unfortunate Miss Janvier.

Kemp had listened to all this with a mixture of amusement and understanding. He could appreciate the situation, one not totally unknown to solicitors. Gillorns were small fry compared to the magnitude of Eikenberg & Lazard as evidenced by their notepaper but even the junior staff in the Newtown office were carefully instructed on wills procedure. First, you asked the proper questions, and then, no matter what the client said, you checked. Poor little Miss Janvier had possibly been overwhelmed by her responsibilities that snowy evening; she was new, she was eager, and perhaps no one had told her... She had seen only the emergency, the necessity for action, the woman in front of her was going to die...

'Go on, Dale, tell me the rest of it.'

'She took it with her.'

'What, the original? The engrossment?'

'If that's what you call it. Yes. Said she wanted it by her. To keep it safe... Oh, Miss Janvier protested about that but Muriel was adamant. She took that newly-made will away

with her in her handbag. Miss Janvier—downright pleased
with herself no doubt for the speed with which she'd handled the matter—scribbled the attestations on the copy, and
went off on holiday.'

'Not even a photocopy of the original?'

'The photocopying room was locked up by then. Everyone in the office had gone home.'

'So now you have two wills, one superseding the other,'
said Kemp briskly, 'but the later one must hold up in law.'

Van Gryson reached for his glass. He drank deeply and
refilled it.

'There's worse to come.'

'Don't tell me,' said Kemp, who had already guessed.
'You can't find the new will. You know it was made, you
have a perhaps inadequate copy in your office, the client
took the original and now it's missing.'

'How did you know?'

'Happens all the time,' said Kemp airily. He was beginning to feel the effects of the wine. 'Nine times out of ten
when a client takes an original will from their solicitor's office it's gone when they come to die.'

'You're a cynic, Lennox.'

'No, just realistic. How did this one disappear?'

'God only knows. It wasn't in her handbag when we
looked, and it wasn't anywhere in that apartment. We're her
executors, damn it, don't think we didn't ransack the place.
Besides, the staff swear Mrs Probert never went anywhere
in the house except her own bedroom and the adjoining
bathroom... She used the same rented limousine every time
she went to the hospital, and the same chauffeur. He says
she went nowhere else on these trips except for that one
evening when she had him stop by our office. And that was
only a couple of weeks before she died.'

Kemp sat still for a moment, deep in thought.

'Muriel took the will away with her,' he said carefully,
'and she returned to her apartment with it. She must have

had a reason for doing so. She had been happy to let you keep the other one so why would she want to take the new one? Perhaps to show it to someone . . .'

Van Gryson shook his head.

'She was having no visitors at the time. And she never left the apartment again—of that we're absolutely sure. According to the doctor, her condition suddenly deteriorated—he'd been expecting it and was keeping an eye on her. She could hardly move from her bed. When he advised hospitalization she wouldn't hear of it, said she wanted to die in her own house so he ordered home nursing to see her through to the end . . .'

Kemp pursed his lips.

'Reliable man, this doctor?'

'Absolutely. Don't think we didn't check.' Van Gryson was terse.

'What about the servants and the nurses?'

'Lennox, you gotta remember we couldn't go around badgering folk. It was a tricky enough situation for our firm. There was a bit of time-lapse before we—er—discovered about the second will.'

Kemp raised his eyebrows. 'How come?' He felt he might as well slip into the idiom.

'Well, as I said, Miss Janvier went on holiday that night. Her secretary didn't get round to doing the filing for a week or two . . .' His voice trailed off.

Kemp could barely hide a smile. So things like that could still happen even in the best-run offices.

'And in the meantime your firm assumed there was only the earlier will and so took no action?'

'In the meantime—' Van Gryson gulped as if he'd swallowed a draught of bitter medicine—'Mr Eikenberg and I attended the funeral flanked on either side by Messrs Madison and Horth in good black overcoats with velvet collars . . .'

Kemp let out a soft whistle.

'Showing a proper respect as the heirs-at-law . . . I can restrain my curiosity no longer, Dale. Indulge it before it bursts out of me. You have a copy of this later will?'

Van Gryson withdrew a single sheet from his folder, and held it out between thumb and forefinger as if it was a leaf of stinging nettle. Kemp reached over and took it from him.

'OK, OK,' said the big American. 'I guess you can stand the shock.'

Then he got up and took his hunched shoulders for a walk round the room like a boxer who had just put his man on the canvas.

It was a simple carbon on flimsy with the name of the testatrix and the names and addresses of the two witnesses written in hurriedly beside the attestation clause. The will itself was brief and to the point:

After cancelling all previous dispositions, Muriel Probert, widow, left everything of which she died possessed to her ex-husband Lennox Kemp, of Newtown, England, in recognition of the great service he had rendered her in the past. It was dated the fifth day of April in the present year.

# THREE

LENNOX KEMP HAD ONLY just seated himself at his desk the following morning when Elvira brought in the mail. She looked down at him with mild disapproval. 'I waited,' she said, 'because you're late. You don't look very well.'

'If you must know, I've got a hangover, and I didn't get much sleep.'

'Well, if you will go out on the town...' She put the letters down in front of him. 'Black coffee's what you need.'

Despite two strong cups of it, Kemp still found it hard to concentrate on his correspondence; there were too many other things on his mind. He wanted a clear head, he wanted a second opinion. He thought of Tony Lambert, his most intelligent colleague and an expert on probate, but dismissed the idea. He couldn't talk it over with anyone else, not yet. The last thing Dale Van Gryson had said to him before they parted enjoined confidentiality.

'Give us time, Lennox. Let us get this thing straightened out at the New York end. It's only six weeks since the death, we can procrastinate for a while...'

'But there's got to be a showdown at some time,' he'd told the American, 'it can't be kept under wraps for ever. Not unless...' Kemp hadn't finished the sentence, watching the expression on the other man's face.

Van Gryson had said nothing but Kemp grinned to himself now. He knew damned well what was in that astute counsellor's mind—perhaps even in the corporate mind of his firm:

'Unless I, Lennox Kemp, disclaim any interest in the estate of the late Mrs Probert, and no meeting has ever taken place between myself and any of her trustees...'

It had gone unsaid, and might very well remain so, but the very idea of himself running a clutch of dubious gambling dens in Las Vegas was enough to make him choke over the breakfast table the two of them had shared in the hotel that early morning.

They had discussed the matter more soberly than on the previous night, Kemp probing for information, Van Gryson prevaricating and, in Kemp's view, revealing the depths of his ignorance. Kemp had been struck by the difference in their approach. The American's main concern was how to keep his firm out of trouble, which meant carrying out the duties of trustees and executors while keeping the snake in the basket by sitting firmly on the lid. Kemp, who was often ruefully aware that he'd have made a better detective than a solicitor, was more taken up with the investigation possibilities.

He had been careful, however, to lay fairly and squarely before Van Gryson his own view of the position at law.

'I don't know whether it's the same under the United States legal system,' he'd said, 'but here in England a will contained in a copy or even a completed draft may be admitted to probate on an application to the Court if proper evidence as to its being made can be adduced, supported by the necessary affidavits—in this case those of Miss Janvier's and the two witnesses.'

'Madison's lawyers would counter that by saying how could they be sure it was Mrs Probert. We haven't even got a photostat copy showing the signature.'

'Sworn statement by the chauffeur confirming time of the visit to your office,' said Kemp promptly, 'along with identification of the deceased from photographs shown to Miss Janvier. I think we can discount any suggestion of an imposter should they bring it up.'

'What about evidence of the existence of the second will after the death?'

'That's where the crunch will come... I have to admit it's crucial to any such application on a lost will to the probate courts in this country.'

'The other side would have a field-day on that one,' Van Gryson agreed gloomily. 'They'll say Mrs Probert had second—or even third—thoughts. She destroyed the new will after she got home.'

'Could she have done that without someone on her staff knowing? You say she could scarcely rise from her bed... Even torn-up paper has to be dealt with.'

'She could have burned it.' Van Gryson was by now entering into the spirit of playing devil's advocate; presumably it made a nice change from government contracts.

'Do you know if she smoked? She used to when I knew her. It's unlikely, of course, in a cancer patient but even doctors indulge such foibles when all hope has gone. How else would she have a lighter or matches at her bedside?'

Van Gryson had begun to take notes. He looked up.

'I'll make inquiries, Lennox. As to her flushing the will down the john, Miss Janvier gave her the will in one of our special envelopes. Difficult to dispose of—the fibres would've blocked the pipes.'

'What if she simply got rid of it on the ride home from your office? Having had, as you put it, third thoughts?'

'We'll have to question the driver again. He'd have noticed. He knew her well from all those trips to the hospital. The car was ordered from the security desk downstairs in the lobby of the apartments and she always had the same chauffeur because she liked him. She had become sensitive about her appearance on those visits to the hospital and he was a sympathetic man.'

'Right. Now, what about those servants?'

'Florence Hermanos had been with Muriel for many years in Las Vegas as her personal maid, and latterly as her trusted friend and companion. That's why she took her with her when she came to New York.'

'Was she the one called Florence Bate mentioned in the
first will? I saw her name above mine.' He quoted: 'To my
personal maid and friend, Florence Bate, all my jewellery
except the ruby necklace.'

'You've a quick memory, Lennox,' said Van Gryson ad-
miringly. 'Yes, she's the one. And under that will it meant
a considerable fortune. Apparently your Muriel was a collector of jewels, mostly rubies. She told us Leo Probert gave
them to her on each anniversary.' He hesitated. 'I didn't like
to tell you this before, Lennox, but we found no rubies,
neither your necklace nor anything else, not in the apartment nor in the bank. There was some stuff in a box on her
dressing-table but nothing of great value.'

'So the rubies are missing along with the will? Interesting, don't you think? Tell me more about Florence. How'd
she get to be Mrs Hermanos?' .

At that point Dale had thrown down his table napkin.

'I told you before... We'd no cause to go prying into the
affairs of the servants. It was a delicate enough matter for
us without blowing it up out of all proportion. We had to
tread very softly, and the last thing we wanted to do was al-
ienate these people.'

'I'd have gone through them with a fine-tooth comb,' said
Kemp succinctly. 'You said José Hermanos and Florence
were a married couple, she was the housekeeper and he was
a sort of handyman-cum-butler—an unlikely combination.'

'Apparently she met and married him soon after coming
to New York. He's a spic—sorry, a Spanish or Mexican
American. Didn't take to him myself...'

'But he's married to Muriel's trusted companion so he
gets a job on the staff. And the others?'

'Just a girl who did the cleaning and gave Mrs Hermanos
help in the kitchen. There was no need for more servants,
Mrs Probert was ill, she never entertained, and the building

itself has its own security staff, doormen and concierge—well, you know how we live in New York nowadays...'

'I don't but I can guess. That's why you're so sure of Muriel's comings and goings?'

Van Gryson shrugged. 'Makes it a lot easier to keep track of people's movements. No one could get in or out of that lobby without being spotted. If there had been visitors they would have been announced. There was no one during those last two weeks except the doctor and the nurse he'd engaged.'

'Just the one nurse?'

'That was all he considered necessary—and only for night duty. During the day Mrs Probert insisted that Florence look after her. And, as you seem to have a suspicious mind, Lennox, there was nothing in the death itself or the manner of it to justify further investigation. All Mrs Probert's medical records were always available to us as her financial advisers. She had cancer, neither the operations nor the chemotherapy could save her, and the nursing during her last days was meticulously documented. She had drugs to alleviate pain but in the end it was the disease which killed her.'

Perhaps Van Gryson thought such plain-speaking was necessary but he had been surprised to see his breakfast companion wince.

'I'm sorry, Dale,' Kemp said after a pause. 'My curiosity for the moment overcame my better feelings. I'm sure Muriel's death was due to natural causes as they're called, although cancer to me has always carried the connotation of an evil thing working in the dark, a malignancy at odds with the good... I'm sorry,' he said again, 'it's just that I'm trying to see the Muriel I knew, and wondering how she would have reacted to her impending death. I think she did right when she came to you and made that first will. Never mind whatever other pressure she was under, all the riches and luxurious living she had gained for herself had been through

Leo Probert. She was not a woman who liked power over others. There was an essential sweetness in her nature. She would have been unhappy with the consequences of that power. Whatever you may think of the characters of her late husband's partners, the first will is a fair one.'

'You're saying it should stand?'

Kemp had laughed. 'I'm in a cleft stick,' he said. 'I mean what I have just said. On the other hand, I'm a lawyer like yourself, and we have been taught, have we not, that a testator's wishes must be paramount? And if we can be certain what those wishes were we have to use all our powers to uphold them. Oh, I appreciate the tricky position your firm would be in if it had to come to court—two trustees of a will in dereliction of their duty towards a client...'

This time it was Van Gryson who winced. 'Too damned right it wouldn't look good, but we could ride that one out. Sure, if we'd known about that visit of Mrs Probert either Julius or I would have been round there on the hour to see what the hell was going on, was she in her right mind, or was it just a whim... But there's worse things where we have to operate, Lennox. It's Prester John Madison and his cronies we have to worry about. There's going to be one helluva row from that quarter if they find out there's another will. They've got plenty of shyster lawyers in their pockets, and they're not above using strong-arm methods.'

'Dear me. How different from the home-life of the English judiciary... Sorry, I can see it wouldn't be a joking matter. Have you managed to stave them off so far?'

'Prester John's too smart an operator to go in with all guns firing at this stage. But don't think there haven't been hints. Julius is dealing with them. The estate will take time to be wound up, blah blah... legatees have to be traced, etcetera etcetera, and there's always the goddamned taxes to the government to be settled. Oh, we can give them the runaround for a while yet.'

At that point Van Gryson had leant forward and said with the utmost seriousness: 'You see how it is. No one must know about the other will back home in New York. Miss Janvier won't talk, that's for sure. It was her blunder and she doesn't want it advertised. The two witnesses are dumbos—they can hardly remember whose will it was anyway, and they're not being encouraged to try. And we whisked that file copy out of the cabinet before anyone got a peek at it. Believe you me, Lennox, we've been thorough.'

'So it seems. Which only leaves me. You didn't really have to contact me at all, did you, Dale, unless you had found the original of the second will?'

Van Gryson had assumed his honest counsellor's face, candid to the point of piety.

'Ethics of the profession, Lennox. Straight dealing as between men of the law. Julius Eikenberg and I, we discussed the situation at length and came to the conclusion it was only right that you should be told. No, we didn't have to tell you. We couldn't afford even to hint at it in a letter. Instead, I came over specially to put it to you.'

Once you had me summed up, Kemp thought, and found me maverick enough to just possibly do whatever you might find expedient in the future.

To take the American off his soapbox for a moment, he had murmured: 'You really couldn't afford not to. You'd have been pretty hard-pressed for an explanation if the second will, all neatly typed up on your firm's paper and still in its special envelope, was discovered stuck up the chimney after you'd already disposed of the assets in accordance with the terms of the first...'

'There aren't any chimneys,' said Van Gryson tersely, deciding to ignore the rest of Kemp's perfectly cogent observation. 'And there were no loose floorboards in any of the rooms or loose tiles in the bathroom. We inventoried all the furniture, gave us the excuse to rake the whole place over. You couldn't have hid a matchstick in that apartment.'

'I still think you should investigate those servants.'

Van Gryson's eyes were bland. 'You thinking of coming over and doing it for us?'

Kemp had shrunk back in horror at the suggestion.

'Not me! It's only in fiction that the hero hops on a plane and does his stuff in a foreign city. I can't even read a street map of London, never mind find my way to the subway in New York. No, I'm staying right here where I belong. But it mightn't be a bad idea if you employed a private eye—is that what they're still called over there?'

Dale Van Gryson put on a sly look. He pursed his lips rather primly.

'Mr Eikenberg has that in hand. We're keeping an eye on anyone who was around at the time of Mrs Probert's death. The rental on the apartment's paid for another three months and we've retained the servants as caretakers. I admit you've got me a bit rattled on Mrs Hermanos. Seemed a nice woman to me...'

'I tend to be suspicious of nice women. And it might be a good idea to have another talk with that doctor. Sound him out on Muriel's state of mind... And the night nurse too, you haven't said much about her.'

'There's nothing to tell. She came from a highly reputable agency, and had been recommended by the doctor himself. We didn't get to speak to her as she's gone upstate to nurse her own mother who is dying, but don't worry, we'll get round to her in due course. We do have some very discreet people we use from time to time on the financial side of matrimonial cases, that kind of thing... No, I don't think we'd call them private eyes. We have to be careful, you know, we're a very respectable firm.'

'Whatever you call them, I'd be obliged, Dale, if you could let me see their reports, if any. After all, I'm an interested party...even under that first will I get a ruby necklace.'

'Those damned rubies!' Van Gryson exclaimed. 'D'you know what happened? They were safe in her bank up till a few weeks before she died, then on one of her trips to the hospital she goes and gets them out. The bank showed us the receipt. Now they've vanished into thin air.'

'I put my money on the butler,' Kemp had said, cheerfully before the two men went their separate ways. 'In English detective fiction it's always the butler who dunnit.'

# FOUR

THE FIRST CONTRIBUTIONS to what Kemp liked to call his Letters from America arrived at the same time as an area of high pressure also from across the Atlantic which brought hot weather to Newtown in mid-July. The compliments slip from Eikenberg & Lazard seemed to distance itself from the other contents despite being marked by the initials 'DVG', the envelope itself was designated Private and Confidential and sent to Kemp's home address. He felt like the recipient of subversive mail.

There were photostat copies of five reports, two by Alfred Orme and three by Bernard Shulman. Fortunately the package had arrived on a Saturday morning so Kemp was able to spread them out between the butter dish and the marmalade jar and give them his whole attention.

Glancing over the typescript, Kemp guessed that Alfred Orme must be as old as his machine—surely no one had called a child Alfred for some fifty years. Reading confirmed this, the style was pedestrian and the material set out without frills in a manner with which Kemp was familiar as he had perused plenty of police statements which had the same lack of literary merit. Orme was probably a retired officer augmenting his pension by doing routine investigative work for legal firms. He would be thorough and discreet but possibly unimaginative. He was no great typist judging by the pepper-and-salt effect on the paper which hadn't been improved by photocopying.

The first report was dated 7.2.89. which Kemp took a moment to work out; he could never see why Americans,

who were supposed to be logical people, should put the
month first, then the day, then the year.

*Tuesday, July 2—Report by Alfred Orme*
Called at Argus Automobiles, a firm known to me as a reputable rental car agency. Spoke with Frank Miner, aged
forty-two, clean licence, no police record, employed by Argus five years. No complaints by employers. Wears chauffeur's uniform, peaked cap, a clean, tidy, well-set-up man
of honest appearance.

Showed no reluctance to answering questions about Mrs
Muriel Probert when I disclosed my interest as an old friend
of the deceased who had lost touch and been shocked to
hear of her death. As instructed, I produced photograph.
Though taken over two years ago Miner recognized it immediately, commenting the subject was thinner and the
features more lined when he knew her. During the last six
months he had driven Mrs Probert to the Mount Sinai
Medical Centre at least once a week.

Engaging him in conversation Miner said she was a nice
lady, and talked to him when she was well enough. Because
he had been sympathetic to her condition it got that he was
the driver she always asked for. (Confirmed by Mr Sher-
rett, Manager for Argus, who said Miner was in fact the
only driver Mrs Probert would have.)

'Did Mrs Probert make calls anywhere else on these
trips?' I asked Miner.

'Not often. Lately hardly at all except mebbe she'd ask me
to stop at her bank—that's Chase up by the hospital. Early
on she used to do some shopping and get me to wait at the
department stores for her. But not for the last month or so.
She got pretty low what with the treatment and all ...'

'I just wondered why she didn't stop off and visit with
some of her old friends.'

'I suppose the treatments just tired her out... I'd help her
into the cab when the nurse at the hospital brought her

down, and all she'd do was wrap that Scotch rug of hers round her knees and say: "Get me home quick, Frank." She'd probably just about had enough. She weren't in no fit state to go visiting.'

'I brought the conversation round to the weeks immediately prior to Mrs Probert's death. Miner remembered she'd visited her bank. It had been cold and she'd put the rug round her shoulders when she went in because she said she might have to wait, and she had it over her arm when she came out. (I didn't press the questions here as I understand the visit to the bank has been confirmed.) My instructions were not to arouse any suspicion in Mr Miner that this was anything more than the concern of an old friend. He volunteered the information about the rug because he'd told Mrs Probert that his aunt had brought one like it from Scotland, but it did give me the opportunity to ask if Mrs Probert was ever forgetful and left it in his cab. He was indignant at that and said she was never forgetful—and not like some of his passengers.

I then asked him about her last visit to the hospital. Without any prompting from me Miner told me what happened.

'Surprised me no end when she wanted me to make a stop on the way home. I'd taken her to the hospital, usual time of two o'clock. I was to be back same time as always, three-thirty. Nasty day, it was, there'd been snow and the streets were slushy, so I was a bit late getting back but it didn't matter, she wasn't ready anyhow. When she did come out the nurse had to help her. She looked really done up. Anyways, once in the car she said to take her to these lawyers, Eikenberg and something, and gave me the address. Like I said, it was slow driving so it must have been well after five when we got there. I got her out of the cab and in at the door but she wouldn't let me take her no further. Said I'd just to wait. She weren't in there more'n half an hour. When she came out I helped her into the car and drove her back to her apartment.'

As this was the last time Miner had driven Mrs Probert I was able to press his memory of the occasion.

'I guess she knew it were the last time,' he said, and he shakes his head.

I asked him why he thought that, and at this point he made a series of rambling remarks which I summarize.

Miner had become quite attached to Mrs Probert, said she was a pleasant lady, not like some he had to drive. When the car was not re-ordered he telephoned the apartment to be told by the Concierge that his services would no longer be required as Mrs Probert was now too ill to go out. Miner said he was not surprised. When she left the hospital that afternoon the nurse had said goodbye to her, usually she said see you next time. He thought that meant they had told Mrs Probert they could do no more for her, and that was why she made the visit to the lawyers. Stands to reason, he said, she wanted to make her will. I was able to ask him at that point if she was perhaps carrying anything like that when she came out of the door at Eikenbergs. He said she was carrying nothing except her crocodile-skin handbag, and that was closed. He had jumped out of the car as soon as she appeared in the lobby and taken her arm to help her across the slippery sidewalk.

'Just the weather for that tartan rug,' I said to him, which made him stop and think.

'Funny you should say that... She never had it with her that day... I don't remember seeing it since her visit to the bank... Anyways, once in the car after visiting these lawyers she just lay back on the cushions as if she were exhausted and she never moved at all on the drive home. I made sure all the car windows were up. It was freezing outside and I didn't want her to get a chill on top of her other troubles.'

As my instructions were to ascertain, if possible, the state of Mrs Probert's mind at the time, I endeavoured to draw him out. This was not difficult, for Miner was only too ready to talk about her and the sadness of her situation.

He said her condition was much worse that day than it had been even the previous week. Miner put this down to the harshness of the treatment—he thinks chemotherapy does nothing except make people's hair fall out—but he did say that on the drive to the hospital she seemed to be angry. He'd never known her like that before. She'd never been bitter about the disease which had come upon her but she'd said to him that day that ingratitude was the hardest thing to bear, and that to find your trust in someone has been betrayed was worse than any illness. Miner had not taken much notice at the time, he was concentrating on the road conditions and anyway he was used to his passengers talking to themselves in his hearing but as I talked to him these words of Mrs Probert's came back. He is a slow-thinking man but in my opinion, honest. I do not think he could have made them up.

When he drove her from the hospital to the lawyers and on the way home Miner says Mrs Probert spoke little, but he scoffed at any idea that she might have been seriously disturbed in her mind. In the way she gave him his instructions to stop at Eikenbergs she was matter of fact and precise.

I terminated the interview at this point as I was afraid he would become suspicious of further questions. I believe he has told us all he can.

*Wednesday, July 3—Report by Alfred Orme*
Mr Orme's second report was short and businesslike. He had interviewed the superintendent, the doormen, porters and concierge staff at the building where Mrs Probert had her apartment. This time he had no need to pose as other than Eikenberg & Lazard's representative checking up on

the safety arrangements for the premises in the absence of an actual owner. The lease still had three months to run, the rent was paid up, and the servants were occupying as caretakers until such time as the furniture could be cleared.

The doormen knew the late Mrs Probert by sight, and confirmed seeing her coming and going to the hospital. They were also well-acquainted with Frank Miner and often passed the time of day with him when he waited for her. The concierge staff produced notes of the times the car was ordered by telephone, and the messages relayed to Argus Automobiles. Sometimes the instructions had come direct from Mrs Probert herself, latterly from Dr Seifel and occasionally from the housekeeper, Mrs Hermanos.

Mr Orme reported that he could detect no slackness either in the record-keeping or the security. The rents of these apartments were high and the occupants expected value for money, twenty-four-hour vigilance and the door never left unattended. Therefore, Mr Orme concluded, if the staff in the downstairs lobby said that the late Mrs Probert had had no visitors during her last two weeks except for her doctor and the night nurse he had recommended, then there could be no doubt.

Mr Orme's interview with Dr Seifel could not have been easy, and Kemp grinned as he relished the sparsity of the report. Doctors are notoriously suspicious of any inquiries pertaining to their patients—particularly dead ones—and Dr Seifel was no exception. He pointed out to Mr Orme that the late Mrs Probert's lawyers had had full access to all her medical records since he had taken her on as his patient when she first came to New York—indeed it had been Julius Eikenberg himself who had sought out Dr Seifel as a specialist in those cases where malignancy had been diagnosed and might already have advanced. Nothing had been concealed either from her lawyers as trustees or Mrs Probert herself, that was how she had wanted it. Details of the unsuccessful operations and treatment could be obtained from the hospital. Yes, there had been short periods of remission under the chemotherapy but in a case like hers the prognosis had never been other than negative, and she had known it to be so.

Things must have eased off a little—at least for the doctor—when Mr Orme raised the question of Mrs Probert's state of mind immediately prior to her death. This would be a perfectly normal inquiry from a representative of her trustees—though it might have come better from one of them personally. Kemp saw both Eikenberg and Van Gryson keeping it at arm's length.

Dr Seifel had given a robust denial to any suggestion that his patient's mental faculties were impaired. Despite her physical weakness there was nothing wrong with her mind; it had operated normally right to the end. In his interviews with her, on a daily basis during her last two weeks, she was coherent, knowledgeable about her condition and no longer distressed by it. The doctor seemed to have indulged in a small homily, saying that if all his dying patients displayed the same attitude as the late Mrs Probert his own task would be a lot easier.

No, to his knowledge, she had had no visitors. He would not have prevented visits had she asked but she had told him there was no one she wished to see. The doctor understood—at least in part. Any woman who had been beautiful might want to hide herself even from old friends now that the ravages of the disease itself and the treatments to contain it had become so apparent.

Reading this part of the report Kemp was brought up sharply by the intrusion of feelings of his own. Van Gryson had said that Muriel's close friends would have been in Las Vegas, and her circumstances since coming to New York hardly conducive to the making of new ones. When Kemp had inquired if either Van Gryson or Julius had called at the apartment he was told they had not. All instructions to them regarding financial matters, payment of servants' wages,

rent and outgoings of her home, medical attendance there
or at the hospital were received by letter or telephone at their
offices and made directly by Mrs Probert herself. There had
been no such communication from her during the last
month of her illness, and they had seen no reason why there
should have been; the bills from the doctor and the hospital
were paid on a regular basis and there had been no other
expenditure.

Eikenberg & Lazard had been content to keep scrupu-
lous accounts thereby releasing their client from day-to-day
worries, but it did seem there had been a closer relationship
between themselves and her bankers than with herself.

In the light of the circumstances, Kemp had noted an el-
ement of shamefacedness in Van Gryson when this point
had been talked over. Yet Kemp could well understand the
situation. The trustees of Mrs Probert were only part of a
firm of some magnitude. She had put her affairs in their
hands but they must have many such clients as rich as she—
and some of them with a great deal more potential. She was
not the wife of an influential senator, nor the mother of an
up-and-coming politician, she was merely the widow of a
man who might well have been a gangster, at any rate one
who had made his fortune out of the gambling proclivities
of others. Muriel had had neither connections nor status in
New York, whatever her position might have been back in
Las Vegas.

Lonely, Kemp thought... She must have been so lonely...
Was that why she had turned back the years, and remembered him?

He continued reading.

No, Dr Seifel had never discussed personal affairs with
Mrs Probert, although he commented—and it sounded tes-
tily—that the body is as personal a matter as you can get and
it was only her body and its freedom from pain that concerned him.

Asked if she had ever mentioned her will, Dr Seifel said he made it his business never to talk about wills with his patients—that was strictly the province of another profession and he understood Mrs Probert was well supplied with lawyers.

Kemp felt himself warming to Dr Seifel.

Yes, the patient had been upset that evening when she returned from her last visit to the hospital but more at his suggestion of hospitalization than anything else. She had been firm that she would not go into a hospital, on that point she had been resolute. Dr Seifel felt there had been a new force in her which he put down to the fact that she had been told the worst. He had hurried round to the apartment that afternoon to await her return because the hospital had already notified him of the results of their last tests. He had been rather worried because she was late but she explained that the car had been delayed by the snow.

He put it to her that if she was to remain at home then she must have nurses, day and night. He was surprised that she immediately agreed, hitherto she had been against it, saying that Florence Hermanos could take care of her.

Once his patient was in her bedroom the doctor had had a word with Mrs Hermanos, and found her surly; she had looked after her mistress throughout her illness and would do so till the end.

'I wasn't going to have any nonsense from a servant,' Dr Seifel had said at that point, 'but I had to recognize her devotion. I agreed to her continuing her daytime duties so long as it was under my supervision but I must engage a properly trained night nurse. I told her to get a room ready—there were plenty of empty ones in the apartment.'

Dr Seifel had telephoned the Nursing Agency he always used in these cases, requesting the services of a suitable nurse as soon as one was available. As Mrs Probert began to go downhill more rapidly than he had anticipated he had had to get in touch with the woman in charge again, stressing the urgency, and telling her that in his opinion the nurse would be required for no longer than a week. He did not add, as he might well have done, that subsequent events bore out that opinion.

He was well pleased with the person sent from the Agency. Dr Seifel had found Miss Smith to be a quiet, dependable and competent trained nurse.

'She was not a chatterer,' he said, 'and they're the worst kind in a sickroom. Nor of any great personal appearance but that's of no matter. Miss Smith was experienced in the care of the dying, in fact her presence seemed to soothe my patient. Miss Smith went about her duties without fuss, and she carried out my instructions to the letter. When she knew Mrs Probert was sinking she called me, and we were both present when she died in her sleep with peace and dignity.'

The records of attendances and the medication given during those last days had already been handed over to Eikenberg & Lazard, and Dr Seifel was satisfied that, so far as he and Nurse Smith were concerned, they had each carried out their respective duties with the proper professional skill. He hoped he would hear no more of the matter.

On that brusque note—introduced, Kemp decided, by the doctor—the interview had ended.

From the attendance notes, complete with dates and times, it was clear that the registered nurse from the agency had been in constant attendance, and had not herself left the apartment, her daytime needs being met by the other staff while at night she had remained by the patient's bedside.

THE REPORTS of Bernard Shulman were much racier documents than Orme's. Told in the first person and the present tense like an ongoing tale of city folk, the individual voices split through the narrative. The typescript showed that Shulman was no mean typist and used more than two fingers. Kemp figured he would call himself Bernie.

*Report by Bernard Shulman. July 7-15*

Got me a stand-in doorman's job at the ———Hotel on the same block as the apartment building and keep a watch on the entrance. Leonie Rojas comes in mornings at seven-thirty and shows again about eleven when she buys groceries round the corner. Give her the eye a few times as she passes and get a smile from her. So I wait a coupla days, then I'm in the shop when she comes in and I help her load her basket. Buy her some bagels and we go into the Park to eat them.

She's no great talker, kinda slow in the head, I guess, nor's she much of a looker as she's got a yellow skin and bad teeth—not much of a start, that, for a girl still under twenty. She says to me she has the job almost a year and wishes it'd go on for ever as the place is clean enough to eat off the floor and all she's got to do is keep it that way. She tells me the layout and when she's not vacuuming the carpets and dusting the furniture she helps the housekeeper in the kitchen.

'Ain't there no one else there?' I asks.

'Not since the lady went and died. I liked her. She gave me things, clothes and stuff... Not that I could wear them.'

She hardly could, with her figure. She's sort of squat with thick legs but mebbe its only puppy-fat and she'll grow outa it. No, she never got no jewellery, Mrs Hermanos saw to that. Leonie had to show anything she got to Mrs Hermanos before going home.

'Those Hermanos,' I says, 'they're OK to work for now the lady's gone?'

'She's all right, I guess. Never did see much of him. Calls himself a butler...' She giggles at that. 'I ain't never seen a butler 'cept in the movies and he sure don't act like them.' She's quiet for a bit, then she says: 'They fight, the Hermanos... and when they don't fight they hardly speak.'

I pretend surprise. 'Hey, I heard they were a nice middle-aged couple that cared for the lady 'fore she died.'

'She cared all right, Mrs Hermanos. I'll give her that...
Why, only the other day I see her crying her eyes out in the
lady's bedroom while she was sortin' out the clothes that's
to go to some big cancer charity. Crying her eyes out, she
was, all over that nice rug Mrs Probert used to take in the
cab when she went to the hospital. I guess the death just got
to her...'

I said Leonie's a slow talker and it's heavy going getting
anything from her but I'd made sure we'd walked a fair ways
so's we'd have to take a bit of time getting back. So, the girl
likes the attention. Probably not much had happened to her
before she got the job at Mrs Probert's apartment and,
though she's no fast thinker, she's kept her ears and eyes
open.

'They was all lovey-dovey at first, the Hermanos...
They'd not been married long. Guess she thought herself
lucky to get a man at all. She's forty if she's a day, and he's
a handsome spic if you like that kinda thing.'

I'd put Leonie down as Spanish-American herself but
didn't like to say so. Anyways, what she's getting at is José
Hermanos is part-Mexican which in Leonie's book is spic.

'Love's young dream can start at any age, Leonie,' I says,
'Mebbe the dream didn't last. When did the quarrels start?'

She had a long think, and finished the bagels. 'When the
lady was near to dying. Mrs Hermanos was with her a lot in
the bedroom. I wasn't never let in there 'cept to carry trays
and clean up, and get the bedsheets for washing. Nothin'
went to the laundry. Mrs Hermanos said all the bedlinen had
to be done by us, laundries make it too stiff for sick folk...
Anyways, one day I'm in cleaning the bathroom and I could
hear Mrs Probert got angry.'

'So, she was sick. Sick people get irritable.'

'Mrs Probert weren't like that. She weren't the com-
plaining type. I'd never heard her raise her voice like she did
then. I heard her say, *Is it true, Florence?* That's what she
called Mrs Hermanos. *Is it true about José?* That's what I

heard her say. I never did get to hear what Mrs Hermanos said because she rousted me out that bathroom quick like she didn't want me hearing no more.'

I says it must have been embarrassing for a nice girl like her to hear the Hermanos quarrelling in front of her.

'It was Mrs Hermanos that got embarrassed, he just carried on like I wasn't there.'

Leonie's turning things over in that slow mind of hers, and it's coming out like a dripping tap.

'He says to her once to forget the damn jools, that wasn't the job they were there for. He started to throw plates about. I could hear him from upstairs. Then the nurse went down, and that stopped him.'

So I says: 'Did Mrs Probert have a nurse?'

'Only for the nights that week she died. Mrs Hermanos didn't like it but the doctor insisted. He always passed the time of day with me when he came, never ignored me like some. Polite, he was . . .'

'And the nurse, was she polite?'

'So-so. Never had much to say to anyone. Anyways, she were on nights when I'd gone home. I'd clean her room in the mornings when she was with the lady but she always left it tidy, nothing lyin' about.'

Leonie sighs. ''Spose that's how nurses get to be. Tidy. They don't leave no mess around for other folk to clean up. When I goes to clean her room it's like nobody's ever been in it. If I'd the education, I'd sure like to be a nurse . . .'

So I tells her she's meant for better things than cleaning up after people. I'm trying to get around to whether she's seen any papers being burnt, but I'm careful, so I says, 'like emptying out their dirty ashtrays and such . . .'

'You gotta be joking. There ain't nobody allowed to smoke in that apartment. Mrs Probert, she never smoked even when she was well and sat in the living-room reading or watching TV. When she got real sick she kept to the bedroom. That chemical stuff they did to her at the hospital, you shoulda seen the hair that come out on her brushes, the poor thing! There'd be nothin' but hair in the trash can when I'd empty it.'

'Guess cancer treatment's worse'n the disease,' I says, going along with her notion. 'Pretty nasty for you, tho', clearing up after a sick person.'

'Wasn't what you'd think 'cept for the washing. Kept that bedroom neat's a pin, Mrs Hermanos did. She was in and outa there all day 'specially the last two weeks, hardly left the lady save when she were asleep.'

'Guardian angel, huh? But Mrs Probert must have known she was near her end. Most folks be preparing for it... Making their wills and so on...'

'Weren't anything like that to do. Was all settled with the lawyers, Mrs Hermanos told me once. That's why the lady didn't have to worry her head about such things when she got so ill. There weren't no papers like that I ever saw, and anyways all the writing stuff's in the desk in the living-room and Madam hadn't been in there in weeks. All that furniture just lay around gatherin' dust.'

So we're walking down our block by now and I'm not getting any more from Leonie Rojas so I stop at the Hotel door and say, 'See you around, babe,' at which she looks hopeful, poor kid. As instructed, I let two-three days go by before I takes her for another stroll in Central Park. She tells me she's got another job, waitressing in a glitzy restaurant over on Broadway. I know who's arranged that for her but I just say I'm glad, and mebbe I'll be in touch. Unlikely; she's too young, and she's not my type but I'm not closing the door in case I get the word to call on her again. I get the message: my way's been cleared to approach the next two subjects, Mr and Mrs Hermanos.

*Report by Bernard Shulman. July 16*
I'd shaved off my moustache which was temporary as my doorman's job and I call at the late Mrs Probert's apart-

ment with a card from the rental agency. I'm wearing my best suit, custom-tailored slubbed silk with the pale green stripe, and black tasselled loafers that cost me a fortune. I guess I look the part OK, young businessman on the up-and-up seeking property to rent for my Momma and Poppa about to arrive in the Big Apple to share my good fortune.

Mrs Hermanos lets me in. 'They rang, Mr Hyams. Said you wanted to look at the apartment. I'll show you round.'

If she's the forty Leonie thinks then she's taken good care of herself. I put Florence Hermanos at nearer thirty. She's got olive skin, chestnut-coloured hair just not turning grey, scraped from her forehead and done in a bun, a smallish figure broader in the bust than the hips, and she talks with an educated—possibly self-educated—accent.

Off the right-hand side of the hall double doors lead into the living-room—which is huge. Mrs Hermanos pulls back the drapes at all four windows, two look out over the Park, two over the street. Furniture stands around like sheeted gravestones waiting for the resurrection. Through an archway there's a dining-room also clad in gloom and dustcovers. At the far end an open door shows a step down, I guess to the kitchen premises.

'You can view the kitchen later,' she tells me briskly as she goes back in the hall and starts up a short flight of stairs to the upper floor. So I looks at the three bedrooms, all with bathrooms adjoining, and at the tall linen closet stacked with household stuff like it was in a department store ready for a sale. The biggest bedroom's over the living-room and the same size. Here nothing's covered up, the canopied bed's still there, so's a dressing-table, a great wall of wardrobes and various oddments of furniture including a couple of tub armchairs you could spend an easy afternoon in.

'Everything here belonged to Mrs Probert,' Mrs Hermanos says, 'so it doesn't go with the apartment. She took the place partly furnished. I'm sure the agency will have given you an inventory of the other furniture.' So, she reels them off like she was selling the stuff.

This sure is one competent woman. She's been around and I guess she's the sort can look after herself. She's wary, though, and I'll have to tread real careful if I'm to get anything out of her.

All the time she's talking she's looking around to see if she's missed anything, as if she's got every floorboard, every shelf, dusted off in her mind, like she's been over the place a hundred times looking for specks of dirt—or mebbe other things.

I nod, as if I know what she's talking about. I'm not really up in this sort of thing. I'm not married and it takes me all my time to keep my three rooms down in the East Village from looking like a shack in the Everglades. Now this apartment of the late Mrs Probert, it's big, the decor's stylish and, like Leonie said, it's neat's a pin. But there's a funny feel in that bedroom, for all its lavish drapes and a carpet you could lose a cat in it's so thick...

A damned lonely place to die in, just hearing footsteps clicking on the landing outside the door—like Mrs Hermanos' who's trying to hustle me out. But I takes my time, looking around, thinking. That nurse would've been padding in and out from her room next door, but no friends came a'calling... There was a photograph on the white-and-gold tallboy, a frail blonde with good bones.

'Was that Mrs Probert?' I says, politely.

Mrs Hermanos comes back to the bedroom door. She's tight-lipped, and only nods.

I takes another look. 'Pretty woman,' I says, and close the door behind me. I'm not much of a one for imaginings but that lonely feeling sure got to me where it hurt.

Kemp stopped reading for a moment. He could have stretched out a hand to Bernie Shulman; it seemed they had

more in common than their occupation of three-room
flats... He took up the copy report again.

I NEED Mrs Hermanos' confidence if I'm to get anywheres
with her so the mention of the woman leads me into a long
spiel about Momma's sister who died of cancer in spite of all
that treatment. By the time we're going down to the kitchen
(a short flight of stairs goes off the main hall with an off-
shoot to the dining-room) we're getting friendly again. She's
either anxious to make a good impression or she wants to
make sure the Hyams family take the place. Whatever it is,
she's got anxious eyes. They're small, dark and snappy but
behind them there's a real worry.

The kitchen's a cavern, gleaming tiles, neon lights and
every appliance known to man. She shows me their own
quarters, a living-room and bedroom, but I don't intrude,
keeping to my role as the gentlemanly sort. She falls for it,
offers me tea, so I sit down at the big pinewood table and
prepare to do a little digging. There's no sign of José but
that don't bother me. I've already put the feelers out on him
around the neighbourhood and I'll soon know as much
about him as she does—mebbe more.

'You wouldn't consider staying on, you and Mr Hermanos? I mean, this is a big place for Momma and Poppa, and
there's me and my young sister Rachel. They might want
some help settling in...'

She said definitely no. The arrangement with Mrs Probert's lawyers was that they would only remain as caretakers
till the apartment was rented.

'And have you another place, Mrs Hermanos?'

On that point, too, she's definite.

'We'll not be servants any more,' she says, 'we're going to
open a restaurant of our own.'

'Gee, that's great,' I says, 'and very enterprising. I'm always glad to hear of people getting on. Sounds like you've
had a stroke of good fortune.'

'We hope so,' is all she says as she pours out the tea, but her hand's a bit shaky.

'Something come from the lady, eh?' I accompany this with a nice broad smile to take away the cheekiness. 'Only right and proper, I'd say. You said you'd been with her a long time.'

She'd already told me she'd been with Mrs Probert for fifteen years. Now she seemed to want to get away from the subject of future plans and was happy to talk of the past. I don't think she lied about any of it—I'm pretty cute at spotting that kind of thing.

They'd met in Vegas. Florence Bate was the child of a cleaning woman and an English derelict who'd died of drink and gambling debts. Florence was bar-girl at one of the casinos and got badly roughed up one night. Muriel Probert covered the hospital expenses and afterwards took Florence into her household as lady's maid. 'Because I was half-English, I think... Muriel never forgot where she'd come from.'

Florence Bate had been happy in the Probert mansion and Muriel was good to her, so that when Mr Probert died she stayed on, by that time more as friend and confidante than servant.

'It was a bad time. Her husband had left her everything, the casinos, the franchises, the lot. She wasn't a business woman, Mr Hyams, it was too much for her...'

'Too much for any woman,' I readily agrees. 'Sort of thing only a family can handle. My Uncle Meyer, he's in that line himself but he's got four sons to keep the business going. Mrs Probert would've needed menfolk around.'

'She'd none of her own. Mr Madison and Mr Horth, well, they ran the places. Mr Madison, he'd have married her like a shot but she didn't like him much and she said no. She was a lady, Mr Hyams, and he wasn't her kind... It wouldn't have worked out. I don't know what would've happened if she hadn't got ill and had to come to New York.'

It was in New York that Florence met José Hermanos, in fact at the little restaurant on the East Side where she'd go for lunch on her day off. She was as much alone in the Big Apple as her mistress, and I guess she welcomed the attentions of the handsome Spanish waiter. Not that Mrs Hermanos tells it that way. She even flushes when I suggest he must have found her an attractive woman. She's evasive now when talking about her husband as if she's having second thoughts. From what I've learned already on the subject of José Hermanos, this isn't surprising.

Anyway, it seems to have been a whirlwind romance—within a month of meeting, they're married. Someone wasn't wasting any time. He tells her one of his jobs was butler in a mansion on Long Island. She swallows this and so apparently does Mrs Probert, who doesn't need a butler but wants to keep Florence happy.

I'm not going fishing in these waters right now. I can hook José whenever I want him through other sources, so when she clams up on the subject I drop it and get back to her relationship with Mrs Probert.

'In the end, she'd only me,' she says, 'all her friends were in Vegas and they weren't the sort to be much help in a crisis anyway. Muriel was rich, see, and rich people don't get a lot of sympathy when they're ill. People get to thinking you can buy anything, even good health. When she came to New York first a few of her women friends would call but when she told them the malignancy was spreading they dropped her. You'd have thought it was contagious, wouldn't you?'

I give this the solemn nod. 'Terrible,' I says, 'the way some people take others' misfortune. She could have done with some company with her on those visits to the hospital you were telling me about.'

'She never wanted anyone with her. Not even me. She was stubborn about that. I offered to go, specially when it was for chemotherapy, but she'd never let me ... I tried to make her see the sense of it during the last weeks, that she ought to have me with her...' Mrs Hermanos looks like she's trying to puzzle something out. 'And when she got home sometimes she'd be exhausted, she'd go straight up to her room and ask me to bring her tea... It was just as if she wanted to be alone for a while.'

'Cats are like that,' I says, 'when they're ill. They find a place to hide away...'

She's not looking at me. She's got some thought of her own and it worries her.

It was sounding to me like Florence Hermanos hadn't talked this way in a long time. Seemed natural, with her lady so recently dead and her having no one around now to listen to her. All the same, I'm getting to delicate ground and don't want to push things too far, so I go back to Auntie Rose and the cancer.

'Some know right away,' I finishes up, 'and some don't want to know even when they're told. Which was your lady?'

'Oh, she knew early on. After her first mastectomy... And she wanted to know how long she'd got. They gave her a year, maybe two.'

'She sure was a brave lady. Aunt Rose, now, she wanted to know nothing. What a time that was for the family! Rose had the money, see? And would she make her will? She would not. Caused no end of hassle when she died...'

Mrs Hermanos is sitting with her chin cupped in her hands. She doesn't speak for a minute or two and I begin to think I've lost her. Then she says:

'Muriel wasn't like that. She put everything straight. She said she was unhappy at turning Mr Madison down and she'd do the right thing by him in the end. He and his partner would get what they wanted when she died.'

'She told you, Mrs Hermanos?'

'She confided in me.' Florence Hermanos says it with pride. 'I wasn't just her maid, I was her friend. She made her will in their favour.'

'Would that Aunt Rose had been so sensible!' I'm starting to think my time is up. The last thing I want is for Florence to get suspicious; this mightn't be my last call on her. I get to my feet and say I've got to be going.

'Well, I'm glad your good lady didn't forget you when she came to make that will... I suppose you'll have enough to start that restaurant?'

Mrs Hermanos pushes her chair aside. The worried look is back in her eyes. 'The lawyers say it'll take time... You see, she's left me her collection of rubies, they're worth a fortune. But there's got to be an evaluation, they tell me. For the probate, I guess...' She gives a nervy laugh. 'I hope it doesn't take much longer.'

We're in the hall by now.

'Rubies will look just fine on you, Mrs Hermanos, with your colouring. I congratulate you on your good fortune. Though it must be sad in a way when you must have seen your lady wearing them many times.'

'Oh, not since she was so ill, Mr Hyams, though she used to enjoy getting them out and looking at them... She used to keep them in the bank.'

'Quite right, too, even with all the security you have in this apartment building. Why, even Aunt Rose had the sense to keep her diamonds safe in a bank vault.'

She turns and gives me the straight look so's I think mebbe I'm overdoing the Auntie Rose bit. She hesitates, like she's summing me up.

'Mr Hyams,' she says, all confidential, 'you seem a young man that knows about these things... Would a bank tell someone—someone who had an interest, not just anybody—would a bank say to that person whether things that had been deposited were still there? Those lawyers of Mrs Probert's, they keep putting me off...'

So she's worried about the rubies. She's wondering if there's been a hitch.

I got to play this real careful, so all I say is:

'A name I have for lawyers, Mrs Hermanos! If they're not shysters, they're tight as ticks. Tell you nothing till they're good and ready. And a bank'll talk to nobody unless you got the authority.' I give her a reassuring pat on the arm. 'Don't you worry, Mrs Hermanos, you'll get your rubies one day if it's what your lady wanted. They can't stop you, not like it's she went and made another will...'

That makes her stare till her little black eyes they seem to pop outa her head.

'Mrs Probert never did that. She'd have told me...'

I do a cover-up act. 'Sorry. Didn't mean to startle you. It's just that with Aunt Rose's estate that's all the lawyers kept on about. Had she made a will nobody knew about with some crummy backstreet attorney... A rare old shemozzle that caused in the family, I can tell you...'

But Mrs Hermanos ain't interested any longer in my relatives. She's shaking her head. 'Muriel did not make another will,' she says. 'She couldn't have. I'd have known.' She snaps her lips tight shut.

I thank her for showing me around, and say I'll be reporting back to Momma and the agency. I'll pay another visit to the apartment again when things are sorted out.

Whether I will or not depends on my instructions, but in the meantime there's things I'm sure of:

1. Mrs Hermanos knows about the will that left the lot to Madison and Horth. She'd accepted Mrs Probert's explanation for it.
2. She knows she was left the rubies in that will.
3. She hasn't got them, and doesn't know where they are, though she's suspicious of everybody.
4. She doesn't know about any other will. The suggestion came as a complete surprise to her.

5.   Something happened between her and José
     before Mrs Probert's death that makes her mis-
     trust him. She doesn't want to talk about it.

Bernard Shulman's last report was brief and at first sight it
didn't look as if it would give much scope for his distinctive
style.

*Report by Bernard Shulman. July 18-20*
I'd put the word out on José Hermanos around my Spanish-American contacts on the lower rungs of the Upper East
side café society, the cooks, dishwashers and waiters who
serve our ravening hordes of mobile eaters.

Kemp grinned; he'd underestimated Bernie. Perhaps the
man was taking a course in creative writing.
   He read on.

JOSÉ HERMANOS IS just one more Hispanic among many
but he's new to the neighbourhood so there's plenty of talk.
Rumour is he's come from Vegas, though he's never said.
Now he's picked up a broad and married her. She's supposed to be well over his age and no knock-out so there must
be money in it. Then he's not seen around for a while, some
say he's been reformed by a good woman, others that he's
been on vacation in the State Penitentiary.
   Opinion favours jail, and it wouldn't have been the first
time.
   I get this from Fernando Sanchez who runs the Esper-
anza Restaurant.
   'Sure I knew he'd been inside. But José was a smart
worker, never gave me no trouble. He's here a few weeks
then he spots this broad, one of our lunch-time regulars.
She'd been coming on and off about a month, I guess. They
get friendly and he starts taking her out.' Sanchez shrugs.
'No skin off my back what my waiters get up to so long as

they don't con me... Bit surprised, though, when he comes and says he's outta here for a better job.'

One of the staff who knew José also described him as smart. 'Been around, I reckon, back there in Vegas. Knew the rackets but kept his mouth shut. I'd say he's got a nasty temper, though he acted smooth.'

'Who'd he hang around with?'

'Nobody around here... Kept himself to himself. Just as if he thought he's better than us... Talked about movin' into the big time... Well, who doesn't? It's hope that keeps us goin'... You know what I think?'

I signal I can't hardly wait.

'I think José's an errand boy. Like he's workin' for someone, and it ain't Sanchez. He's a sharp dresser, is José, and you can't be that on the money we get...'

Hermanos may be every bit as smart as they say but he hadn't been smart enough to avoid the cops in Las Vegas, which gives me my cue.

I'm not usually given the red carpet by the New York Police Department but this time I gets in to see Detective Dan Rice at the precinct station by merely producing my calling card. I should be so lucky—someone up the line must have influence.

I even get to see the file on José Hermanos, and it's a beaut. He's been put away three times, two for robbery and extortion, one for embezzlement. All the incidents took place in Vegas, the last was five years ago.

'This record's from Vegas,' I says.

'I know that,' says Detective Rice, who tries to stare me down. 'We sent for it.' He doesn't say why.

'And his name's not on the blotter of any precinct in the city?'

'So far he's clean, but there's always hope... We're keeping an eye on José Hermanos, Mr Shulman, no sense in duplicating the job, eh?'

I can take a hint. Seems I'm off this one. I hands the file back after taking a closer look. When Hermanos came before the court on that last embezzlement charge the bail money was put up by one Clive Horth.

BY NOW Bernie Shulman was running out of steam. There was only a brief note on the next page:

Called the St Theresa's Nursing Agency again. Told that Nurse Smith who attended the late Mrs Probert is still not available. They thought it was some family illness took her out of town. I gets her home address from their register, and follows it up. It's a two-room apartment down in Flatbush, Brooklyn, but when I go there the place is shut and no one's home. Neighbours say various things: she's away on another case, she's gone to nurse her sick mother, or she's on vacation. Don't know whether it's worth following this one up. Seems like a long shot.

KEMP TURNED OVER Eikenberg & Lazard's slip which accompanied the reports. On the back Dale Van Gryson had written:

*The Smith woman was vouched for by Dr Seifel and the Nursing Agency which is a highly respected outfit employing only persons of good character. See no reason for further inquiries in that direction.*

In a further note Van Gryson advised that if Kemp should have any comments to make on the investigator's reports he might contact him at his private address in Long Island, which he gave, rather than at the New York office.

Obviously the matter was still to be kept under wraps.

# FIVE

LENNOX KEMP HAD the whole weekend in which to digest the reports from New York, and indeed by late Sunday night he did feel he'd been on some new kind of diet—full of meat, not all of it wholesome.

Normally he did not like receiving material at second hand, preferring to watch people as they spoke, noting the shifting of their eyes, the movements of their hands, listening to the small prevarications or changes in emphasis, the patterns of speech that are used to hide, to deceive, to impress. Words on paper could never convey the subtle nuances which lurk behind all conversations, but words on paper were all he had.

Nevertheless he was eventually able to note down certain things to his own satisfaction, and come up with what, to him, seemed a plausible working hypothesis.

From the accounts he had heard and read he accepted some facts as incontrovertible:

Muriel Probert had cancer, and she died as the result of the disease. She had made the first will to put things right between herself and her late husband's business partners. That Van Gryson deduced a different reason for her decision from the one given by Florence Hermanos didn't alter the fact that the will in 1987 was made by Muriel of her own volition and without undue influence. It was executed in the presence of her trustees and subsequent executors. Perhaps Muriel had not wished to give them details of any more personal relationships she'd had with Madison. Mrs Hermanos's version only strengthened the view that the casino operator might have turned nasty—as a rejected suitor he might well have done.

That the second will had been made Kemp also accepted as fact. No matter that it caused embarrassment to Eikenberg & Lazard, their Miss Janvier had indeed drawn up a proper will two weeks before Muriel died, and it had been executed and attested in the correct form.

Between these facts lay unknown territory, wide open to surmise and the hazards of speculation. Muriel had evidently changed her mind; what prompted that change, what made her act in the covert way she did could only be adduced by a careful analysis of the events leading up to it. Muriel was dead; the trend of her thought could only be imagined.

Kemp tried another tack.

According to Van Gryson, Messrs Madison and Horth had been told by Muriel that she was seriously ill, she had been given two years at the most to live, and she had left them the whole casino empire in her will. In the meantime they were to continue to run the enterprises.

Kemp put himself in her shoes—shoes he devoutly hoped he'd never have to wear.

Would men like them let Muriel go off to New York and out of their sight, even if they did believe in the inevitability of her early death, without taking some precaution to guard their inheritance? Not on your life. What if a dark stranger should cross her path? It's not only in sentimental films that marriage vows are exchanged from hospital beds . . . What if the doctors found that miracle cure every researcher in the world was seeking? What if she recovered and some old flame came loping back with ideas about her fortune? No, Madison and Horth were in the gambling business but that didn't mean they were chancers. They'd cover themselves against every eventuality by their own cast-iron insurance policy.

They'd put a man in.

It had to be José Hermanos. Already he'd a link with Horth; it was Clive Horth who'd put up his bail money. And José was just the kind the casino operators would choose, an ex-con, he'd ask no questions, he'd do whatever they wanted of him. And it had been easy. José was smooth, handsome and a fast worker. It hadn't taken him long to infiltrate the household by marrying Florence Bate. The question was: had she too been suborned? Kemp left that to one side for the moment.

When she had first come to New York Muriel was still seeing old friends from Vegas. They would have reported back the whole sad saga of the unsuccessful operations, the worsening of her condition. When even these friends dropped away and she began to spend more and more time in the apartment, the need had arisen for a closer watch to be kept on her. How better than through a member of the household, the living-in butler-cum-handyman?

The arrangement worked well for Madison and Horth. With their man's position secure they would have instructed him to report visitors, and to keep a special eye open on any lawyers or men of business who might have influence over her. He would also be free to scout around the apartment in Mrs Probert's absence to scrutinize all her correspondence and personal papers. At these times, either with or without the connivance of his wife, he would even have access to the bedroom.

But in the month before Muriel's death something had gone wrong...

To put himself in Muriel's place required a greater power of empathy than Kemp thought he possessed. Yet he tried. After all, he had known her once, and, though it was a long time ago he hadn't quite forgotten.

Coming to terms with her illness must have been hard for her. She had never, when he knew her, faced up to reality, never been content with things as they were. For her the grass was always greener in the next field...

But she had a stubborn side, a childlike faith that all would go well if she stuck to her own aims, such shallow aspirations as they had been then—to be richer, to have lovely clothes, to live in luxury. Yet somehow she had got exactly what she wanted, that small gritty pebble of selfishness carried her forward. Even her suicide attempt she'd bungled as if something within her would not let her go...

Perhaps she felt it was Nemesis when they gave her only two years more to live. The old Muriel would have rushed off on a world cruise, gone on a spending spree for her beloved silks and velvets... But this was a different woman, one already weakened by the disease, and she would do exactly what her medical advisers told her, accept whatever treatment they offered, not because there was hope in it but because they were the experts.

Feeling himself closer to her now, Kemp realized that the loss of her beauty would devastate her, so much so that other things would seem trivial. It would be like her to want to clear the decks before facing the worst. She used to say she hated her mind getting cluttered up. (In the old days she'd cluttered it with very little.) Settling affairs with her late husband's partners would be part of that clearance. Once done she wouldn't give it another thought, it was in the hands of her legal advisers.

Then Muriel had had a jolt.

Kemp looked at what had been said by the chauffeur, Frank Miner. Muriel had always got on well with such people. For all her love of high society, she'd never been snobby; anyone who'd ever worked for her and been pleasant was her friend. He'd said she'd never been bitter but that day, the day she'd asked him to stop at the lawyers, she'd been angry... It took a lot to make Muriel angry, Kemp remembered. She was not a deep thinker, she had no social conscience, she was, if anything, phlegmatic about injustice, poverty and deprivation—the things that, in their circles at the time, roused others to invective.

No, whatever had happened to make her angry had been of a personal nature. She had spoken of ingratitude, of betrayal... These would not be words normally used by someone like Muriel. She had been hurt, and badly hurt. She had been let down. Muriel had always made a great fuss when anyone let her down even over the smallest thing like a friend's failure to come to one of her dinner-parties or keep an appointment to go shopping. It was generally her women friends who bore the brunt, she had a more tolerant attitude to men. It was all part of her vanity, she was egocentric to a degree; sensing a snub where none was intended and resentful of an imagined injury, she could not let the matter lie until she had made the offender suffer in return.

Her petty revenges would be swift and sure. Then, having, as it were, got it out of her system, Muriel would relent and expect sweet harmony to follow.

Remembering all this now, Kemp could see what had possibly happened. The only person who had remained close to Muriel in those last months was Florence Hermanos. She had put her trust in Florence, and somehow that trust had been shattered. Kemp went back in the reports to what Leonie had overheard, Mrs Probert asking angrily if it was true about José. Of course it might have been she'd found out that he had a prison record but Kemp did not think that Muriel, after all her years in Vegas, would worry too much about that, particularly if Florence had vouched for him.

No, it was something else, something far more serious. She must have begun to suspect the truth, that José was tied in with Madison and Horth. If that was it, then her mind would leap to only one conclusion. Florence too had been under their thumb. The woman she had taken into her house, the woman she had treated as a confidante, was in league with the casino operators, keeping a watch on everything Muriel said or did.

It could have happened so easily. Leonie said there were rows, José shouted a lot around the apartment; he was probably one of those men who think that invalids, like the elderly, are stone deaf.

For all her lightness of character Muriel had never been a fool. Life in a gambling society, even at a level high above the drifters and grifters who swarmed in the streets of Las Vegas, would have sharpened rather than blunted her wits. If she had overheard just one snatch of conversation between José and Florence, recognized just one name casually uttered, Muriel would have been alerted to what was going on.

And she would have acted swiftly in the same way she used to, without hesitation or proper thought, her only instinct to hurt in return those she suspected of conspiring against her.

Muriel had made that second will out of nothing but spite: Florence Hermanos had let her down, so Florence wouldn't get the rubies; Madison and Horth had intruded upon her privacy so they wouldn't get their casinos. It was as simple as that. Kemp couldn't stop himself smiling; Muriel had remained the Muriel he had known, right to the end.

# SIX

KEMP REALIZED that arriving at a theory of why the second will was made did not help to solve the mystery of where it had got to, whether it was still extant or had gone up in smoke.

He shuffled the reports together, and went out for a walk.

The streets of Newtown were not at all like those in Manhattan but he supposed the people hurrying off to see Hertfordshire take the field against Essex or chivvying their toddlers round the shops would have much the same hopes and aspirations, be burdened by the same woes and worries as the joggers in Central Park or the window-gazers on Fifth Avenue.

As that line of thought only took him into a cul-de-sac of banality, he switched his mind back to the city they called the Big Apple. He must sometime look up where it got that name from, for it seemed to him vastly inappropriate. Apples should be fragrant and sweet and from what he'd heard New York was neither. However, he did allow that once you got the taste of it in your teeth you'd want another bite and something in those reports of Bernie Shulman's had given him the flavour of it.

He was thinking now that he would like to take a long, cool look at Florence Hermanos from a distance of no more say than the breadth of a desktop. As this was not possible he would have to see her through Bernie's eyes.

Van Gryson thought her a nice woman. Further questioning had merely produced the information that she was nicely-spoken, quiet and polite. As Van Gryson came from Boston—where it seemed gentlemen were still gentlemen—

these somewhat negative qualities sufficed in his view to make her a nice woman. Van Gryson might be a hot shot as a corporation lawyer but Kemp suspected his knowledge of women of another sort was minimal. His wife too was a Bostonian.

Bernie Shulman had also mentioned Mrs Hermanos's speaking voice. Educated, he'd said, then with a shrewd stab, 'probably self-educated'. Any voice in America which sounded even remotely English would be termed educated. Florence was half-English and she had been with Muriel a long time; accents tend to rub off.

The account of herself she'd given to Bernie tallied with the known facts. She had shied away from the subject of José, surprisingly for a bride of some eight months who might still be expected to be in a state of rapture. Lovey-dovey, they'd been at first, said Leonie, but not lately. Florence must have found something out about him which was not pleasing to her. Maybe that he worked for Madison?

Whatever it was, Florence had ceased to trust him. Muriel too had talked about trust on that last ride with Frank Miner. It didn't sound as if she was talking about José Hermanos. He was a relative newcomer into her life, hardly the kind to engage her deeper feelings... No, the person she was bitter about, the ingrate who had betrayed her trust, had to be Florence.

But, whatever Muriel might have thought in a surge of spiteful temper, it did not necessarily follow that Florence was also in cahoots with the casino operators. Kemp was certain that she had not been when she was picked up by José in the restaurant, she was merely a pigeon to be plucked.

At this point Kemp wondered why he was beginning to think in Bernie's argot, and decided it was an infection, something you caught from reading American thrillers or watching them on television.

For a cure, he went to the cricket match where he knew he would not have to think at all.

BACK HOME THAT NIGHT, after supper, he started to write things down.

At the top of the paper he put the question: Who knew about the second will?

He took the various characters and put them in columns, hoping this small exercise would clear his head.

Julius Eikenberg and Dale Van Gryson did not know until later, although they certainly wished they had.

Miss Janvier knew. He put a query beside her name but only a faint one. She had not known who Mrs Probert was, she did not know of the first will and had nothing to gain by the second. Even if she had been later suborned by Madison and Horth—Kemp had to admit here that he was influenced by Van Gryson's dark hints as to how far gangster methods would go within their legal system—she would keep silent. In any case there was no way she could have entered the apartment and made off with the will. Kemp drew a line through her name.

He didn't list Leonie Rojas at all, even as an accomplice. He accepted Bernie Shulman's account of her at its face value. He did not read her as the kind of material the casino operators would use on a delicate mission such as this. She was only a kid, and she had spilled out to Bernie all too eagerly her impression of the household. Five minutes of her conversation and you would know she wasn't bright and she was indiscreet—a combination certain to wreck any conspiracy.

He wrote down the name of Dr Seifel and looked at it. Certainly the doctor had been about the apartment a lot during Muriel's last days. He had been there the afternoon she returned from her visit to the law firm. Might she not have said to him: 'I've just been and made my will'? He had disclaimed very smoothly any knowledge of such things but

he was a much cleverer man than Mr Orme who had interviewed him and who had been obviously intimidated by the
doctor's superiority. On the other hand, what had Dr Seifel
to gain? There was nothing in it for him under either of the
wills. It also struck Kemp that Dr Seifel was much too busy
a man and too highly paid to allow himself to be used in any
way by the likes of Madison and Horth.

Nor was there any gain for the night nurse, Smith, whom
he had engaged. Yet she too was living in the apartment
during these vital last days, and had been, as it were, in at
the death. She remained as anonymous as her name, and
Kemp would have to wait for Bernie's further report on her.
She was on the register of what was a reputable and highly-
regarded agency which Van Gryson had checked up on at
the same time as he had Dr Seifel. St Theresa's only employed properly trained nurses with impeccable references
and of good standing in their profession. Again, the nurse
did not appear to be the sort of person who could be approached to do sinister work for Madison. She had only arrived on the scene at the last moment; to use her would not
be the way of the men from Vegas who would have had
plenty of time to plan whatever skulduggery they were up to.

Which brought Kemp by logical progression to the name
of José Hermanos, the right man in the right place at the
right time. José had gained entry to the household, he had
a hold on Mrs Probert's maid and only friend, he had the
full run of the place, in Mrs Probert's absence, even of her
personal possessions.

Did he know that a second will had been made?

Kemp took it now as a premise that Muriel had brought
the will home with her in her handbag. If she wanted to
conceal it—for whatever purpose—she might well have
hidden it in her room. Where do women hide things? Under layers of lingerie in a dressing-table drawer, at the back
of a wardrobe full of dresses, in a shoe box, or with other
private papers in a bureau? Kemp struck out the last; the

only desk was in the sitting-room and Leonie said Mrs
Probert no longer went in there after she became so ill. Even
if the will had remained in the handbag that too could be
searched by a creeping José when his employer was in the
bathroom or safely asleep.

It would be easier still if the searching was done by an accomplice and who better than the last name on Kemp's list:
Florence Hermanos.

If Kemp's theory was correct and Muriel had made the
second will in a fit of pique, why did she bring it home? The
answer to that lay also within her very nature. She wanted
to take her full revenge, to face the one who had offended
her with retribution. She wanted to show the document to
Florence and cry: 'See what you've made me do! Now you'll
be sorry...'

That would have been Muriel's way.

At first she would have kept the will hidden, just as she
had disclosed to no one that visit to Eikenbergs. Not that it
would have mattered had they found out; she would merely
have said she was there to check her funds or pay a bill...
She would be waiting, then, for the opportune moment to
confront Florence.

But the cancer had been waiting too, and now took its last
giant stride. She had a relapse, and was overcome by her
weakness. Death had come closer than she had thought, and
all other things were diminished by it, to become as nothing. She would no longer care...

# SEVEN

THE NURSE HAD done well to get rid of so many of the rubies in the first few weeks. It might be seen as a personal triumph but she never thought of it in that way. She had a single-minded purpose, and she stuck to it. Speed was vital. Those lawyers would have been on to it immediately; a list of the items in the suitcase would have been circulated by the police to every jeweller and pawnbroker in the country as stolen goods the moment they were missed. She had some, but not much, respect for the police but she knew from her experience that even juvenile crooks could get away with things because they moved so fast...

So, she travelled. It was what she'd spent most of her life doing, she was good at it, and she knew the routes.

First to Philadelphia where she'd once worked, and where she remembered the name of a dealer who had assessed that old lady's gems for the insurance company. He bought some of the rings and a bracelet when she told him they'd been left to her by her grandmother. He'd quizzed her, though, saying the settings were modern. The family had them re-set, she said, and eventually he took them—perhaps because the price she asked wasn't high. But it was a warning to be more careful in the future.

She took a Greyhound bus to St Louis. There she sold the big necklace, telling the shopkeeper it had been a present from a man whose wife she'd nursed when she was dying. She couldn't possibly wear it, she said, she wasn't the type, and she would prefer the money but she didn't want the man to know she was selling his gift and be offended. The proprietor of the shop had looked her up and down. She knew what he saw: a dowdy woman in a reachmedown coat and serviceable hospital shoes, and he might well be thinking he wouldn't mind her nursing his own mother. Her voice helped, soft and kind of dutiful, a voice that would be soothing to hear around a sickroom. She even managed a titter of gratified surprise at the amount he gave for the necklace...

She never stayed longer than a day in any one place, checking in at cheap downtown lodgings for single nights only, and using a different name each time. Everywhere she went she travelled on public transport, avoiding the airlines. She'd get on bus or train, put her holdall carefully on the seat beside her, take a paperback from her handbag and bury her face in it. She'd dumped her first lot of clothes— the ones hurriedly packed in her Brooklyn apartment—and bought others, equally nondescript, equally suitable, at the cheaper stores. She looked like an ordinary housewife, sale clerk, or worker in a factory. If anyone did get into conversation with her she was on her way to the next town to see her sick mother, an uncle who was dying, a cousin who was having a baby. She neither encouraged nor snubbed such chance acquaintances, she was simply a rather dull fellow-traveller whom no one would ever remember.

She did well in the Mid-West. People there had money; they liked nice things and the dealers knew their market and were not too particular about the source of their wares. Once she had taken the glittering pieces from their satin and velvet nests she burnt the little boxes with their dangerous, well-known names, and wherever she stayed the night she left nothing in the garbage cans. She never haggled over the price she was offered for the jewels, she never repeated the same story.

Coming back East, she kept to the small towns for fear that the list might already be out in the cities, but she still knew where to look in the better districts for the smart jewellers' shops. She was aware of the fact that she presented herself well at these places. The circles in which she had moved—though hardly socially—once she'd taken up private nursing had shown her the virtue of talking refined, and it was as a refined, modest type of woman that she hesitated and stammered through whatever new role she saw fit to use.

A glowing, flamboyant ruby pendant and a pair of matching earrings had been given her by an elderly lady for whom she'd worked as companion-housekeeper. The young shopkeeper had looked at them with some awe.

'She liked extravagant things... She wanted so much for me to have them. But how can I wear them in my position? I'm still in domestic service. And the earrings, well, they're for pierced ears...'

She had seen the doubt in his face, so she fumbled in her bag.

'Look, I've even got the letter she wrote me.'

She showed it to him. It bore a good Boston address, and was signed Anna Cohen.

'*My dear,*' it said, '*you have been such a comfort to me in my illness that I want to give you these jewels as a reward for all your kindness...*'

The letter was, fortunately, undated and Mrs Cohen had been dead for years, but it was genuine enough—which was more than could be said for the jewels mentioned as a reward; they had proved to be paste not diamonds.

As she left the shop, stuffing another fifteen thousand dollars into her bag (she knew the pendant alone was probably worth more than that but she never pushed her luck) she was moved by the thought that perhaps she had now levelled the score with the late Mrs Cohen who had fobbed her off with paste. It had never been her intention to do so; she had only kept such letters out of sentiment, she had never anticipated they would turn out to be so useful.

She would have to take a chance on Chicago but she needed to be in a big city again, one with an airport and the busier the better. When she came out of the Greyhound bus station at noon a strong wind was blowing from the lake. She remembered that wind and the clinic up on the shore where she'd once worked. Buses ran out there to bring the visitors for the patients, and it would be a good place to dump the last bit of evidence, the brown suitcase.

No one took any notice of her on the afternoon bus. The other passengers clattered out and headed for the white buildings of the clinic across the green lawns. She strolled along the lakeside until she came to a deserted spot, and threw the suitcase into the muddy water along with the last of her holdalls. She'd gone through a lot of these on her travels, disposing of them in ditches or canals whenever she bought another. But it was with almost a sense of sadness she watched the brown suitcase wobble and sink; it had been her constant companion these last hectic weeks, it was like losing a friend and she'd never had many of those. All she had now was a big new shoulder-bag she'd bought in a downtown market at her last port of call.

She had booked in at a nondescript hotel on the outskirts of Chicago for two nights under the name of Bethia Bruce, and she hoped fervently it need not be for longer than that for by now she was in a fever to be gone. And it was there the night before she had at last emptied the contents of the suitcase, spreading them out on the faded counterpane. Up till then she had never looked properly at what had lain snug beneath the glorious little boxes. She had deliberately ignored all these envelopes and papers, she had put them right out of her mind, afraid they might deflect her from her chosen course of action.

Not till I get rid of the rubies, she'd told herself, not till I'm rich, and free to go wherever I want. She stifled what conscience she had by recalling Mrs Probert's words, that they were no concern of hers. Indeed she had said they didn't matter any more.

She knew she had taken a risk that morning in Chicago. At the last jeweller's shop the proprietor had been suspicious. He had taken her into his office and kept her waiting. She knew what he was doing, checking lists of stolen property, yet she had sat on, prim in her black clothes, the cloche hat pulled over her hair, dark-stockinged legs tightly together to steady them as she stared down at the black lace-up shoes bought a month ago in St Louis. They had served her well, these shoes, walking long streets, running up station platforms...

She had raised her eyes when the shopkeeper came back smiling, and she knew it was going to be all right. He was pleased to be able to make the purchase of such valuable rubies from this poor widow of an impoverished businessman.

'Josh gave them to me in our good years, but when he died last month there were only debts... I feel obliged to pay them off. I need the money to do that...' Stumbling words, spoken through unshed tears...

Had the man come in frowning, she was ready. She had measured the distance to the other shop door, and she was prepared, once again, to run for it.

But luck—flowing with her for the first time in her life—had held. Only now did she allow that feeling of suppressed panic to rise and spend itself, dissolving as afterthoughts do when the moment of fear has passed.

She had been careful in her tour of the banks, crisscrossing the city to different districts in order to change her accumulated hoard of dollar bills for large denominations more easily carried. Careful too in her choice of a travel agency, picking the most congested with people booking their holidays in the sun... She was surprised to find how easy it all was—once you had money.

Back in her hotel room she opened the last of the boxes. It contained a gold brooch in the shape of a holly-leaf with a cluster of tiny rubies for berries. She was relieved to see there were no markings on it, nor had there been on any of the other pieces. Mr Probert had obviously not been a sentimental man, even at Christmastime, or, more likely, Mrs Probert bought the jewellery herself, indulging her preference for the one gemstone. She took the brooch out of its box, wrapped it in a tissue and put it in her bag. She set light to the box with a match, flushing the charred remains down the toilet as she had done with all the others. It was routine by now and routine was something she had been trained to follow.

Only then did she look once more at the other contents of the suitcase.

She picked up the photographs. One she knew was of a younger, prettier Mrs Probert—there had been a similar photograph in the bedroom of the apartment. Another was of a swarthy middle-aged man, presumably the late Mr Probert. The third was bent at the corners as if it had been carried around for years. It showed a youngish man with hair fluffed up on a high forehead who looked out with cool, amused eyes. The rest were old snapshots in some of which he appeared again, leaning on a tree-trunk in a wood, on the doorstep of a house surrounded by trees. Mrs Probert was in some of them too, a slim girlish figure with light hair against the same background. These must have been taken during the English marriage of which the patient had spoken when she was restless at night.

She could not bring herself to burn them, although she hardly understood what stopped her. Some innate sense of decency told her that to do so would be a kind of sacrilege. Besides, think what she owed to the late Mrs Probert . . .

The rest of the papers weren't of much interest to her, some theatre programmes, some newspaper cuttings about the death of Mr Leo Probert who seemed to have been a person of standing in Las Vegas, and a few receipted bills, including those for the purchase of many of the rubies. She'd already looked at these but hadn't dared use them although they had helped in her estimate of the prices to ask. She'd no scruples about burning the lot.

Which left the stiff official-looking envelope. From its cover she knew it contained a will. She was familiar with wills, indeed had often been called upon to witness them at a death-bed, and she knew that they were of considerable importance—particularly to those who'd crowded round the dying person at the end though they hadn't visited for years. She wondered about this one. Mrs Probert had been clear enough that night when she had said the papers in the suitcase didn't matter any more...

She took it out of its envelope for the first time, and read it through but it meant very little to her because it didn't even mention the rubies. She put it back in its cover, and considered whether she ought to send it to those lawyers whose name was on the envelope. But to mail it from Chicago would still be dangerous, the police could trace things like postmarks...

It can do no harm to wait, she thought. Those lawyers would have a copy anyhow and know what was in the will, and anyway the probate of wills takes a long time. Nursing in the homes of the rich, she'd heard enough complaints from relatives, and listened to many an acrimonious quarrel about the slowness of attorneys... It was scarcely six weeks since Mrs Probert had died, there would be time enough to think about what to do with the will once she herself was safe from pursuit. She tucked the will into her shoulder-bag along with the little brooch. I'll not sell that one, she thought, it's not as good as the others, I'll have it as a keepsake. I've already made a fortune from the rubies. All I have to do now is get away...

She glanced up at the calendar hanging squint from a hook in the stained wall of the hotel room. Tomorrow would be the Fourth of July. My independence day, she thought. No more running around for other people, no more being at everybody's beck and call. I've got my freedom at last. The freedom only money can buy.

# EIGHT

In AUGUST Kemp took a short holiday as the High Court had gone into vacation, and even the Newtown villains seemed to find the weather too hot for criminal activity.

He packed a bag, heavier with books than clothes, and went walking in Suffolk where the scents of summer in the little roads off the beaten track suited his mood of lazy contemplation. He read Henry James and, for balance, a choice selection of American detective fiction, and pondered on the diversities of style. Perhaps the urge to familiarize himself with the two opposite ends of the American scene—even if only through its literature—was an unconscious one—but, for good or ill, he had become linked to both... It might be a long haul from *The Bostonians* to the Eighty-Seventh Precinct (as it was from Dale Van Gryson down in Long Island to Bernie Shulman's flat in the East Village of New York) but people moved to the same old tunes of greed, passion, jealousy and hate...

Kemp felt he had an affinity with Bernie Shulman, for he too had once plied the same trade, knocking on closed doors, prodding at reluctant memories, setting snares for the unwary—a Paul Pry of the back streets... Thinking of Bernie now while sitting at an inn for lunch, Kemp took out the papers he had brought with him and read again that interview with Florence Hermanos.

Unless she was a born actress, a species he discounted for he held the view that even little girls are innocent creatures at birth, Florence came out of it rather well. She had, of course, no reason to doubt Bernie's credentials. He was good at his job despite the variance in his writing skills; Eikenbergs would pay enough to employ only the best in the field.

Florence had talked surprisingly openly to that nice Mr Hyams but Kemp gave credit where it was due; Bernard Shulman had played his role as to the manner born—perhaps his real self was not too distant. He was young—that was evidenced by Leonie's willingness to spill all over a bag of bagels in the Park—he was Jewish and might well have a Momma and Poppa like those he'd adopted as part of his persona, he might even have had an Auntie with cancer and a clutch of diamonds... Exuding warm charm and an honest face, he had broken down the barriers between himself and Mrs Hermanos, who did not take him as other than what he presented.

What emerged from his report was that she was a lonely figure, beset by anxieties. She missed Muriel Probert. Two women who have lived together over the years, even in the relationship of mistress and maid, must have grown companionable. Now Muriel had gone, and Florence was left with no one to talk to, for she saw her husband as untrustworthy. Mr Hyams, the nice young visitor, had shown an interest in her situation, she became drawn to him—so much so that she had spoken of what was uppermost in her mind.

Those damned rubies...

Kemp stared out through the casement window at a tangle of honeysuckle, and thought about Muriel's ruby collection. She had always been a great collector of objects, though it was a far cry from modest porcelain thimbles to gems worth a fortune... But the existence of those rubies— or rather their present non-existence—blew a hole right through any theory that José Hermanos and Florence were in this together.

Florence was relying on the rubies to provide herself and José with the means to achieve her ambition, which was to have a restaurant of their own. But if José was in the pay of Madison and Horth it would be to them he looked for re-

ward. Not that the jewels were of no consequence to him; as
Florence's husband he would share in her good fortune. She
would inherit them under the first will, which also gave his
masters the properties in Vegas.

It looked as if she and José had the same end in view but
that did not necessarily mean they shared the same knowledge, or even that they were acting in concert. Florence had
been flummoxed by the very idea of a second will. She had
been speaking more to convince herself than to her visitor
when she said it wasn't possible for Mrs Probert to have
made one. If she had known of it, or even suspected its existence, her reaction would have been very different.

Here Kemp had to trust Bernie's powers of observation,
and his exact recall of words. As he would have been instructed that this was the crux of the matter he would remember and write down at the earliest opportunity what she
had said. Kemp, when in the same line of work as Bernie,
had learned the value of a verbatim report. Possibly Bernie
had studied Rex Stout's Archie Goodwin in this respect, and
he could not have chosen a better model.

What concerned Florence Hermanos was the whereabouts of the ruby collection. She knew Muriel kept it in the
bank but took it out from time to time. What she did not
appear to know was that Muriel had taken it out not long
before her death. Reading again Frank Miner's account of
that stop at the bank Kemp wondered if this also had been
connected with Muriel's new distrust of her maid. Mr Orme
had not pressed the driver as to the date but it seemed to
have been during the week previous to the visit to Eikenbergs. Perhaps this too was part of Muriel's plan to discomfort Florence, she would flaunt the jewels in her face
along with the new will... Depending on Florence's attitude when she learned she'd been disinherited—grovelling
in repentance or stoutly denying any offence—Muriel might
even then choose to forgive, perhaps throw the rubies at

Florence's feet and make her pick them up... But the scene Muriel might have prepared for never happened...

Whatever had been in her mind when she removed her precious collection from the bank there seemed little doubt that she had concealed it—at least from the eyes of Florence. Muriel had had that tartan rug over her arm when she came out of the bank. She could easily have hidden the jewel case under it until she was in the privacy of her bedroom.

Florence must have taken it for granted that the rubies were safely at the bank when Muriel died. But, despite Eikenbergs' careful hedging, she had begun to have doubts. Leonie found her weeping one day over that Scotch rug... Had the thought just struck her that Muriel had never taken it out with her on those last drives to the clinic despite the cold weather? Had the rug suddenly turned up in some unexpected place while Florence was sorting out the clothes? That might have been enough to set her already anxious mind off in all directions.

And not only Florence's mind...

Kemp's too had taken a leap.

To hold that collection of rubies supposed to be worth a fortune the case must be fairly large. What better place for Muriel to hide the stiff envelope containing the will than in the jewel case already concealed somewhere in the bedroom?

And so, when the will disappeared the rubies went with it. Or, could it have been the other way round?

At this stage Kemp felt as frustrated as the big bumble bee trying desperately to get out of the window and into the honeysuckle. He opened the casement, and solved its problem. His own was more intractable. He had no real information to go on to test his theory, and there were more loose ends to it than there were fronds on that bush.

If he was right about the will being in the jewel-box then Florence Hermanos was not to blame. Muriel had carefully cut her off from knowledge of either. As for José, if he had seen the hidden case during one of his prowls would he have opened it? Muriel had had it out before while José was around, he would know what it held. Was that what he'd meant when he'd shouted at his wife to 'forget the damn jools'—because he knew they were safe enough in the apartment?

That idea just would not do. José was too smart a man not to open up everything... He would have discovered the will, and either destroyed it himself or handed it over to the men from Vegas, who would put a match to it without a second thought. José would probably have left the rubies intact. Or would he? Perhaps he had ideas of his own about them. He'd only latched on to Florence as part of his job, he wouldn't want to be tied to her forever, he'd want younger, prettier women in his life... No need for him to tell Prester John just where he'd found the will, they'd be so god-damned pleased he'd found it at all. He'd have his own insurance policy against future trouble with them if he managed to annex a personal fortune in gems.

Kemp sighed. It was all much too hypothetical, and he had a shrewd suspicion that, under the influence of Suffolk sun and American literature, he was letting ideas run away with logic. What he needed when he got back to Newtown was a long talk with Dale Van Gryson.

THE OPPORTUNITY CAME sooner than he expected. He came home on a Saturday, and late on Sunday evening he was phoned by the American.

'Stop right there, Lennox,' he exclaimed as Kemp began to ask questions, 'stop right there. I've been trying to get hold of you. The whole thing has blown up in our faces. The New York police found the body of Florence Hermanos in the East River... Yeah, Florence Hermanos... Sure, they're going to pick up the husband but that doesn't let us out. No way can we keep the lid on this any longer... Not when we sent our Mr Shulman to see her only a few weeks ago. We've

just gotta come clean on that one, and the rest besides...
The police are going to be round the office like flies.'

'Mrs Hermanos was meant to be a victim,' said Kemp, 'at
least that's my theory. She knew nothing about the second
will—and I've a pretty fair idea why it was made—and she
didn't pinch those rubies. I'm sorry she's dead. I think you
were right, Dale, she was a nice woman.'

But Van Gryson wasn't interested in Kemp's theories right
now. Eikenberg & Lazard were up to their high collars in
trouble, and it was going to take more than shuffling of paper to get them out of it.

'It looks like suicide, Lennox. They generally are from
that locality... Oh, and another thing for your ear alone.
Our friends Madison and Horth are more than impatient,
they're talking of taking us to court if we don't get a move
on with the probate. Julius has had to take the matter of the
second will to the Bar Association under advisement... He'd
no option, we think the men from Las Vegas got wind of it.'

'I'm not surprised,' said Kemp. 'When and if the cops
pick up José Hermanos I bet they find he was working for
your Prester John.'

Van Gryson grunted. 'I've been too damned busy to look
at these reports, Lennox. Now we've got to satisfy the New
York Police Department that we got into this mess by sheer
accident. It's no fault of ours that Florence Hermanos is
dead... We were only following perfectly correct procedure in questioning people about the disappearance of a will
and some jewellery. We never hounded the woman... She
kept phoning our office about her inheritance. That's common enough when people think they're getting something
under a will, and they imagine the executors are stalling...'

'But they were, weren't they?' said Kemp sweetly. 'And I
hope by now there's a list of the stolen gems been circulated... That also must be common practice.'

'Yes, yes,' said Van Gryson hastily, 'we've had the inventory from the bank, and given it to the police...'

About time too, thought Kemp.

'Look, I'll get right back to you, Lennox, when the whole thing's a bit clearer from this end.'

On this hopeful note, spoken none the less in a tone of some disgruntlement, Van Gryson rang off.

# NINE

As KEMP AWAITED further news from New York he felt like an attendant courtier forced to hang about in the antechamber while affairs of state were under discussion in the great hall, unhappily out of earshot. Fortunately he was kept busy enough at this time by his firm's involvement with the people of Newtown: citizens who had been swindled, burgled or struck by moving vehicles, those in the sad process of detaching themselves from partners matrimonial or commercial, those locked in mortal combat with the planning authorities, not to mention those accused of nefarious acts committed when they were tucked up in their innocent beds.

Such matters gave him little time to brood on the fate of Florence Hermanos, or wonder if his ruby necklace too had ended up in the East River along with that poor lady and the rest of the collection. What would he have done with it anyhow if it had come his way? He had at present no woman-friend who might live up to Muriel's hope for him. Indeed for the moment his view of the sex was less than romantic.

In her efforts to find a successor to herself Elvira kept producing a string of pretty girls for his inspection as if he were auditioning for a variety show. Or such was his impression as they had twirled their skirts in and out of his door but Elvira assured him they could all type and use word-processors. So far only suitable temporary secretaries had been installed and it remained to be seen whether any of them would be sufficiently struck by the office colour scheme to deign to stay.

A week or two passed before Kemp heard again from Van
Gryson. This time the letter was on the notepaper of Eikenberg & Lazard so obviously everything was now out in the
open. Kemp skimmed quickly through the letter and put it
on one side. He was more interested in the copy statement
attached, a statement given to Detective Daniel Rice of the
New York Police Department by José Hermanos, and dated
the twenty-second of August:

'I had nothing to do with the death of my wife Florence
Hermanos. I was in Las Vegas at the time getting fixed up
with another job. You can check.' (A stapled memo read:
'Checked out all relative times, substantiated by witnesses.') 'I was never near any place that it happened. I got
a shock when the police told me she was dead. I never
thought she'd do it, but she'd been acting odd. She'd been
upset by the death of the woman we worked for, and about
the things said. She got to thinking people were accusing her
of stealing Mrs Probert's rubies, and other things. There
was a lot of talk going on, and Florence was going out of her
mind with the worry of it all.
    I want to put the record straight about those rubies.
    My wife had worked years for Mrs Probert. They'd be-
come friends. In the month before she died Mrs Probert had
become difficult. She was quarrelsome over little things and
made life very difficult for Florence. My wife had to look
after the invalid night and day until the last week and she
often complained to me that she was worn out and that there
was no way of pleasing her mistress.
    Mrs Probert had told my wife a long time ago that under
her will Florence was to get her rubies, but in that last month
things got bad between them and they had a lot of rows. I'd
hear them quarrelling and Mrs Probert taunting Florence
that she'd a good mind to change that will so that Florence
got nothing. Mrs Probert even got the rubies out of the bank

and showed them to her. Florence told me they were still in their boxes and kept in a little suitcase.

When Mrs Probert got really ill and couldn't hardly move from her bedroom she changed towards Florence. She told my wife she was sorry for how she'd behaved, that Florence was the only friend she had in the world and she wanted things to be all right between them. She said that one day when she had been angry over some little thing she'd gone and made another will cutting Florence out. Florence said Mrs Probert was crying and very upset. They were in the bedroom at the time and Mrs Probert got out an envelope and told my wife it was the will she'd made the day she got angry but now she wasn't angry any more and she was sorry she'd made it. She asked Florence to bring some matches up from the kitchen, and when she brought them Mrs Probert burned the will in front of her. Florence never saw what was in the will, Mrs Probert just said it was a lot of nonsense and she was sorry she'd made it.

But after Mrs Probert's death my wife was never the same. She went around in a kind of daze, hardly speaking even to me. She just said she was being badgered by all kinds of people who were saying things about her and that Mrs Probert's lawyers were suspicious of her, so she told me to say nothing about the will nor about the rubies ever being in the apartment. She got me worried about her state of mind, said she'd do away with herself if I said anything so I kept quiet.

My wife had set her heart on getting those rubies, she'd worked hard for them. If you want to know what I think, I think maybe she thought the lawyers would try to do her out of them, or they'd say she'd stolen them, anything rather than hand them over. So maybe she took them herself when Mrs Probert died, and then felt bad about what she'd done and couldn't go on living with it.'

End of statement. Kemp guessed it had been sanitized out
of the vernacular by the attendant officer to keep things tidy.

He turned to Van Gryson's letter which was neatly
headed: *In the Matter of the Estate of Mrs Muriel Probert*.
Although Kemp was familiar with the necessary practice of
parcelling people up and tying labels on them so that the
judicial process can know where it's going, he still felt a
twinge.

Dear Lennox,

Events have moved as rapidly as our system allows
but hardly in the direction of your beneficial interest,
although, as you have been at pains to indicate to me,
that might not worry you unduly. After consultation,
we were advised to file the second will for probate on
the strength of the copy in our possession with sup-
porting evidence from Miss Janvier and the witnesses.
Counsellors for Messrs Madison and Horth immediately moved to have the first will also produced so that
the whole matter could be taken into what I believe you
English call the Contentious Department. This seems
to us the right and proper place for the action at this
moment in time. Other considerations may of course
arise which would merit the withdrawal of the second
will, leaving the first to stand unopposed. Should the
contest go ahead, however, I am sure you would be the
first to appreciate our invidious position as executors
of the first will and trustees for the late Mrs Probert. As
such, we could not of course continue to act for you,
but we should be pleased to instruct counsel from another firm to appear on your behalf. In these circumstances we would recommend you retain Mr Arnold
Benton of Benton, Benton & Curran to whom I have
already spoken of the matter—in confidence, naturally. He is a lawyer of wide experience in the Surro-

gate's Court where the conflicting claims may finally
have to be decided, should the case get that far.

Oh, come on, man, Kemp thought, this is a right piece of
legalistic flummery you're putting out. As a lawyer himself, he had respect for all process of law but he found some
aspects of it tedious, time-consuming and expensive. Court
cases of an adversarial nature with counsel on either side
scoring points off each other were not to his taste; too often the litigants—and sometimes the facts—tended to get
lost in the rhetoric. He preferred his office practice where he
could at least see his clients and recognize them as human
beings.

He sighed, and took up the letter again. Fortunately Dale
Van Gryson had dropped his tone a little. Even so, it wasn't
exactly chatty.

I only mention the possibility of a withdrawal of the second will because we are on such weak ground as to its existence after Muriel's death. See the attached copy of
statement made to the police by José Hermanos when they
eventually picked him up in Las Vegas. He seems to have
been there all right at the time of his wife's demise. The
medical examiner puts her death at between midnight and
four in the morning of seventeeth August when José was
apparently seen by at least three witnesses (calibre unknown) in a casino in Vegas. She had not been long in the
water and from the autopsy report it could have been suicide, no outward marks of violence, etc... Of course she
could have been pushed to it, and not in the way suggested
by Hermanos's statement; our friends from Vegas have
plenty of other employees(!) besides him, but the police are
satisfied and intend no further action.

I should be glad to know what you make of Hermanos's
statement. The timing of it is, to my mind, important, as is
the death of his wife. We filed for probate three days before that event so the other side were by then aware of the

second will. The police had some trouble finding the husband and you will see they did not get a statement from him till five days later. I have spoken to Detective Rice who was keeping an eye on him for us here in New York and he is in no doubt that José was working for the Las Vegas connection but that, of itself, does not entail any law infringement. I can say no more than that but would welcome your opinion on his statement. If it is true, then we have no case.

It may well be that we will have no option but to suspend the kind of inquiries hitherto being made, no matter how discreetly. I have had a private word with the District Attorney as regards the death of Mrs Hermanos and our previous request for surveillance on her husband. Fortunately the DA is a personal friend of Mr Eikenberg's and understood, at least in part, the delicacy of our position, so there should be no repercussion in the matter of our investigator's visit to the woman prior to her death, nor how that visit was facilitated.

Kemp sat back and tried to listen to the message behind these convoluted sentences with their varied tenses and careful phrasing: all this was to be off the record. The New York lawyers were shying, like frightened horses, from the suggestion that they were in any way implicated in hounding Florence Hermanos to her death.

The letter ended with fulsome expressions of friendly goodwill—rather in the manner of Van Gryson's warm handshake—and a request that should Kemp wish to communicate would he do so to the writer's home address in Long Island rather than to the office on the Upper East Side given in the letter-heading. Despite the writer's personal interest in Kemp's opinion, it seemed that Eikenberg & Lazard wanted to keep their well-shod feet out of the more unsavoury aspects of the case. He couldn't blame them; it was from their executorship of the first will that they would draw their fees.

And the soft clink of coin reverberated through much else in Van Gryson's letter. Kemp didn't suppose the highly-recommended Mr Arnold Benton would come cheap, and the mere thought of a bunch of attorneys gleefully battling the issue out before the New York's Surrogate's Court was enough to raise the hair on the back of his head when he considered the astronomical costs of such an exercise.

Besides, did he really want to run a gambling empire in Las Vegas when he'd trouble enough running a small office in Newtown and couldn't even get a competent secretary? He wasn't sure that, as an alien, he'd be allowed to hold the real estate anyway, never mind the franchises . . . Of course he could always sell out to Madison and company but he didn't relish the idea of having any dealings whatsoever with that lot. He'd heard about the Mob, the Mafia—whatever they called themselves—and they seemed fellows to be avoided at all costs.

He had a good mind to write to Van Gryson there and then waiving all claims on Muriel's estate. It was what the New York lawyers were inveigling for—although they were much too polite to say so in plain terms . . .

He re-read José Hermanos's statement, and was at once caught and held by his own restless curiosity. So much tallied with that theory of his as to why Muriel made the second will, out of sudden temper and capriciousness, and even the reconciliation between the two women, the ritual burning of the will, it all seemed true to character. And yet . . .

It was just too pat. It fitted too easily into a scenario which Madison and Horth might have written for themselves. All right, they had had to admit the existence of a second will—just when they found out could only be speculation—but they would say that will had been destroyed before Muriel died. The witness to the destruction was also dead but she had passed on this vital piece of information to her husband, and that husband was their man. It was neat, maybe too neat.

As to José Hermanos 'putting the record straight' about
the rubies, that sounded to Kemp like absolute rubbish.
Criminals of his acquaintance tended to use just such a
phrase when about to set up one of their wilder deviations
from truth. Hermanos must have seen those jewels in their
boxes at some time or another and knew they were kept in
a small suitcase. Easy enough for him to have nicked them
immediately after Muriel died, and then put the blame on
Florence. As to her being frightened by the lawyers, it had
not seemed that way to Bernie Shulman, confused, yes, but
not frightened. If Bernie had got it right she had not known
the rubies were even in the apartment, she hadn't known
about the second will, and if there was anyone she feared it
was her husband ... And with reason. Her death let him
walk off with the jewellery, at the same time as providing his
employers with a waterproof explanation for the extinction
of the second will. Kemp didn't much like the word 'waterproof' but he couldn't get away from the fact that it was to
certain people's advantage that she'd ended up a floater in
the East River.

Thinking about Florence Hermanos made Kemp depressed. He'd grown fond of the woman, the way one does
when reading about someone in a novel, and now she'd been
cut out before he'd got beyond the first chapter. He didn't
feel in the mood to answer Van Gryson's letter which, with
all those parentheses and conditional clauses, also read like
a novel—one perhaps by Henry James.

# TEN

WHEN ELVIRA CAME into Kemp's office one morning in late September he noticed that her stomach arrived first. It was a timely reminder.

'How is the new girl coming on?' he asked immediately.

'Well, she's the only one of the temps who was interested in staying on, and she's a bit slow,' said Elvira, rather grudgingly, 'but she's all we've got. Those legal agencies in London that I contacted, they only seem able to produce high-class secretaries who wouldn't be seen dead in a place like Newtown...'

'H'm. I suppose we're not exactly the hub of the business world. Pity, though. I rather fancied getting a tall blonde with three A-levels and aspirations to study law. You read about them in the magazines, they wear little black suits and big horn-rimmed specs... I have a yearning for a blonde secretary, I've never had one before.'

'You've never had any kind of secretary before except me,' Elvira reminded him bluntly. 'Actually, Miss Blane's coming along quite nicely, but you mustn't call her a girl, she's the same age as me.'

'Is she the Irish one? I've seen her around the office. Well, I trust your judgement in these things, Elvira. If you think she can do the job I'll give up my idea of a dream-girl.'

'You don't have much choice, Mr Kemp. I'll be leaving in November. Not that I want to, of course, but you can see for yourself how it is...'

Kemp looked at her with the affection born of their long relationship. Her new plumpness suited her, and her ginger

hair shone bright as scrubbed carrots. For all his joking, he
knew he'd never find another like her.

'This Miss Blane, where did she work before coming to
us? Has she any legal experience?'

'Oh yes... That's why I think she might be suitable. She
was with a solicitor in Dublin before coming over to England. Shall I write to him for a reference?'

'No, just give me his name and I'll telephone him. You
know I prefer the personal approach. Well, that's that,
then... Now, what breathtaking appointments have you got
for me today?'

'One you probably won't enjoy. Mrs Brinscombe's coming in at eleven.'

'Not again?' Kemp sighed. 'To expect that access arrangement to work would have been the triumph of hope
over experience. There's been more trouble, has there?'

'She sounded upset when she phoned.' Elvira folded her
lips in the prim way she had when suppressing her own
opinion of a client. Kemp was well aware of the reason this
time; Elvira was inclined to feel sorry for Mrs Brinscombe
and thought the divorced husband was a selfish brute.

It had been a contested custody case and an unpleasant
one, with ill feelings on both sides. Dennis Brinscombe had
money, a thriving business and a bad temper, his wife had
nothing except a yearning for independence and an easy way
with tears. The only thing the Brinscombes ever seemed to
have had in common was Belinda, ten years of age and a
handful.

When Vivienne struck out for independence she'd chosen the wrong man, a young artist who fled at the earliest
opportunity once the custody case was settled. At the time
of the court hearing Kemp had been able to present the
mother as having a settled home, with the prospect of a
second marriage. Now that Fritzie had taken off—along
with some of her furniture and half her bank balance—
Vivienne's situation was bleak. Although she had bought a

small flat with her share from the sale of the matrimonial home, and enrolled herself for a course in design, she was finding the fact of independence a lot less enthralling than the idea of it. She had as yet no self-reliance and, with the ex-husband stalking the background with the loud threats of an appeal against her custody of Belinda, her only refuge was tears.

She had been crying now, Kemp noticed as he faced her, but whereas such weeping might make any other woman pale and wan it only brightened Vivienne's blue eyes and flushed her cheeks rather prettily.

'He kept her the whole weekend, Mr Kemp, right till Monday morning. And he gave her a party on Sunday afternoon without telling me anything about it. He was only supposed to have her on Saturday.'

'What did Belinda think of that?' asked Kemp. Although he didn't like the man, he had to admit Dennis Brinscombe was playing his cards well.

'Of course she loved it—especially as he'd bought her a lot of new clothes that I can't possibly afford. But he should have told me he was going to keep her another day. This is the third time he's done it to me.'

Her wording showed where the real resentment lay, the personal affront.

'I had to phone that house late on Sunday night, I was so worried. All he says is he'll drive her to school in the morning.'

Belinda went to a private school, the fees paid for by Dennis who could well afford them. Belinda in fact was getting the best of both worlds and the arrangement could have worked had it not been for the individual temperaments of the parents. From what Kemp had seen of the child he guessed that these irreconcilable elements warring over her head only echoed like distant thunder. Belinda herself was unaffected by them. She had something of her father's steel in her character but her real love was for Vivienne, whom she tended to treat as someone slightly disabled and in need of succour. That was a good relationship and it would be a pity if Dennis Brinscombe carried out his threat. He had already fought at every stage of the custody proceedings. He had come armed with battalions of nannies and live-in housekeepers, and every detail of his expensive establishment down to the Laura Ashley furniture in the child's bedroom. Belinda was part of his property and as such he was determined to keep her.

When his lawyers lost the case he was outraged and vented his spite on them and the Court itself, but his harshest abuse he reserved for Kemp personally. On the steps outside the courthouse he had stormed:

'I'll get you for this, Kemp. Don't think you can get away with it. You've not heard the last of me. You're all soft soap in there but I know what your little game is. You'll be worming your way into my ex-wife's bed next and then we'll see what those bloody fools in there have to say about her fitness to bring up my daughter.'

Kemp simply turned on his heel and walked away. He had enough experience of thwarted spouses not to be unduly perturbed by this one blowing off steam, and the insinuations were too stupid to be slanderous. Kemp quite liked Vivienne Brinscombe and considered her capable of a wan courage if only she could come out from behind her veil of tears, but he was not in the habit of bedding his female clients no matter how attractive or available.

On the other hand, Dennis Brinscombe had a reputation for resorting to violence that was more than verbal when his interests were at stake. As head of the large, powerful construction company responsible for the large, powerful buildings which crouched along Newtown's skyline like giants at a hunting, he and Kemp had locked horns before. Being on opposing sides in planning matters had already soured their relationship, although that was the inevitable outcome for any lawyer in the town who came up against

Brinscombe's grand design for the future of the landscape. The unsatisfactory case of one of the company's workforce who had come to Kemp with a complaint of physical assault had been more serious. Before charges could be brought the man had melted away—helped, it was said, by further threats to his wellbeing or some compensation for his injuries, possibly both. The construction industry breeds hard types and Dennis Brinscombe was a masterpiece in his class.

Kemp wondered idly if poor Fritzie Neumann had been seen off in similar fashion and as the thought came into his mind he spoke of him to Vivienne.

'I was sorry to hear that Mr Neumann has gone. Is there any chance you can get back some of the stuff he took?'

'Oh, Fritzie...' Mrs Brinscombe dismissed her former lover with a careless shrug—surely a good sign? 'He said he only wanted some bits and pieces for his room. And he'd pay me back the money when his artwork starts to sell.' She looked at that one for a moment as if it was something beyond her horizon. 'You know, Mr Kemp, I've been trying to come to terms with my feelings for Fritzie. Perhaps he was only an excuse for me to leave my husband and all I really wanted was a life of my own...' Her great melting eyes rested briefly on Kemp as if offering him a share in it. 'If Dennis would stop being so beastly mean about the maintenance payments I'd be the one to buy nice things for Belinda. As it is, he's spoiling her and I can't do anything about it.'

To prevent another overflow of tears, Kemp hastily took up the subject of Belinda. 'Your daughter's got a good head on her shoulders, Mrs Brinscombe. She's not going to be spoiled. And do try not to get upset over these access arrangements. There has to be some measure of give and take.'

'With Dennis it's all take.' A hint of vindictiveness crept into her voice. 'But if he just once gives Belinda a smack for

being cheeky, that'll be the end of his little game. She won't
stand for it any more.'

'Is he in the habit of smacking her?' Kemp was startled;
nothing like this had come out in court.

'Dennis had a favourite saying: "I'm not a violent man,
but..." Seems to think that makes him hitting out excus-
able. And it was always Belinda who got the slap. For putting on make-up, giving him cheeky answers and once for
using swear words. I took care to keep out of the way when
Dennis was in a temper, and I made sure it was never me
who upset him...'

Except of course by running off with an impoverished
artist... Kemp was rather amused to be further enlight-
ened about this Niobe of a wife, and he could see how things
had been. Dennis Brinscombe wouldn't lower himself by
striking a weeping woman, that would be beneath his dignity. His daughter on the other hand was a modern schoolgirl, and pert with it. She would stand up to him, and so
become a target for his hand. All the same, the circumstances as related by Vivienne certainly warranted some reaction on the part of any fond father, though actual
chastisement might have been going too far. It confirmed
Kemp's view of Dennis as a man who kept his temper on a
short leash; perhaps Kemp ought to look behind him on
dark nights in the streets of Newtown.

It didn't help either when Vivienne now told him, somewhat archly, that her ex-husband was under the impression
that she and Kemp were having an affair.

'That's absolute nonsense!' he exclaimed, though he
could see that his client was rather taken with the idea.
Having hopped out of the matrimonial cage, she was putting her wing feathers to the test. A flight of fancy indeed,
thought Kemp grimly, and told her so in no uncertain terms
even at the risk of denting her nascent confidence as an attractive freewheeling *sole femme*. He wasn't sure if she got

the message; her sapphire eyes had widened but not with any conviction.

'By how much is Dennis behind with his payments?' he asked, to get the interview back to ground level.

'He's paid nothing into my bank for over a month. It's quite deliberate. He wants to keep me short so that all the presents and treats for Belinda come from him. He thinks that way she'll come round to wanting to live there.'

'No chance,' said Kemp briskly. Belinda was a perceptive child for her years, he was sure she'd cast a cold eye over both her parents and would cleave to the one who needed her more. 'But I'll get a letter off today to Mr Brinscombe's solicitor about the arrears.'

Might as well do it when it's fresh in my mind, he thought, when Vivienne had taken her blinding blue eyes out of his office. He asked Elvira if Miss Blane could take shorthand.

'Of course she can. I know you and your urgent letters. Mary had never seen a word-processor before she came to us but her shorthand's all right. She says Mr Cafferty in Dublin dictated his correspondence in the old-fashioned way, and didn't hold with what he called talking machines. Did you have a word with him?'

Kemp nodded. 'He gave her a good reference, if you can put up with a lot of Irish blarney. Said he knew her family, the Blanes, down in Enniskerry. Thinks she's a great worker, and he'd have kept her on but she wanted to come to England like all the others. He made a little joke about spinsters over thirty in Ireland needing to go abroad, otherwise they're on the shelf.'

Elvira sniffed. 'Mr Cafferty sounds a right old bigot of a man... I bet it's not really like that. Anyway, I don't think our Miss Blane's the marrying kind.'

With this feminine opinion still in his ears Kemp took a closer look than he'd done hitherto at the woman who might possibly be his next secretary as she sat herself down on the other side of his desk, notebook in hand.

Elvira could well be right. Mary Blane was certainly unremarkable in appearance, a rather dumpy woman only saved from downright plainness by soft, dark, wavy hair pulled into a knob at the back of her neck.

She smiled for the first time when Kemp had finished the dictation and asked her if she liked being in Newtown.

'It's faster than Dublin.'

'Is that where you're from?'

'Near enough. Enniskerry's a wee bit to the south.'

'And why did you want to come to England?'

Her smile broadened. 'Mr Cafferty thinks it's because I'd like to be married.'

'And would you, Miss Blane?'

'I would not. Not everyone does, Mr Kemp... Will that be all?'

*Touché*, thought Kemp. He himself hadn't been married for a long time, and the single state didn't seem to have done him any harm. He watched her push the chair back neatly into its place with the unconscious gesture of one used to keeping things tidy in a confined space—perhaps the kitchen of an Irish cottage.

Having netted Mary Blane firmly into her background, he continued to see her against some misty green landscape where the roads ran south from Dublin. With this picture in his mind's eye he could put up with her lack of dexterity on the office machines, accept her slowness, and even come to appreciate her aptness in conversation, the right placing of words, something he tended to believe the Irish had the gift for.

If she was not exactly his dream girl, she was at least pleasant, and the very quietness of her life up till now had given her an air of serenity which might well be a godsend in an office sometimes sorely in need of it.

# ELEVEN

KEMP WAS SURPRISED to receive an airmail letter from Bernie Shulman, addressed to his flat in Newtown. He had thought Bernie would be off the Probert case by now and back to whatever other work there was for young private eyes in the City of New York.

As had happened before, Bernie's thoughts seemed to march with his own, and his query was immediately answered in the man's unique style.

Dear Mr Kemp,

I hope this is OK with you but I don't much like unfinished business. Mr V.G. says he don't need me any more but I guess all it is he don't want the legal side getting its paws dirty. How I got your name, well, I've got a thing going with one of his secretaries, a right doll she is too with china-blue eyes and talks like she's got bells on her teeth, so I gets to take a peek at the file. This is off the record as you lawyers say about things you don't want uttered.

When I do a job I like to keep it neat, loose ends bother me and there's enough loose ends in this one to knit a coupla sweaters.

First, there's Mrs Hermanos going in the river. She never done that on her own, not the woman I saw. She don't strike me as a suicide, and believe me, I've seen plenty. They've a look about them, a look that says they're going nowhere, they can't go back and the road ahead's closed. You can see it in their eyes. They've gone blank with nothing out there worth seeing. Now this Florence Hermanos, she ain't got that look. From what she told me she's never had no easy life. A girl like her growing up in Vegas the way she did, she'd have learnt early that life's no bowl of cherries. Sure, she wanted those rubies real bad but she wasn't the sort to drown herself over them.

What Hermanos says in that statement about her running scared because folks was talking about her, that's a lot of bullshit. Hermanos gave those flatfoot cops just what Prester John Madison wanted him to give them. With all respect to Mr V.G. he's got no idea how the system works out there in Vegas. I've asked a few questions in that quarter and I can tell you Madison and Horth have powerful connections. I'm not saying Leo Probert wasn't squeaky clean but he'd be the one out front, the respectable citizen who owned the real estate, but it's the gambling concessions that really score along with the prostitution, the drugs and any other racket that keeps the shekels rolling. In Britain you got your Royal Family, here I guess we just got the Family, if you get my meaning. Madison was Maderoni before he changed his name for health reasons. What I'm saying is, you gotta watch your back with the connections those two have... My guess is they dumped Florence Hermanos in the river because she'd become an inconvenience, and they wanted to make sure they got their boy out before she squawked.

I'm getting zilch outa Dan Dare—Detective Daniel Rice to you—and don't expect to. The New York Police Department got enough murders and suicides on their hands right now, they're only too happy to close the book on this one. Mebbe they've had their orders, I figure from a different source this time. No one wants anything messing up things in the Surrogate's Court. The hearing's down for some time in October but that's Mr V.G.'s headache not mine.

Kemp took a breather there. Keeping up with Bernie's running style was like accompanying him on a sprint. I bet he goes jogging in the park every morning before breakfast, thought Kemp, who didn't.

He made himself some more coffee, and took up the letter again. Fortunately it was typewritten; he would have hated to have to decipher Bernie's handwriting.

You remember that Miss Smith, the nurse brought in for night duty before Mrs Probert's death? Well, before I was taken off the case I went back to her address in Brooklyn. She's never turned up there again, and the landlord's repossessed the apartment. I talked with him, a big Swede with more houses than brains. Gave him the soft sell—my mamma needed a nurse and Miss Smith'd been recommended. He let me look at the apartment, nothing there 'cept for clothes, including her uniforms, stashed in an old cupboard. Not a scrap of personal paper, nothing to show where she'd gone. Looked to me like she left in a hurry. Talked with neighbours on the landing. Nobody's seen her since May, but they say she often went off like that—she'd be called out to urgent cases.

'But it's three months,' I says, which puts them in a spot.

'She never done that before,' says Mrs Pizzey from next door. 'Miss Smith would come back on her off-days, she'd do her laundry, get fresh uniforms... We'd see her about. Funny, her letting the flat go... She musta moved on.'

'She mighta let me know,' Mr Jorgensen grumbles, 'the rent was only paid to the end of May. I give her another month, then I got an eviction notice. I gotta clear the place now for another tenant.'

The Swede hadn't seen Nurse Smith since she took the apartment over three years ago. He'd never had trouble before about the rent, which was paid from her bank round the corner.

'What was she like?' I asks Mrs Pizzey.

'Quiet... Never one to talk... Never really got to know her.'

'Tall, short? Fair, dark?' I keep plugging away.

Mrs Pizzey's a bit helpless, she's not very bright. She turns to her husband but he's not much help either.

'Blessed if I know. Seemed nice enough to me. Soft-spoken... But kept a close mouth. She was kinda fairish, not exactly a goodlooker, but there was something about her. She was pale, like she was never out in the air enough... Well, I suppose nurses get like that, don't they, working in hospitals and sickrooms.'

I go round the corner to the bank but of course they're tight as clams. What I do get, however, is that Nurse Smith did have an account with them, it's never been closed, and there's a credit balance though they won't say how much.

What I reckon is this: Miss Smith took to her heels not long after leaving Mrs Probert's apartment. She packed up some clothes—the neighbours say she always carried a kinda totebag with her and there's nothing like that left in the apartment though there's an old trunk and a big suitcase, both empty—but not her nursing uniforms just as if she's finished with that profession. She must have money with her since she never come back to clear her bank account, and she never meant to come back to Brooklyn so she wasn't bothered about the rent...

I goes to St Theresa's Nursing Agency once more. No, there's been no word from Miss Smith, and they're a bit huffed so they've taken her off their register. I shakes my head and says how sorry I am to hear it as my Aunt Rose is sick and Miss Smith had been recommended...

'We are sorry, too, Mr Shulman,' says the woman in charge. 'We thought we could always rely on Miss Smith but now she's gone without a word to us. She hasn't even picked up her fees for her last week's work... Nor can I help you at the moment as all our nurses are out on duty.'

There's a babe in reception, though, who's not a nurse and next morning I goes in with a bunch of flowers, and I take her to lunch.

Yes, Karen as she's called, knows most of the agency nurses.

'Including Miss Smith?' I says.

'Madeleine Smith? Well, I don't know her like the others. They're a friendly lot but she never mixes much with them either.'

'That her real name, Madeleine Smith? Madeleine Smith was supposed to have poisoned her lover with arsenic.'

Karen looks startled.

'Oh, I don't think...'

'Skip it,' I says. 'It happened a long time ago. What's she like, your Nurse Smith?'

'Nothing to look at, if that's what you mean. She acts as if she's always on duty even when she's not, and I've never seen her out of uniform. She'll smile occasionally but most times she's stiff as starch. Why the interest? She's not your type, and she's certainly no chicken.'

'I go for older women,' I tells Karen, who's all grown up at twenty and has an engagement ring to prove it. 'But it's her professional status I was asking about. I understand she's a good nurse?'

'Sure. Lots of the doctors ask specially for her. She's an expert on the care of the dying.' Karen shudders. 'I wouldn't want to take that on whatever they pay.'

'I should've thought Nurse Smith was paid rather well. But didn't your lady matron say she never collected her last wages?'

'That's right. She's got a week owing. We just thought she'd trouble at home, her going off like that. But she did tell me once she'd got no folks left, her mother and father were dead. They'd both had cancer and she'd nursed them. That's what started her off on dying cases.'

'Is she from New York?'

'She trained here at Cornell, she's got good qualifications, but I think she was from some backwoods originally. She never talked about it so I guess it was some hick town she'd had to get out of... It's funny, though, her going off like that without her money.'

I broaden the subject and talk about private nurses, how they're around people's houses at times of crisis, like they're not servants but neither are they family. Must be tempting sometimes to take advantage...

'You mean they could blackmail people, or steal things? What line of business you in, Bernie? You've got a very nasty mind... Anyway, none of St Theresa's nurses could get mixed up in anything like that. One black mark and they'd be out on their ear. And the word would get around, they'd never get another job. Stands to reason if they work for us they're only sent to the best class of homes.'

When I'm escorting Karen back to her desk she tells me one other thing.

'You're not the first person come inquiring about Miss Smith. A man came in last week asking for her. Got told the same as you, that she'd left us.'

'Did you see him? What was he like?'

'Sure I saw him. Big and burly. Not like you—and he'd not got an Auntie Rose. Mebbe he's Madeleine's boyfriend, though I never heard she had one. But then she's the secretive sort... And she's older than the rest. I got the impression she only came to nursing lateish... Most go straight from college but I don't think she did—if she ever went to college at all. I'd say she'd knocked about a bit before she began training, did all sorts of other jobs first. I don't want to sound snobby but she wasn't the same class as our other nurses. She'd certainly no sense of how to dress or make the best of herself. It was almost as if she'd come from a background she didn't want anyone to know about...'

'Perhaps she's gone back into it,' said I, giving her my card. 'Will you do me a favour, Karen, and let me know if Nurse Smith turns up at the agency?'

She looks at the card and says she knew all along what I was up to, but she shows me her dimples and promises to ring me. Strikes me she won't have any occasion to do it; my guess is Madeleine Smith won't be coming back.

Looks like I'm not the only one on her trail.

You thinking what I'm thinking, Mr Kemp? Nobody's seen Nurse Smith since she left Mrs Probert's apartment the day that lady died, and the reason for that's plain: she took those rubies and went on the run, covering her traces as she went. No call at the agency, no call at her bank, a quick trip to Brooklyn and then she's off. She could be lying low somewhere, mebbe in her hometown wherever that is, or she could be travelling.

When I was still investigating for Mr V.G. I asks him when that list of the ruby collection got put out. He's never the man for the straight answer, Mr V.G. Guess he's been around courthouses too long to know what a straight answer is. But from what I think I hear him say I gather there was a serious delay. The lawyers got themselves into such a tizzy about the will they never got on to the rubies being gone till they were checking the assets at the bank. That'd be weeks later. It'd be a clear month before they told the police to circulate the list of missing items.

Any day now one of these pieces'll turn up all bright and shiny in some jeweller's shop but the bird that's dropping them, she's already flown the coop. I can't even get a proper description of her. I did ask that Supervisor at St Theresa's if she'd a photograph of Miss Smith. She looked at me as if I'd spat on the carpet and told me with the frost on her lip that this wasn't a dating agency...

What I ask myself is this: should I go on with this investigation? I've been put off the case. Paid off, in fact—and

I'll admit handsomely by Eikenbergs. Mebbe I should be taking my talents elsewhere, though there's no great call for them in the foreseeable future so all I can do is kick my heels in my three-room apartment and reflect that Philip Marlowe had the same problem.

That's unless you want me to go on.

You've got some claim on these missing rubies, and if I'm right that she went off with them then I bet she's got your will as well—and you've certainly got an interest in that.

I guess I'm just plain curious. Also I don't like being screwed-up by a smooth spic bastard like that Hermanos who's getting away with mebbe murder. I kinda liked his wife even though I had to pull a dirty trick on her... I guess I'm not making much sense, Mr Kemp, but what I'm saying is, I'd go on looking for Miss Smith but it's going to cost me. I've a living to make, same as the lawyers. But if you was my client then I'd have the backing. I'd send you proper bills and receipts for the work, and it'd be strictly kosher business... What d'you say? A small retainer into my bank account at Chase Bank on East Houston would give me the right credentials.

The letter was signed Bernie Shulman; Kemp had been right about the name.

Bernie, too, had got it right. Although they had never met, he had picked his man. Kemp grinned to himself. They had a lot in common but the main thing at this moment was insatiable curiosity. Of course he was going to go along with Bernie, he couldn't stop himself—short of taking the next flight to New York and doing the job personally.

He wondered what the going rate was these days for private detectives in the States; it was over twenty years since Lew Archer had been asking a one-hundred-dollar starter, Spencer up in Boston was already getting two hundred a day plus expenses.

The next morning Kemp went into his Newtown bank and arranged to cable five hundred dollars into the account of Mr Bernard Shulman at the address he had been given. Then he wrote to Bernie.

# TWELVE

LENNOX KEMP WOULD have repudiated any suggestion that he had fads, but certain practices arising from his professional work as well as from more private pursuits had resulted in small obsessions that might merit the term. Of course he would not have called them fads, rather he would have said they were merely sensible precautions. One of these was to be meticulously tidy with personal letters and papers.

Most lawyers tend to view with horror their clients' carelessness with the written word. The days may have long gone when letters to and from 'my darling little pumpkin' or what have you were read aloud to an appalled audience during divorce proceedings, but legal advisers can still be dismayed at what people will put down in black and white and then leave around for anyone to read.

Because he had been at first enjoined to secrecy by Dale Van Gryson, Kemp had kept Eikenbergs' letters and reports, and his own notes, out of the office. They were nothing to do with Gillorns, whose filing cabinets in any case were already stuffed full of confidential matters both civil and criminal.

In the flat there was an old desk of his father's which Kemp used for such personal correspondence as he had—and, until the American imbroglio, it hadn't amounted to much. But he was well aware that his flat had never been secure. In the course of at least one of his cases it had been thoroughly gone over by men from a branch of the Intelligence services who knew their business—and by the end of their rummage, his also.

Now that the affair of the two wills would have become public knowledge—at least to anyone interested enough to notice proceedings in the Surrogate's Court in New York—Kemp transferred the papers to the office, where he now corresponded officially with Dale Van Gryson. In the matter of Bernie Shulman, however, Kemp had reservations. It wouldn't do for Dale to know that Kemp was pursuing his own line of inquiry, particularly through Eikenbergs' original investigator. The ethics were questionable, though that was unlikely to deter either his or Bernie's curiosity.

He decided to keep the Shulman stuff and his own theoretical notes either in his pockets or at home, thereby achieving a split between theory and practice as nicely balanced as the whole thing was in his mind.

He entertained no desire to inherit Muriel's share of vast gambling markets but he would like to let the second will be tested in the courts just to see which way the rabbit jumped. He could always agree to withdraw it in a magnanimous gesture at the appropriate moment to the great relief of Messrs Madison and Horth and, he suspected, of Eikenbergs also. In the meantime the procedure could go ahead without any harm to himself.

Or that was what he thought...

He had enough to worry about at present on his own patch. He'd had another run-in with Dennis Brinscombe, or rather with Brinscombe's foreman on one of his building sites. Kemp acted for the previous owner who had complained that the builders were breaching certain conditions entered into when the land was sold. Kemp went out to have a look.

Lea Valley clay being what it was, the terrain resembled the battlefield of Ypres but there were still clear indications that boundary posts had been moved and demarcation lines obliterated by piles of rubble and waterfilled trenches. Whether it was intentional or not, Kemp's client had reason enough for complaint, and Kemp took a polite protest first to the foreman's office.

As it was raining the hut was crowded with hard-hats but he'd no difficulty picking out their leader, a large moon-faced man called Mark Cutler.

'Yeah, I'm foreman here. What d'you want?'

There was hardly room to get in, never mind spread out the plans he'd brought, so Kemp used his elbows to get to the man's desk, and stated his business, remarking in passing that they wouldn't need an audience. Several of the men eyed him sourly as they took themselves and their boots out of the door.

'Just bring it to Mr Brinscombe's attention, will you, before the matter goes any further.' Kemp took a red ballpoint and re-outlined the disputed boundary on the wall-plan behind Cutler's chair. 'Save a lot of unnecessary correspondence between solicitors.'

Cutler was on his feet by now, pawing the ground like an enraged bull. He had cold, blue, aggressive eyes.

'Don't come in here telling me what to do. I know all about you, Kemp, you're a trouble-maker...'

And I could return the compliment, thought Kemp. He suspected Cutler of roughing up the workman who had since left, although no names had been mentioned.

'There'll be no trouble, Mr Cutler, if your men will simply reinstate those boundary posts. That's all I have to say.'

'Get out! I run things around here, and nobody tells me what to do. If you know what's good for you, you'll clear off... Now!'

The only decent path back to where he'd left his car took Kemp close under scaffolding already up for the first building. Picking his way carefully through the mud, he felt something whizz past his ear.

A second later a piece of lead piping splashed into a puddle at his feet.

'Sorry, mate...'

Kemp looked up at the grinning face, and could think of nothing to say by way of rejoinder. Nobody had offered him a hard hat.

Of course it had not been meant to cause him serious injury, except perhaps to his pride. Indeed from the cackle of laughter up aloft, and the sudden withdrawal of the grinning face which disappeared faster than the Cheshire Cat, it was obviously seen as a great joke by somebody. Kemp was not amused. Dennis Brinscombe must have put the word about that there was a grudge to be settled between himself and Lennox Kemp, and who better to ram it home than this bunch of his building buddies?

He was not in the best of moods when he returned to his office and found Mary Blane busy with a duster and a tin of furniture cream.

'What do you think you're up to? The cleaners do that...'

'No, they don't, Mr Kemp. I'll not be giving them the bad word, mind, but they only move the dust about... Anyway, I had a spare minute.'

'Well, you shouldn't have... If you're going to be my secretary, then it's high time you started reading the files instead of dusting them.'

'Whatever you say, Mr Kemp.' She had a voice flat as her shoes but with a lilt to it now and then which lightened its tone. She seemed quite unruffled by his show of temper.

He was annoyed at himself for speaking roughly. Actually, Elvira had reported Mary Blane as gaining in confidence in a sphere to which she was not accustomed, and Elvira was already seeing her as Kemp's future secretary. Kemp had visualized difficulties—taking a somewhat wry view of his female staff who were not above petty jealousy and the bickering that goes with it. It said a lot for Miss Blane that she had been accepted so easily, had slipped into her place without fuss, proving she could deal with the work and also get along with her colleagues.

It's probably because she's an older woman, he thought, and rather plain; to the other secretaries she's no threat, while to the skittish juniors she probably reminds them of their mothers...

'Sorry,' he said, feeling an apology was needed, 'but I've just been on the receiving end of a lump of lead piping, and it irked me.'

'Irked you?' She stared at him, and he noticed that her eyes were the same colour as his own. 'Irked you?' she repeated. 'You mean somebody dropped it on you?'

'Oh, it was on a building site. Could well have been an accident. No cause for alarm.'

'I'm not alarmed, Mr Kemp, it wasn't me they dropped it on. Should you not be more than irked?'

To make light of the matter he went into an inconsequential line of chatter, ending up with telling her that in his business there were often unfriendly people around. 'Life is full of such little hazards, Mary, one learns not to take them too seriously...'

Perhaps in a small town in Ireland one had had to... But Kemp had visited Eire several times and found it a more peaceable place than Newtown. He must remember that Mary Blane had probably lived a quieter life than he had, and was not used to the hostility he sometimes encountered. Thinking of her background now, he spoke of it.

'Have you still got relatives over there?' he said.

'In Enniskerry, you mean? There's not a Blane left in the place. Maybe the life there was too quiet for them.'

He wasn't sure if she meant it as a joke but the way she said it made him smile, and, suddenly, he felt better. He was surprised to hear himself say:

'I hope you will decide to stay with us, Mary. Have you fixed yourself up with somewhere to stay in Newtown?'

'I've a decent flat in a Mrs Beresford's house. I saw it advertised in your local paper when I was with the Agency.'

'Lydia Beresford's an old friend of mine. I always said that house was far too big for her. Of course your salary will be upgraded when Elvira leaves at the end of next month.'

'You mean, I am to have the job?'

'I don't see why not, Mary Blane, if you want it.'

'I do that.' She smiled at him using her name the way he had. 'I never thought to have a chance at it. I've not the experience like your other staff. Mr Cafferty's office was a bit of a backwater, and I've not been one for quick learning.'

'The pace of life in Enniskerry? Well, there's a lot to be said for it, and I'll try not to get impatient. When I'm irritable just yell at me the way Elvira does.'

'Oh, I wouldn't do that, Mr Kemp. I'm not like Mrs Jenkins. I can only be myself, and that's a quiet kind of person.' She gathered up the cleaning materials and stood for a moment with them in her hands, the very picture of domesticity. All she needs is an apron, Kemp was beginning to think, when she forestalled his irritation by saying meekly: 'I'd already done all your tapes before I started cleaning-up. Maybe I'll go now and put my head into your files like you said.'

She walked out, leaving him feeling he had been put nicely in his place.

He had got himself a new secretary, and certainly not the sort he had had in mind... Neither a dolly-bird nor a bright intellectual but a rather frumpish spinster—somehow the word suited her—who wore the wrong length of skirt for low-heeled shoes. Pity about that, her legs weren't bad... He had noticed them casually as she crossed the floor, and been reminded of that Irish melody about the girl who moved through the fair like the swan in the evening... Mary Blane certainly had an unhurried gait as if she had all the time in the world. It would make a change from Elvira's brisk trot.

He wondered why he had thought of that Irish tune—
must be the romantic side of his nature... All the same,
when Mary Blane's nice dark brown hair escaped from that
silly knob on her neck, it did curl up quite attractively...

# THIRTEEN

A FEW DAYS LATER Kemp's flat was burgled—or that was
the way he was told it by Mrs Higgins, his cleaning lady,
when she phoned the office just after eleven.

'You've had the burglars in, Mr Kemp.' She made it sound
like the decorators but Bessie Higgins had been brought up
in London's East End where burglars cut no ice—sometimes they were close relatives..

'Are you all right, Bessie?'

''Course I'm all right. They been and gone. Place'll take
some cleanin' up, I can tell you.'

'I'll be there in fifteen minutes. Don't you touch a thing.'

He called at Newtown Police Station on the way, and
picked up Sergeant Cribbins.

'Save you a journey,' he explained.

'Oh, aye? This ever happened before, Mr Kemp?'

'Once or twice. It's a professional hazard. Some clients
think I take their secrets home to brood over... But I gather
there's been a spate of breaking and entering lately. No offence to Newtown's finest.'

Cribbins nodded. 'The press, they call it an epidemic. You
can say that of the common cold. You got anything of value
at the flat?'

Kemp shrugged. 'Only the meagre home comforts of a
lone bachelor. Sorry, no family silver, no priceless manu-
scripts, and no money except for the ten pound note I lay
out for Bessie. This is one of her days for scouring the place.
They must have been quick off the mark this morning,
though, whoever they are... I leave at nine and she gets in

at eleven when she's done my shopping. But every crook in the district with half an eye must know that by now.'

Bessie was standing by the kitchen sink lapping strong tea from her usual mug. 'Leastways they never chucked food about,' she said. 'Last place they young devils done there was flour all up the walls.'

In the sitting-room the furniture had been upturned, drawers pulled out and paper scattered everywhere. In the bedroom it was the same, clothes torn from hangers, underwear all over the floor.

'A man no longer has any privacy,' murmured Kemp. He made a rapid survey. 'All that seems to have been taken, Sergeant, is a radio and the video.'

'Par for the course,' said Cribbins glumly. 'The telly, it'd be too heavy for them. They gave that old desk a good going-over. How long you had it—since World War One?'

Kemp went over and had a look at his maligned possession. The desk had not been in good health the night before, now it was past caring. Someone had smashed the lock with a heavy blow, splintering the wood—it must have been like using a hammer to open a packet of cigarettes. The contents lay below in sliding little heaps as if each item had been thoroughly fingered before being dropped almost with contempt on to the carpet.

'Just as well I am circumspect in my love-life,' said Kemp, 'and have no cherished correspondence.' By a lightness of tone he tried to ward off his sudden surge of outrage.

'You've been lucky,' the Sergeant observed, 'that's the only bit of real vandalism. Anything missing?'

Kemp shook his head. There had been nothing worth taking, but it had all been read. He saw the Sergeant's point. 'This, and the outside door.'

Sergeant Cribbins had already taken a good look at that.

'Clean job,' he said, 'they just broke open the lock.'

'That's what I seen when I came in,' said Mrs Higgins. 'Didn't need my key, did I? I saw all this mess, and I phoned you, Mr Kemp. You leave my money out on the kitchen table same as usual? Well, that's gone... Young scallywags, that's all they're after, quick cash and stuff they can sell round the corner.'

Sergeant Cribbins seemed to agree with her. He snapped his notebook shut. 'One radio, one video cassette-player, one ten-pound note—not much of a haul but if it's the usual gang of young tearaways they'll reckon it's a fair hour's work. Fingerprints, Mr Kemp? No point... They all wear natty woollen gloves these days, keeps their thieving little hands from getting dirty.'

'You won't find no dirt around this flat,' said Mrs Higgins truculently, 'and if you've quite finished, Sergeant, I've got work to do—and so've you if you want to catch up with them that done this...'

As Kemp gathered his scattered papers together, Bessie grumbled on in the same vein as she followed him round the floor with the vacuum cleaner. Bessie held the somewhat naïve view that as standards of living rose so the crime figures should fall. Although she'd done a bit of shoplifting in her disreputable youth, she was now socially and economically secure in Newtown and therefore on the side of the angels. Like a reformed drunkard inveighing against the evils of alcohol, she had only bad words for streetwise youngsters who considered petty pilfering a way of life in the affluent 'eighties.

'We stole for bread to eat, we did,' she cried now, above the steady hum of the Hoover.

Kemp was amused. He wondered why it was that people who talked like that tended to mix their generations; it was quite possible that Bessie's father had helped himself to the odd loaf in the depressed 'thirties but it would be cosmetics nicked from Woolworths by the time Bessie reached her light-fingered teens.

Anyway, Kemp didn't believe that local youths were responsible for this particular break-in. It had been made to look like their work, the theft of easily-disposable consumer goods, the taking of Bessie's money, the forenoon timing of the visit, all these were supposed to stamp it with their *modus operandi*.

To Kemp the explanation was simple; someone had wanted to take a look at his personal papers, hoping to find . . . well, what?

There was Dennis Brinscombe, a man fuelled by resentment and suspicion, eager to find further cause for complaint. What would he expect to discover—his ex-wife's nightdress under a pillow, torrid love-notes in a desk drawer? It was true that Vivienne Brinscombe had visited Kemp's flat one night when overcome by misery at Fritz's departure, but all she had left were traces of tears, soaked into the sofa cushions. Kemp had told her in no uncertain terms that the visit must not be repeated.

Brinscombe was a powerful man who held his workforce in the hollow of his hand. They were rarely local men. Rumour had it that he had gathered in the remnants of 'the lump'—building workers who went from site to site all over the country, owing allegiance only to the highest payer, and Brinscombe paid over the odds. Such men would not be over-sensitive about breaking the law if the price was right. They could have been told to get something on Kemp just as they had been told to frighten him off the building site. Well, if that was all, thought Kemp grimly, they went away empty-handed; his life was an open book, he didn't even fiddle his income-tax.

The idea that the break-in might be connected with the American case struck a note deeper and colder than any threat from Brinscombe. It opened up possibilities that were, to say the least, unnerving.

Kemp sat down in his armchair with a cup of coffee at his elbow—Bessie's tea was too strong a brew for him—and considered the implications.

If a conservative corporate lawyer like Dale Van Gryson could take seriously the likelihood that strong-arm methods could be used by the gambling promoters to regain their property it was no good brushing it aside just because it was all happening on the far side of the Atlantic.

But surely, he reasoned, not here in England...

He looked out of his high window at the line of roofs smudging the gold October sky, banal, innocent platitudes of some obscure architect.

Not here, in Newtown...

Yet he had Bernie's word also that Madison and Horth were backed by powerful connections, might even be cogs in the giant mechanism which went variously under the name of the Family, the Mafia, the Mob. Kemp shifted uneasily in his seat. He had to admit he had never really considered that network to exist outside of books and films. But of course it did, it was a very potent actuality, particularly in the very fields into which he himself had all unwittingly been drawn.

The next logical step along the way was one Kemp was reluctant even to think of, but it was inevitable. If he really was an object of attention here in England rather than simply a name on court documents in New York then he must be suspected of having something they wanted. No matter that the judgement might go in their favour, Madison and Horth could not safely enter into possession of those properties if the second will was known to still exist, hanging about somewhere, suspended perhaps like Mahomet's coffin in a limbo between heaven and earth. And why should they have believed José Hermanos's statement any more than Bernie did? It would get them off the hook for the moment, strengthen their case in court—and they weren't likely to communicate their doubt to the lawyers—but an undestroyed second will remained a time-bomb liable to blow up in their faces if it ever came to light. Being men of resource—and if their back-up was as rumoured, of infinite resources—they would put ears to the ground to listen for the ticking... And along whatever subterranean channels they operated, one must inexorably lead to the man who would gain most from the ultimate explosion.

I'm making all this up, Kemp told himself sternly, getting to his feet and handing over his cup and saucer to Bessie Higgins. It's time I went back to the office and got on with some real work, or I'll be getting paranoia...

He had known some clients develop this unfortunate state of mind in the course of even the most minor of legal actions. All too easy to imagine everyone against you when you're faced with a bundle of unflattering allegations impugning your character or your bank balance when all you've done is damage your neighbour's fence or run over his dog. A nasty lot of accumulated spite looks bad when it's written down, and sounds even worse when it comes out in court. Win or lose, there's nothing like a lawsuit to bring out the worst in people, and for a time afterwards a certain vulnerability remains.

In the days following the break-in Kemp found himself affected, in a mild form, by the very kind of paranoia he'd noticed in others. Partly it was the result of the unwelcome intrusion into all that he had of private life but, without letting his imagination run too deeply, there was the more unwelcome idea that he might be under scrutiny. He just hoped that if someone was keeping an eye on him they would also keep their distance.

He had put a new lock on the door of the flat but was under no illusion that it would render the premises any safer than they'd been before, and he was relieved that his hands were the first to pick up the envelope from Bernie from the doormat a few days later.

The correspondence from Bernie was growing bulky; either he'd have to find a safe place for it or buy an overcoat with poachers' pockets...

He fortified himself with a drink before opening the envelope; letters from Bernie tended to require a measure of relaxation. This one appeared to have been typed at high speed in a state of considerable excitement, the keys must have hopped across the pages like a frog with tin toes.

Bernie acknowledged Kemp's retainer. It had come in the nick of time as there had been a breakthrough . . .

I suppose you'll hear from Mr V.G. when he gets his wits and words together but it's me for the first shot since I sees more of the action. I gets it on the blower from the china doll at Eikenbergs that some pieces of that ruby collection turned up. A coupla rings and a bracelet goes through the hands of one Amos Zachary in Philadelphia around the end of May. He's got a jeweller's shop on Chestnut, strictly kosher business, which is why he looks real close at stolen property lists—most don't bother—and he spots these items from the description. 'Course he'd sold them before that list got put out but he keeps proper books and the things are on record. A woman brought them in and from what my doll tells me the police think it was Florence Hermanos and mebbe that's the line Mr V.G. takes too, but me, I don't go for it.

I'd been doing some scouting around in Philly anyway— I'll come to that later—so I goes and sees this Mr Zachary. He's an old guy but been in the gem trade long enough to know what's what so he's suspicious at first till I tells him I represents a client who's got an interest in the rubies and he opens up.

'Respectable kind of woman she looked to me. Softspoken, educated accent, thirty or forty years of age, difficult to say since she was dowdily dressed . . . Cheap clothes and shoes . . . Shabby-genteel, as if from a family down on their luck. That fitted her story the items had been her grandmother's . . . I'm rarely taken in, Mr Shulman. I blame myself . . .'

'Fair or dark,' I asks but he shakes his head. She'd a felt hat on, one of those close-fitting kind that's been out of fashion for years.

He tells me he puts her down as someone used to waiting on other people, a patient sort of person, possibly a nurse... I keep on trying to get a description that might fit our nursie but I ain't got much to go on there.

I gives him a full-bosomed lady with little black eyes, as I sees Florence Hermanos in my mind, but he's sure on this one. She was flat-chested under a coat that had seen better days. He never got a real look at her eyes but he reckoned she was kinda fair...

'And a good liar,' he adds. 'I'm not used to being conned. That tale she spun... How she was trying to keep the family together now all their money'd gone and all they had were Grandma's jewels. There was the son they were putting through college and a girl wanting to get married...' He shakes his head, poor old Zachary, she'd sure taken him for a ride.

Of course he'd given what description of her he had to the two cops that come down from the NYPD to interview him but he kinda peers at them with those little eye-glasses he has and they think his sight ain't too good. Me, I know he wouldn't be in business if he was as half-blind as they think. Anyway all they seemed to want from him was that it was a woman in her thirties so they could pin it on Florence Hermanos. That bugs me. A female can pad herself out in the bust department but what she can't do is take away what's there, and Florence was well-stacked.

The entry in this guy Zachary's book shows a date two days after Mrs Probert's death, and that fits the lady we're after. She's smart. She stops for nothing, not her wages, not her bank balance, she's off like the bat that got the hell out, and she starts flogging the jewels before either the cops or the lawyers catch on. I reckon there's rubies scattered like birdshit from here to the Pacific, but if even half the dealers are honest as Amos Zachary I'll run for President... She never asked the big price off him so there's fat profits for all. Strikes me she'd be cautious as a cat in the night—and about as conspicuous.

Which brings me to what I was doing down in Philly. Well, I goes first to the hospital where Karen said Madeleine Smith trained. She did, too. Records show she enrolled about seven years ago, age given as twenty-four, home address Vineland, Pennsylvania. She got her RN, did some time on the wards and left in 1986. She registered with St Theresa's in 1987, so a year's missing. Nobody at the hospital remembered Madeleine Smith, seems she's the kind people forget easy.

So I take a trip to Vineland to check out that address. It's in seedy farmland, old frame houses, broken-down shacks, scrubby fields and vegetable gardens, but the quarter given for the Smith address had been up for urban renewal so the whole place is gone to shopping malls and motels. Ten years, that's the blink of an eye in the demolition business. So I draw a blank. No joy either at the schools, though Madeleine would have needed a high school diploma at the very least to get started in nursing. But Smith's a helluva name to check up on in the records of the schools I visited, even with the approximate dates. There were hundreds of Smith families in the town, and too many M. Smiths went through local education, Marys, Marthas, Mamies and Mays but never a Madeleine. Come to think of it, it's a bit high-sounding for a dump like Vineland which isn't exactly a centre of culture. Mebbe she chose it herself, mebbe she chose the Smith too. I get the feeling this lady's been covering up the whole of her life just the way she's doing now...

If it's true as the tale goes she nursed her parents when they were dying of cancer, then it's likely they died at home, which home has long gone under the wheels of the bulldozers, but I check the hospitals just the same. And get the same no go—far too many Smiths, and I don't even know their Christian names. Local doctors, likewise. I'm up to my ears in Smiths, and mebbe it wasn't even the family name.

But that address in Vineland sticks in my gut. It was real enough ten years ago, the place existed then. She must have come back to it when her folks were ill, and if she'd been brought up there it'd be her background. But not Vineland, there'd be nothing there for a girl already into a profession. She'd go somewhere bigger, and the nearest is Philadelphia, so I try the City of Brotherly Love, and have my first stroke of luck.

I go the round of the nursing agencies and at the third I hit the jackpot. Mrs Brunner who runs it has been there twelve years. She's an amiable person, which helps. I spin the story that a Madeleine Smith once nursed my aunt years ago in this city, now my aunt's died in New York and left the nurse a keepsake.

'Funny,' she says straight out, 'Madeleine was often being left things. Nothing of value, you understand, just bits and pieces... I guess you could say she had a way with her.'

So we gets talking and I learn a few things. Madeleine Smith was on her register for six months in 1986. She was fully trained, and a good nurse, quiet and well-spoken, according to Rachel Brunner, so she got sent to the best families.

'She was never impressed, though,' says Mrs Brunner, 'like some girls are... There was a hard streak in Madeleine, almost as if she judged people by a standard of her own. I never got to know her well, she was always somehow on guard, but I was sorry to lose her.'

'She didn't stay?'

'She only came because she needed the money. She was quite blatant about that. She'd had to nurse her mother at home, and the family was poor. Then she looked after her father when he was dying and it's my opinion it was only Madeleine's earnings kept the home together. Not that it was much of a home.' Mrs Brunner gives a shudder. 'Have you seen that place they lived in out in Vineland? A pig-sty it was... The father was a drunk...'

'The place is all gone. Was Smith really their name?'

'She called herself Smith. It was on her certificates. She never talked about her family and I respected her reticence. I think she'd a hard life, Mr Shulman... When her mother died there was a tribe of little ones left, and the father was a no-good layabout. I think Madeleine took responsibility for them all...'

I says mebbe that explains why she lived so poorly in Brooklyn despite the private nursing. Mebbe she was still keeping that family back home.

Mrs Brunner kind of sniffs. 'They were trash from what I hear. Always in trouble, in and out of the juvenile court. If she was saddled with them she'd have her hands full.'

At last I get a physical description though it's hardly startling.

Madeleine Smith's middle-sized and as Rachel Brunner never saw her out of uniform what sort of figure she has remains a mystery. Though nurses don't wear caps any more, Madeleine stuck to the old-fashioned ways and pushed her hair up underneath so that even its colour was uncertain. 'She's got a light complexion so I'd go for fair,' says Mrs Brunner, 'and she's got a mouth that's wide when she smiles—which wasn't often when I knew her.'

It's nothing much to go on. This kind of woman's not going to stick out in a crowd. There's millions just like her.

She'd left the agency in a hurry. Seems to be a habit with her. She just phoned in one day and said she'd not be back. Rachel Brunner's a bit hurt.

'I quite liked her,' she tells me, 'but she never let you know much about herself. She made no friends among the other nurses so it's no good you asking them. She was a solitary person, very self-sufficient.'

'No men friends?'

Mrs Brunner shakes her head. 'It was almost as if she hadn't got time for anything like that. As if she was waiting for something to happen...and it wasn't marriage. I'm sorry I can't help you, Mr Shulman, but I've not heard from Madeleine since that phone call. But it's odd you should ask about her now. There was a man called about a week ago to know if I had a Madeleine Smith on my register. Of course I didn't talk to him the way I've talked to you. He was brusque in his manner, so I just told him no, I didn't have a Miss Smith on my books.'

Looks like my nice nature paid off again. Mebbe I oughta develop it ... Anyway, I thanks her as if she's my own kin. She's given me the first real light on this Madeleine Smith character. I guess I was starting to think she never existed.

What worries me is I'm not the only one looking for her. Those hotshot supremos from Vegas they don't buy that story of Hermanos about his wife mebbe taking the rubies, and they'd have cottoned on to the nurse before we did—a crook can smell one of their own kind through a wall. So they've gotten a head start on me, and they got the means to trail somebody a lot faster. Me, I've got to operate legit, they ain't so particular. And they don't give a damn whether she's got any leftover rubies, they'll figure when she took them she took the suitcase as well, and the will was in it. So mebbe she tore it up but she's had a sight of it, and that's enough to make her a dead duck as far as these hombres are concerned. You get what I'm saying here? When they catch up with Madeleine they're gonna kill her. She's witness to the fact the will existed after Mrs Probert was dead, and if I'm right about the guys that's after her she's got as much chance as if she rode through Dallas in an open car...

Kemp put down the letter at that point; Bernie's mordant humour could sometimes strike like a blow between the eyes.

He went into the kitchen and fiddled about for an hour or so making supper to give himself time to recover. It was in the end a good supper since a lot of care had gone into its preparation while Kemp whistled through his teeth and thought about the contents of Bernie's letter. It had made quite enjoyable reading until the last part.

He returned to it when he was eating his pear but there were no further startling revelations in the final paragraph, just an assurance that Bernie would keep up the good work and be in touch. Keeping up the good work seemed to mean Bernie combing every city in the United States for this eponymous female who called herself Madeleine Smith, rattling off his report on the typewriter at his East Village apartment, and presumably finding time in between for meaningful relationships with Karen of the agency or the china doll at Eikenbergs—probably both.

What a slow life I lead compared to his, thought Kemp, not without envy, what a slouch I have become . . .

For there had been a time when he too had followed the mole's way, probing at mysteries beneath the Sunday calm of suburban streets, pushing an inquisitive snout into litter-bins of discarded secrets, rooting about in the dry wreckage of other people's lives for the specks they would prefer hidden. It had been a sleazy way to earn a living but Kemp still had the flavour of it in his mouth, and could stretch out the hand of fellowship to his American colleague.

IT WAS ANOTHER AMERICAN, however, who brought him to the telephone just before midnight. As Kemp said: 'Hullo, Dale . . .' he glanced at his watch. The day's business would have ended for Van Gryson and he would be home in the quiet presence of his Bostonian wife out on Long Island. Kemp pictured her as a large, spoon-shaped lady in a high-necked velvet dress but perhaps he was being influenced by Henry James again . . .

'There's been a development, Lennox.'

'Oh yes?'

To Kemp it was a twice-told tale though Van Gryson's version lacked entertainment value. There was one additional piece of information.

'...and before I left the office this afternoon the Police Department told me they'd had a call from St Louis. Local senator bought a ruby necklace for his wife. Now she's a lady who knows her gemstones. She says the thing was set by a well-known jeweller in New York so she packs her husband right back to the shop to get its provenance. The shopman plays dumb of course...but when he's shown it's a listed item he comes clean.'

'Are we talking about my necklace?'

'Hell's bells, Lennox, I can't say who the damned thing belongs to at this moment in time...'

'It's mine under both wills, Dale,' said Kemp reasonably. 'Whether it passed as stolen property or not doesn't alter the ownership...'

'A lot of money changed hands, Lennox. The senator is one very angry man, I can tell you.'

'He'll get his money back. The shopkeeper should have been more careful but he's probably got insurance against fraud. I suppose my necklace is in the hands of the police in St Louis... Well, it's better than at the bottom of the East River. Was it the same woman as in Philadelphia?'

'Hard to say from the bare description. Could've been a series of accomplices getting rid of the stuff. And it was done real fast—within a few weeks of Mrs Probert's death.'

'Someone on the run. You're not still thinking it was Florence Hermanos?'

'Who else knew about the damned rubies? My guess is the Hermanos were in this thing together, with the backing of Prester John Madison... She got frightened at what she'd done and took a jump. Her husband's been selling the jewellery bit by bit and making a small fortune out of it. That seems to me a perfectly logical assumption. You got any other ideas?'

'Plenty, but I'll keep them to myself for now. Any advance on the legal battlefield?'

'In view of the discoveries concerning some of the missing assets from Mrs Probert's estate your counsellor, Mr Benton, has moved for a continuance—an adjournment I think you call it—for a month in order to make further inquiries.'

'In the hope the second will turns up wrapped round some more rubies?'

'Now, now, Lennox, you're getting sarcastic...' Van Gryson's tone was admonitory.

'Sorry. Thank Mr Arnold Benton on my behalf and tell him that now I know my necklace is safe I'll probably be able to meet his fees.'

Dale's laugh was delayed, and not altogether hearty. However, he assured Kemp that his interests would be taken care of in the Surrogate's Court and he would be kept informed of further developments.

In the meantime—as if to show that he had at least done his homework—he confirmed that the procedure in a contested matter over there would not differ greatly from the same action under the English legal system. He pointed out that under the New York Surrogate's Court Procedure Act, Section 1407, a lost will may be admitted to probate if the execution thereof were proved in the same way as an existing will, and if all the provisions in it were clearly and distinctly proved—New York law was more stringent in this proviso than other states—and if it could be established that the will had not been revoked.

'And that's where we're left still up a gum tree,' Kemp responded succinctly. 'The copy will would answer the other conditions without any trouble...'

'Counsellor Benton agrees with you. That's why he's asked the Court for more time. But I can tell you right now,

Lennox, the gentlemen from Las Vegas are foaming at the mouth. The matter is creating a very nasty atmosphere in our office...'

In Van Gryson's good night, goodbye, Kemp detected a certain frostiness. Perhaps winter had set in early over there on Long Island. Eikenberg & Lazard would be a lot happier if I dropped the case, he thought. They don't mind a straight civil suit when both sides have ample means and their costs are secure, win or lose, but the merest hint of criminal skulduggery has them running for cover. They're scared stiff of Prester John and his hoodlums because of their well-funded connections, and they would be glad if that aspect went quietly away. They want to see the Probert estate settled and put to bed so that they can get on with clean living, Government contracts and other more salubrious matters like multi-million-dollar anti-trust litigation...

When he put the phone down Kemp wondered why he had not mentioned Madeleine Smith, or told the New York lawyer that he had begun an investigation of his own. Somehow he knew Van Gryson would be displeased... But it was not only that: Eikenbergs were custodians and executors of the first will. They owed a duty to divulge information to the beneficiaries under that will no matter what their opinion of the said beneficiaries might be. Kemp had been shaken by Bernie Shulman's blunt view of Madeleine Smith's chances should Madison and Horth catch up with her.

There had always been in Kemp's nature a tendency to sympathize with the underdog against whatever forces of society were ranged against it. It might seem ludicrous now to retain such feeling for this woman who had stolen and was on the run... Yet he could not help himself indulging in a reluctant admiration for her.

He would be glad to get a good night's sleep. Re-reading Bernie's letter made it seem like a very long day.

# FOURTEEN

IF IT HAD SEEMED a long day it was certainly a short night for Lennox Kemp. The telephone wakened him at half past six.

'John Upshire here. Sorry, Lennox, but it's time you were up.'

'What the hell...' Inspector Upshire at this hour of the morning!

'Your office premises in the Square have been broken into. Reported by the constable on the beat ten minutes ago. As it's you, I thought I'd go round there myself.'

Personal attention from the Inspector was a compliment to their friendship but did nothing for Kemp's morale—never very high early in the day. He threw on some clothes, and arrived at his premises just after seven o'clock.

He found Upshire and a constable standing in the reception hall which looked as if it had been struck by a snowstorm, papers lying everywhere, chairs and tables upturned.

'The station tells me they did your flat a few days ago,' the Inspector observed laconically. 'You been making yourself more unpopular than usual?'

'Just give me the details,' said Kemp tersely.

The constable obliged. He had been going past on his regular beat when he noticed that the lock on the outside door of Gillorns looked insecure. That was an understatement; it had been well and truly smashed. The constable had entered, taken one quick look round, and called the station where the Inspector had just got in.

'I've a case on with the Met this morning so I was early. I could have done without this kind of mess on my own patch.'

'But I've got an alarm system!' exclaimed Kemp.

'Cut,' said Upshire, 'and cleanly, by someone who knew what they were up to. It might have gone off for a second or two, but who's to hear it? That's the way these chaps operate.'

'By the chummy way you see these chaps I gather you've had others?'

'A few. What'd they want here?'

'Blessed if I know. Solicitors don't keep money around—we even put the stamps and petty cash in the safe at night.'

'Never touched the safe. Well, they wouldn't, would they? Great old-fashioned Chubb thing of yours, it's like concrete. No, they weren't interested in your safe.'

'Well, thank God for that. At least all the title deeds are still with us—though who the hell steals title deeds nowadays when we're all on registered land. But don't disparage my safe, John, it's big enough to hold all my clients' wills and trust documents—they're the last thing any solicitor wants to find missing...'

Inspector Upshire shrugged his shoulders.

'Maybe someone just turned the place over for kicks... Have a peek at some of the juicy secrets you keep in your files.'

'They're welcome to them. By the time they're reduced to lawyers' prose they wouldn't raise a blush on your maiden aunt.'

Kemp was walking gloomily through the various rooms kicking aside the scattered folders and spilled-out files as if they were autumn leaves.

Upshire followed him. 'I suppose it'll take you time to see what's missing?'

'A day or two, once the staff and I get down to it. Funny, though, it doesn't look as if they've actually destroyed much.'

'Your telephones are OK, sir. They'd been thrown about a bit but the system's working.' The police constable was busy with his notebook.

'Is this the same kind of pattern as others you're seen?' Kemp asked him.

'Well, generally with offices there's more vandalism... They break things up, see, if they don't get no cash right away. And they'll lift anything not nailed down. Calculators, cash registers, even typewriters...'

Kemp looked in at the cashier's room. 'No, they've touched nothing here. They haven't even been at the account files so it wasn't an auditors' spot check.'

John Upshire was glad Kemp had recovered sufficiently to try a small joke.

'I'll be off then, Lennox. You'll let the station have a list of anything missing. I'm a bit puzzled myself. Experienced burglars don't do solicitors or accountants' offices, there's no money to speak of, and few disposable valuables unless they're safe-breakers—and that takes time and planning. If it's just pure vandalism, there'd be more damage. That alarm, now... I've had a look at it. They knew where it was and how to sever the wires. Mind you, in my opinion a security system's only as good as the men who fitted it. It's not the first time the word's been put around to the villains that so-and-so's had an alarm installed—and how it works.'

'Could be someone in the building trade?'

'Depends who your clients are. I think this job was done by someone with a grudge against you—might even be personal. Could be the same lot did your flat...'

A similar thought had occurred to Kemp. It had been in his mind since he had been woken up to hear the bad news.

All Brinscombes' new buildings would have alarm systems, from office blocks to private houses—they were practically *de rigueur* nowadays like smoke detectors and double-glazing. And Kemp had taken the Inspector's point: technical skills and knowledge were no longer confined to

the honest workman, there would always be other interested parties bent on keeping up with the times.

The thought was not consoling, except in the sense that
if this was Dennis Brinscombe's doing it came from
straightforward spite and nothing more; at worst an attempt to wreck Kemp's practice, to discredit him with clients who believed their business safe from prying eyes; at the
least a desire to cause maximum inconvenience.

It would do that all right.

Once the two policemen had left Kemp took stock of the
damage. His own room had been singled out for the most
attention from the intruders and looked like a second-hand
store in which giants had been having a pillow-fight. John
Upshire had helped him straighten the furniture but the
floor was knee-deep in paper, the steel filing cabinets were
empty and openly gaping down at what had been their
neatly-aligned contents now covering the carpet in a flabby
mass of spineless cardboard.

Whoever had done this part of the job had been meticu-
lous. Every file had been extracted, the papers ripped out
and scattered. Some of the correspondence had actually
been torn across but from what Kemp could see at a hasty
first glance more substantial documents were intact. The
search, if search it was, had been hasty but systematic. He
guessed the other parts of the office had simply been turned
over to make the whole thing look like a run-of-the-mill
break-in, but it had been in here, in his room, that the real
purpose of the visit had been sustained.

Once they had, in their various ways, expressed astonishment and horror at what they took to be vandalism, the staff
began clearing up. Although none of the office equipment
had suffered, there were small breakages, some of the girls
had lost personal items from their desks, and boxes of carbon paper and typewriter supplies were missing from the
stationery cupboard which had been ransacked.

'Just list everything for the insurance,' said Kemp, leaning up against Peter Carruthers's door. 'It all looks a bit of
a frolic to me . . . You're lucky they left your room alone.'

'They didn't, actually. Someone's had the staff files out,
and the account books. They put them back, but in the
wrong order.'

'Clients' accounts?'

'No, the partners' personal files, including yours. The
ones with your lists of investments, share transactions with
the bank, and your deposit balances. Maybe they thought
you'd had a windfall and you'd be good for a loan . . .'

'Or I was handing out bribes to our planning authorities.
You can't buy a drink for a councillor in this town without
somebody saying he's on the take . . .' Kemp made a joke of
it but he had misgivings. It was a good thing that cheque for
Bernie Shulman had been written at home and gone through
his private account without record in the office. Perhaps his
paranoia was not so ill-founded after all.

He went back to his own room where Elvira was sitting at
his desk directing operations. Mary Blane and Polly, the
post girl, were crawling around on the floor gathering up
paper.

'Hello . . . picking the daisies?' said Kemp. Elvira frowned
at him. Already there were a stack of folders in front of her
as she took the handfuls of letters from her attendants and
sorted them into neat piles. Elvira knew exactly where everything should be, even torn-up documents were being
carefully mended with Sellotape as she went along.

'Doesn't look as if I can see any clients in here today.
They'd get a fine impression of our security arrangements
and be off like a shot,' Kemp grumbled, feeling as out of
place as a man at a spring-cleaning. He gazed about him
helplessly, and noted that Miss Blane had strong calves
where the dark skirt was rucked up behind her knees. She's
like a peasant gleaning in a cornfield, he thought irrele-
vantly.

'You're due in Court in ten minutes,' said Elvira sternly, 'so you can leave all this mess to us. And there's been a panic call from Mrs Brinscombe. She's coming in at four-thirty. Mr Lambert's out, so you can use his room. Here's your file for the Court. I've put it together and nothing's missing.'

'Elvira, what am I to do without you?' He stuffed the file in his briefcase, and dashed for the door. Newtown's magistrates—mostly retired gentlemen with time on their hands—took a bleak view of lawyers who were late, no matter that there was cause...

As he left the office, Kemp reflected that prospective motherhood was bringing out an imperiousness in Elvira that had not been noticeable before; she was already treating him like a wayward child.

In fact the Bench were disposed to be lenient today when he had explained the reason for his lateness, he won his case and was in a better temper when he returned. By then the files were neatly stacked round the walls of his room in alphabetical order, and Elvira was sitting back with a glass of milk in her hand. Mary Blane was carefully dusting the inside of the cabinets before putting in the folders. Kemp raised an eyebrow at Elvira.

'Let her be,' she said, sharply. 'No one's done that since we moved in here six years ago.'

Kemp felt the need to exert some authority. 'Right,' he said, 'I'm taking you straight home, Elvira. I don't want that infant of yours suing me for negligence...'

Elvira looked exhausted, and she complied meekly.

'We've been through all this before, Mr Kemp,' she said when they were in the car, 'when we've had local cases of murder and I don't know what else, but you've nothing like that on at the moment... Except the Brinscombe affair, of course. They say he's a vengeful man, and Bill wouldn't put anything past those men of his on the building sites. Do you think it could be Brinscombe that's behind the break-in?'

Kemp was non-committal. 'Could be any client with a grudge. Someone who wants to cause me the maximum inconvenience, and perhaps lose me clients.' He didn't quite believe it himself.

'I'd keep an eye on Dennis Brinscombe. He'd like nothing better than to ruin your reputation.' Elvira was shrewd. She had watched Kemp's recovery from the ignominy of being struck off by the Law Society, and recognized the precariousness of his position; anyone with a spark of enmity towards him could hark back to that misdemeanour.

'Well, if it was Brinscombe's boys, they didn't find anything,' said Kemp brusquely. 'And you've got more important things to do now than worry about me. You have to let the past go, Elvira... What I would like to ask you is your opinion of your successor?'

'I like her, Mr Kemp,' said Elvira frankly, 'but I'm not sure she's what you really need in the office... I mean, she's learnt the word-processor and all that, and she's beginning to get a better grip on the matters you deal with, but her mind's elsewhere somehow... I'm not being unfair. Everyone in the office gets on with her, and she's not so shy as she was at first in speaking to your clients. But she hasn't got the sharpness you need...'

'Like the ability to get out a file quickly as you did this morning? I know that. Perhaps, with time...'

They had drawn up at her house, and Elvira was getting out of the car. 'You know what I think, Mr Kemp? Mary Blane would make someone a darned good wife. She's not cut out to be a legal secretary...'

Kemp watched her walk away, her bright hair bobbing in the sunlight. Dear Elvira, he thought, always on the lookout for a suitable mate to rescue him from what she imagined as a lonely existence...

But Mary Blane—that was surely taking matchmaking too far. If he ever did find himself a wife it would have to be one with a strong personality, someone with initiative and character. From what he had seen of Miss Blane she lacked definition, there was a vagueness about her as if she had come late into the modern world and still found it a bewildering place. It wasn't simply that she was plain, in fact her looks were pleasant enough, but in a woman of her age there ought to be something more...

Anyway, he was not looking for a wife, had not consciously done so for many years, and he had far more important matters on his mind.

# FIFTEEN

KEMP WENT HOME for lunch because he wanted solitude in
which to think, the disorder in the office too irritating a di-
version, his normal midday rendezvous with colleagues at
the local Cabbage White too noisy. In the early days of
Newtown's development some whimsical planner had de-
creed that the public houses be named after butterflies. Now
that the hostelries outnumbered the commoner lepidoptera
the custom had died out but the old Cabbage still kept its
lunch-time crowd. He wasn't in the mood for such company.

Making himself sandwiches, heating up soup and opening a bottle of wine were routine tasks for the hands, leaving the brain free for sterner things. He had to admit it had
grown sluggish of late, perhaps on a parallel course to his
probate problem winding its way like a serpent in a laby-
rinth through the judicial process in far New York.

But now his mind had been given a rude jolt. The two
break-ins were ominous, either the perpetrators were looking specifically for something, or they were merely warning
him that he was vulnerable both at home and in the office.
If they had been sent by Dennis Brinscombe then Kemp
could handle it; the motive was simply spite and a desire to
make trouble...

The alternative was more serious. Whoever had broken
into the office could have read the Eikenberg file which re-
vealed the state of play from Kemp's side of the case. They
had also checked up on his personal accounts, and the list
of private documents held at his bank... Did they think he
had the original second will already lodged there, waiting to

spring it at the next Court hearing like a Perry Mason bombshell? Or had they hoped to find the recent deposit of a ruby necklace?

Kemp had thought he could not be touched here in England but he should have known better. The men from Vegas had a long reach. Shakespeare had spoken of the length of Prester John's foot; it was beginning to look as if his namesake's arm was just as sinister. Madison loomed in Kemp's imagination like a menacing black giant even though reason told him the man was probably just a thug of middle size and certainly white...

It was frustrating not being able to fight back because you didn't know who your enemies really were; the outriders of the Mob could be anywhere in the streets of Newtown.

Kemp sighed, and went back to the office. Perhaps Vivienne Brinscombe's troubles would take his mind off his own, as fire drives out fire...

SHE WAS LATE, which allowed him time to do other urgent work, and when she did arrive she was accompanied by a rather sullen-looking Belinda. Seating them in Tony Lambert's room, Kemp watched Mary Blane offer tea and biscuits. This she did with a certain homely air when he had difficult clients—almost as if she was a housewife entertaining the neighbours. He was amused to see her beginning to treat the office like a house, a house to be kept clean and tidy—she'd even mended a tear in his curtains. He wondered if she would get round to the idea of domesticating himself, and had a sudden vision of her vacuuming his flat. Mary, the Irish maid-of-all-work... He pulled himself up sharply, and listened to what Mrs Brinscombe was saying. She was already breathless.

'...and then I had to fetch Belinda from school. It's about her I've come.'

'Since she's the only dispute you have with your ex-husband I'm glad you brought her,' said Kemp, smiling broadly at the ten-year-old girl.

'How do you feel about it, Belinda?'

She was not used to having straight questions put to her except at school where, it was said, she was above average intelligence.

'I hate it,' she said at last.

'Why is that? You must have some friends in the same position?'

'They're not like us. They don't have *my* parents!'

'It's a difficult situation for all parents, and for the children too, after a divorce, Belinda. Do you know what compromise means?'

She thought for a moment. 'Making the best of things?'

'Very well put. And are you making the best of things?'

Vivienne Brinscombe had been bursting to speak. She ignored Kemp's warning hand. 'Oh, what's the sense in talking to her like that? You don't know what she's done. Just wait till you hear, Mr Kemp. She's done something so terrible Dennis will never forgive either of us—and it's me he'll take it out on...' Vivienne's voice broke, and the ready tears started from her eyes.

Kemp looked at Belinda. Her face was scarlet and she was gnawing her knuckles to stop herself from crying. She didn't have her mother's propensity for tears.

'Come on,' said Kemp gently. 'Stop eating yourself and have a chocolate biscuit.'

'I'm not a bloody kid.' She spat the words at him but at least she took her hand from her mouth. 'I'm not going to say anything—'

'—Until I get a lawyer. Well, I'm here, Belinda, and I'm sorry that wasn't even very funny. If you don't want to tell me what this is all about, then that's all right...'

'But it's not all right,' her mother cried. 'She knocked her father down last night, and she stole his wallet! That's what

Belinda did! Now Dennis is really on the warpath. He'll go
to the police and even the Social Services. He'll say she's
unmanageable, and I'm not a fit person to be in charge of
her. He'll get her sent away to some home or other...'

'Come off it, Vivienne.' Kemp felt it was time to put a
stop to this absurd scenario. 'You're letting your imagination run away with you. What really happened?'

'What I told you. She hit her dad, and ran away with his
wallet...'

'Did you really do that?' Kemp asked Belinda calmly.
'Why don't you tell me about it? It's probably not as bad as
it sounds... Have some more tea, Vivienne, and let her do
the talking. Take your time, Belinda, just tell me what happened.'

It did take time to get the whole story out of the troubled
girl but gradually under Kemp's mild prompting it emerged.

Dennis Brinscombe had planned a mid-week treat for his
daughter the previous day. It was a habit of his to do this
when business was slack and he could spare a whole evening. He would ring up on the spur of the moment in the
morning before Belinda went to school, leaving Vivienne in
a dilemma. If she refused she felt guilty afterwards for having perhaps deprived the child of something she couldn't
afford to give her, on this occasion a slap-up meal (according to Dennis) in a restaurant, and a visit to the cinema.
Naturally Belinda was delighted, so Vivienne acquiesced,
though reluctantly.

'You enjoyed having supper out with your dad?' asked
Kemp.

'It was all right—' Belinda was grudging—'if only he
wouldn't show off...'

The restaurant had been one where Dennis Brinscombe
was well known and expected good service. Like most ten-
year-olds Belinda preferred to be anonymous when eating;
too much attention was merely an embarrassment.

Things had gone badly from then on. Even Kemp felt a spark of sympathy for Dennis faced with an unresponsive daughter when all he'd wanted was to demonstrate to his pals how close they were—a cosy idea he'd gleaned from some book on the psychology of father-daughter relationships.

The crux came with the choice of cinema. Newtown boasted two: one which showed popular films, the other the rather more serious kind.

'He wanted to go to some rubbishy American thing about a cop in a kindergarten,' Belinda burst out. 'I told him, no way... That was for kids.'

'What else was on?'

'*Henry the Fifth.*' Belinda's eyes glowed. 'With Kenneth Branagh. I'd seen bits on telly... And I'd read it. I thought that when Dad said he'd take me to the cinema that was the one. Or at least he'd give me the choice...'

'And he didn't?'

'Said I wouldn't understand it. It was for adults only. I knew that wasn't true. It was only that he didn't want to see it. He'd be bored stiff. He never goes to that kind of thing...'

So by half past seven there were two very disappointed people in Newtown. Belinda was as stubborn as her father; she planted her stout little legs on the pavement outside the place where the American film was about to be shown, and told him he'd have to drag her inside. Dennis had given up, and driven her home, his home.

Put a frustrated couple together, particularly if they are kith and kin, in castle or cottage, and what you get is a row. The one that evening in Dennis Brinscombe's house must have been a whopper. He had tried to put a brave face on things in the presence of his housekeeper and the maid but Belinda by that time was beyond polite behaviour.

'He only acts nice in front of them,' she said, scornfully, 'so's they'll think him a wonderful father... I did wait till they'd gone before I told him so, really I did, Mum.'

'What happened then?' asked Kemp.

But Belinda was still looking to her mother for help.

'You shouldn't have said what you did, Belinda...' Vivienne couldn't decide what line to take, she was too deeply involved with her own misery.

'I know now that I shouldn't have. But he was saying things too. About you and the way you were bringing me up...' The girl turned and appealed to Kemp. 'There's nothing wrong with Mum and me, it wasn't true the things he said...'

'He was probably in a bad temper, Belinda,' said Kemp in what he hoped was a soothing tone. 'People say things in the heat of the moment they regret afterwards.'

'It was when I said he didn't give Mum enough money to keep me that he really blew up...'

'How exactly did you say it?'

Belinda went very red.

'I called him a bloody miser. It was then he slapped my face...'

Kemp heard Vivienne draw in her breath.

'And what did you do, Belinda?' asked Kemp.

'I slapped him back.'

'How hard?' Kemp was looking at her sturdy form; she was built like her father.

'Pretty hard. He fell down on the sofa.'

'I see. What happened then?'

'Well...' Belinda was by now getting into her narrative, the worst part over, she was beginning to enjoy herself. 'His jacket was unbuttoned and when he went backwards his wallet fell out of his pocket. So I just picked it up and left. I got the bus home, Mum, but I was ever so careful... There were people at the bus stop under the street-light and I stuck close beside some ladies. Then I watched when I got off and made sure some lady was going in my direction and I walked behind her till I got to our road...' This was the child now speaking, a child well and truly warned about the dangers in the streets of Newtown after dark.

Vivienne was dabbing at her eyes with a handkerchief. For the first time Kemp gave her his attention.

'You have the wallet?'

She brought it out of her bag and gave it to him. 'Nothing's been touched, Mr Kemp. I swear it...'

'Of course it hasn't. You didn't take anything out of it, did you, Belinda?'

She shook her head. 'I only took the wallet because it was there on the floor...' She suddenly looked apprehensive. 'It wasn't really stealing, was it? I'd have given it back. I gave it to Mum soon's I got home.'

'Of course it wasn't stealing,' Kemp reassured her. 'And your dad will get it back quite intact. And I think he'll understand...' Kemp only hoped Dennis Brinscombe had his better side. Kemp tended to hope it for all his clients, and sometimes for his adversaries also.

'What I'm going to do, Vivienne, is this. I shall telephone Mr Brinscombe's solicitors right away.' He looked at his watch. 'Mr Cooper will still be in his office. Let's try and forestall any trouble Dennis is likely to make. Now, just keep quiet, both of you.'

Kemp was glad Alec Cooper kept as late office hours as he did himself.

'Lennox Kemp here, Mr Cooper, it's about the Brinscombes.'

If Alex Cooper wanted to hear nothing more of the Brinscombe affairs that evening he gave no sign of it. He had had an earful that morning from his client threatening all manner of legal action, not excluding police prosecution...

'I did my best to talk him out of it, Lennox, but you know
the way he is. All bluff and bluster. What the kid did was
stupid...'

'He hit her first, Alec.'

'I can well believe it. It's his way and he works with a
rough crew. He thinks he has to use his fists like them. But
he is genuinely fond of his daughter. You say you have the
wallet?'

'Here in my hands.'

'He even gave me a blasted list—everything that was in it.'

'Well, let's go through it, then. Fifty pounds in tenners,
twenty in fives... Got that?'

'OK. That's the money. Now, three credit cards, AA card,
driver's licence, Diner's Card, all the plastic...'

Kemp spilled them out on his desk. They checked with the
ones on Brinscombe's list. 'Some of his own business cards,
several from various manufacturing concerns—I'd say
they're all from reps. I'll read them out.'

They checked.

Kemp turned the last in his fingers. A plain card: 'Mr
Clive Horth, Casino Operator, and an address in Las Vegas.' Kemp was so startled he didn't even begin to read it
out.

'That's the lot on my list. Nothing appears to be missing,' Alec Cooper was saying. 'Though why the hell my client had to go to all that trouble beats me... I don't think it
would be wise for me to ask him to call round at your office
to collect it, not if he's still punch-drunk. Look, Gillorns is
on my way home. I'll pop in and get it. It'll be lateish, I'm
afraid...'

'That's fine with me. I'll be here for a while yet. In the
meantime I'll talk to my client and try to calm things down
this end. I know what Dennis Brinscombe is after, and it's
just not on... The girl is happy with her mother, and no
court is going to change that. I'd like your opinion—off the
record—of his chances. It will go no further I assure you...'

Kemp was speaking quietly but there was no need: on the other side of the room Vivienne and her daughter, now restored to her usual bouncy self, were helping Miss Blane to clear away the teacups.

Alec Cooper was a good lawyer. He had a difficult client but he also had a shrewd knowledge of the local Bench. 'Off the record, Lennox, he hasn't a snowball's chance in hell...'

'Thanks, Alec. I'll do my best to mend fences if you'll do the same.'

'I'll try. Perhaps the way you've handled this sorry little matter today might impress him. I can only hope so. I'll see you later.'

Kemp put the phone down, and turned to Vivienne. 'Mr Cooper is going to collect the wallet tonight and return it to Mr Brinscombe, and then I suggest we say no more about it. Now, Belinda, you've done a wrong thing but I think you know that... You've also done some right things, you told your mother straight off, and you gave her the wallet. That was brave of you. You're outspoken but you are honest. Your temper is something you have to keep to yourself—don't let it boil over again. Henry the Fifth had a temper too, but he kept it for bigger battles... Sorry, I'm moralizing again, but you see what I mean?'

Belinda nodded. She was bright-eyed as she picked up her schoolbag, and she gave her mother's arm a quick squeeze.

As they were leaving Kemp said to Vivienne: 'Does Dennis often go over to the States?'

'Oh yes, lots of times. He's been going for years. I never went because I had Belinda and anyway he never seemed to want us on these trips. They were business, he said, all about learning their construction methods and new materials. I think Dennis admires the Americans. Well, he would, wouldn't he? They're a pushy lot, too...' She smiled, and her eyes were as brilliant as her daughter's.

When they had gone Kemp picked up the wallet and restored its contents. He hesitated over the card not listed, possibly a simple omission on Brinscombe's part, perhaps he had forgotten he carried it. It was not dog-eared as some of the others were, it looked new.

Kemp thought of keeping it but decided against it and slipped it in with the rest, after noting the address and telephone number. Though what good that would do he hadn't the faintest idea, but it was nice to know that Prester John's partner was a real person with a place of residence. Perhaps Brinscombes were thinking of putting up a casino here in Newtown if and when the gambling laws were ever relaxed. With the spirited opposition there had been to the fruit machines in the one amusement arcade, they'd little hope...

There were more sinister implications to be considered, and those not light-heartedly. Once the men from Vegas had knowledge of the second will— *'Everything of which I die possessed to my ex-husband Lennox Kemp of Newtown, England'* —they would look for a contact there, and it had come ready-made. Big construction companies operate worldwide; Brinscombes were not in that league but Dennis travelled to the States where he would have met and mingled with others in the industry, and there must be a lot of building going on down there in Nevada... When they'd probed the network for a name to match the place they'd come up with Brinscombes of Newtown. Right on the spot, the hired help... And the already disaffected Dennis would be only too pleased to help put the boot in when he was told the target.

Kemp went back to his own room where order now prevailed. Someone had worked hard that afternoon, even his desktop had been polished. He took out the American case file. The last letter from New York was a note from his attorneys' office to say that the hearing would be resumed on November 16 which was in five days' time. The accompanying letter from Counsellor Benton was hardly optimistic; he pointed out that without sufficient evidence to rebut the

presumption of revocation, the copy will was a dead duck.
That of course was not what he had written but the meaning was clear enough. Presumably the letter had been read
by whoever was responsible for the break-in and the good
news was even now winging its way across the Atlantic to
cheer the spirits of Messrs Madison and Horth.

If they had suspected there was any clandestine correspondence going on between Kemp and someone in the
States in a last-minute effort to obtain that vital evidence,
they'd been disappointed. It was small comfort...

Kemp got his head down on a draft lease which had been
hanging about too long and was still busy when Alec Cooper arrived. Kemp handed him the wallet, and said: 'I've got
a bone to pick with your client, and it's not about Belinda...

'Now I'm not saying categorically that Mr Brinscombe's
responsible for those break-ins at my home and this office,'
he finished, 'but I'd like you to warn him that if there's any
further trouble I'm going straight to John Upshire.'

Cooper pursed his lips. 'I think you're mistaken, Lennox. Of course I know all about this personal vendetta he
had against you and I've tried to tell him time and time
again to watch his words... But he's not the only one to
blame. He thinks you're sleeping with his ex-wife and it's my
belief she's been encouraging him in the idea. I suppose it's
her way of getting her own back on him...'

'I wouldn't go to bed with Vivienne Brinscombe if you
paid me, Alec. You know that. Ex-wives are high risk business. But this has become a lot more serious than a personal grudge. Your client's mixed up with some very nasty
people... I'll say no more than that.'

'You mean his building crowd? I don't like them much
either but I'm pretty sure Brinscombe himself would never
do anything illegal. He's got too much to lose in this town.
I think you're wrong about him having anything to do with
the break-ins. Why, my office was done about six months

ago—they bust a computer and poured ink all over Hals-
bury's Statutes!'

Kemp grinned. 'Which I bet you hadn't looked at in
years ... I agree that burglaries are all too common in Newtown but there was something about mine which connects
with Dennis Brinscombe, and I think a word of warning in
that direction wouldn't go amiss.'

'He's my client, Lennox, but I'll try... Thanks for holding on to the wallet. I don't know how he'd manage without his pasteboard credentials ...'

When Alec Cooper left Kemp thought it was about time
he too went home. It was after seven, and an early frost had
been forecast. He could feel the cold seeping in as he walked
through the outer office.

He was startled to see Mary Blane come out of the cubby-
hole which housed the tea-making facilities and other domestic paraphernalia without which he was always being
told the office could not function. She walked calmly over
to spread damp dishcloths on the radiator.

'Just finishing clearing-up,' she said. 'It was like Paddy's
market in there.'

He was irritated by her presence, by her treating his place
of business like a housewife's dream of home.

'That's the cleaners' job,' he told her shortly.

'No harm in being tidy,' she said. 'And the cleaners will
have their hands full. Those men who repaired the lock left
enough sawdust for a timber yard.'

She walked past him into the cloakroom, and came out a
minute later struggling into her heavy coat.

'You shouldn't be here so late,' he told her. 'I'll have to
take you home.' He was annoyed and only made the offer
out of courtesy.

'There's no need ...'

'Don't argue. Come on, my car's outside. It's Station
Road, isn't it?'

Before he turned off the lights he looked at her. Bundled up in her tweed she seemed smaller, more frail. Her eyes were an opaque grey, in their colour not unlike his own, and there was little depth to them. He wondered if it was mascara made the stubby eye-lashes so dark but he'd never noticed that she used cosmetics other than a paleish powder now pearled on her forehead.

'You look as if you've been working hard,' he said, feeling some contrition, as they walked to the car park.

'I don't mind,' she said, 'but today was different, wasn't it? I mean, do you have break-ins like this regularly?'

He laughed at the way she put it.

'Not for years,' he said, starting the engine, 'but there's been a spate of them recently in the town.'

'Were they looking for something special?'

'Damned if I know... There's always a lot of confidential stuff in a solicitor's office. Perhaps someone just wanted to see it.'

'Someone here in Newtown?'

'Well... it could have been from further afield.'

She was quiet for a while. Even her silence seemed strangely companionable.

Then she said: 'You have an American case in your files, Mr Kemp. Do you think whoever broke in was interested in that?' Her tone had not changed, it remained level, patient, inquiring.

'Why should you think so?' he asked.

'It's an unusual case, and unlike the other matters you deal with, it's personal to you.'

He wondered if she knew about the break-in at his flat. It was no secret, she'd have heard all about it from Elvira or one of the other girls.

'Yes,' he agreed, 'it does happen to be my own private concern. You've done some letters on it. Does it interest you?'

'It does. The Irish have quite a thing about wills. I learnt that when I worked at Mr Cafferty's.'

'How long were you there?' Mr Cafferty had not divulged this information on the telephone.

'It was my first real job as a secretary... I learned shorthand and typing at nightschool,' she replied, leaving him to see her background as possibly educationally deprived.

'Why did you hit on Newtown when you came to England?'

'I had an aunt who was a maid in a big house here. She's dead now but it was the only place I'd heard of.'

'So you've no relatives over here now. Aren't you lonely?'

'No. You've no relatives either, Mr Kemp, and you're not lonely.'

Her bluntness took his breath away. Elvira and she must have been having one of those cosy talks indulged in by women with men in mind.

He felt the need to change the subject and began to speak quickly before he realized that he hadn't moved it very far.

'You say the Irish have a thing about wills... I'm sure Mr Cafferty never had to deal with a case like mine. You see, Mary, it concerns the estate of my ex-wife and I have to admit my feelings are as complex as the matter itself...'

'You were fond of her in the past, and now the past has caught up with you. Sometimes it is difficult to separate the past from the present.'

As he edged the car through the Newtown traffic Kemp found himself for the first time in weeks talking freely. To no one else had he spoken of his memories of Muriel and their life together, and it came almost as a relief to be able to do so now to someone who was a veritable stranger.

'And that's why this case disturbs you, Mr Kemp? She makes a gesture towards you, like a wave of the hand after all these years, and you're not sure what she meant by it.'

'Something like that, Mary... I find I don't really care whether I win this case or not, and that's unlike me. Usually I go all out to win.'

'Perhaps your Muriel didn't care either... I mean, in the end it wouldn't matter to her who got all those casinos and things. When life is slipping away you have to just let go... You're not going to be there to see happiness or despair on the faces of the people that are left.'

The words were banal enough, but not the way she said them.

They had reached Mrs Beresford's house at 55 Station Road, and Kemp drew the car up outside. He was surprised to find he wished the journey could have been longer. In the comfortable presence of Mary Blane his irritation had quite melted away. She had had a calming influence as she sat there beside him, quietly listening, her gloved hands on her lap. Her responses, in a voice flat as her shoes, were softly-spoken, hesitant sometimes, but always to the point.

Before she closed the car door she leant in and asked him: 'Those break-ins and that piece of piping that just missed you... do you mean you're in danger from these people?'

'Of course not,' he said quickly, 'I'm no use to them dead. But they might want to scare me so that if it came to the crunch I'd hand over what they were after.'

Now that he had put it into words he knew the thought had been there ever since he'd found Clive Horth's card in Brinscombe's wallet.

'Is it the second will you're talking about?'

'You've been through the file, Mary, you've seen Mr Van Gryson's original letters... It's possible the beneficiaries under the other will think I've got it, or that I know who has.'

He could see that she was shivering. 'You get right into Mrs Beresford's nice warm house now... You're cold standing there. I'll see you in the morning, Mary.'

'Good night, Mr Kemp. Thank you for bringing me home.' Like a little girl after a party.

He watched her go up the path between the evergreens before he started the car and drove home.

There was something he had to do there, something that had been bothering him for days. After the burglary in the office it had become urgent. He had taken his own will—one made years ago and never thought of since—from the safe-keeping of the bank, and now he must destroy it.

It was with mixed feelings he watched it flare up as he put the match to it in the kitchen sink, then he scooped up the ashes and put them in the dustbin. The action was almost one of predetermined revenge should the Vegas men seek to harm him, but there was a sadness too, a reminder that he was alone in the world, he had neither kith nor kin, no one to whom he could leave all his worldly goods. He should have married again, had children...

Damn the making and breaking of all wills, he thought fiercely, if they bring one to this deplorable state of mind. He remembered how he had talked with Mary in the car, her pleasant, soothing companionship...

He caught himself saying, 'Dear, dear Mary Blane,' and went to bed to get over it.

# SIXTEEN

MARY BLANE WASN'T the only one to be concerned for Kemp's safety. He had a late telephone call that night from Bernie Shulman, the first time the American had spoken to him direct so it had to be urgent.

'You all right, Mr Kemp?'

'Apart from having had a couple of burglaries, yes. What's the trouble?'

'All hell's broke loose. José Hermanos, he's skipped to Mexico... I get that from Dan Rice. Seems his alibi for the time he's supposed to have been in Vegas when Florence died, it's a bummer... So he figures he'd mebbe be up on a murder rap if he puts his head inside a courtroom and he's made himself scarce. Madison's lawyers, now, they're jumping like fleas, that statement of his it's full of holes like a sieve. Your attorney's gonna throw it out anyway...'

'There being no witness present for cross-examination?'

'Right. Even if Madison's connections down there catch up with him and drag him back by the heels, the damage is done. José's told too many lies... Looks like Madison's known all along that second will was never destroyed, leastways not the way José said. You've been burgled, huh?'

'Sort of.'

'Someone tried to kill you?'

'Doesn't necessarily go with burglaries over here, Bernie. Besides, I'm no good to them dead.'

'How'd you make that out, Mr Kemp?'

Kemp took the greatest pleasure in telling him.

For the moment there was an awed silence on the line.

'You mean Prince Charles would get the lot?'

'Roughly speaking, yes. I have just burnt my only will so that I shall die intestate. My parents are dead, and I am without kin. If the second will should turn up in court, killing me would be the last thing our friends from Vegas—'

He was interrupted by a great hoot of laughter from Bernie.

'Oh boy, oh boy! You reckon they'll start taking potshots at Royal Charlie, eh?'

'Wouldn't do them any good. The British Crown is a continuing institution. Mind you, I don't see it managing casinos in Vegas, though it's an interesting concept... Have you got anything else on the woman, Bernie?'

'Yeah, lots. There's a report in the mail. Now we're talking of someone really in danger from Prester John and his mob. She ain't got a chance. I'm near enough finding where she's gone but the others are way ahead of me.'

'I'll look forward to getting your letter, then. In the meantime, thanks for the warning but you could've saved your breath.'

'I've got myself a contact with Madison's law firm, that's how I know they've spread a wide net—including you, Mr Kemp. They got you in their sights.'

'Well, just you drop the hint to your contact that should anything happen to me the Crown takes all. That should be enough to keep their hands off... I think, Bernie, at present they're out to scare me. If things go wrong for them in that court they want me to do a deal...'

'Yeah, that's the boys from Vegas. They'll show you the big hand... Gee, that's a great trick, the one about Prince Charles... I'll pass the word along. Nice talking to you, Mr Kemp.'

'Likewise, Bernie.'

No sooner had Kemp put the phone down than he had another trans-Atlantic call, one not totally unexpected.

'Of course I shouldn't be talking to you, Lennox, as we're on opposing sides,' said Van Gryson at his most ponderous, 'but I've conferred with Mr Benton and he agrees that in view of the original amicable relationship between you and me—'

'Which I trust continues, Dale.'

'Naturally it does, Lennox. This is no ordinary case... Which is why I'm ringing you. As executors of the will, the first will, we have now been asked by the beneficiaries' lawyers to move for a further adjournment. As you know, the case is down for hearing on the sixteenth of this month, that's in four days. The Surrogate won't like it, and neither Mr Eikenberg nor myself take kindly to the idea. Madison and Horth have been pushing us all the way so far. Now, quite out of the blue, they're the ones seeking further time.'

'How extraordinary,' said Kemp. 'Any idea why they should want it?'

'Seems this witness of theirs, Florence Hermanos's husband, has gone missing. With good reason, I suspect... The New York Police want him for further questioning about his wife's death.'

'I read his statement which you kindly sent me, Dale, the one in which he says the second will was destroyed by Muriel herself.'

'Of course Hermanos's non-appearance does not of itself provide rebuttal of presumed revocation, Lennox.'

'I know that. But it helps. Which does lead one to find this attempted motion to delay rather suggestive...'

Van Gryson was silent for a moment.

'I get your drift. The beneficiaries are concerned that the second will might still come to light...'

'And they're going to leave no stone unturned to make sure it doesn't.' Kemp tried to keep his tone only slightly sardonic.

'Have you reason in making that observation?' Van Gryson was wily when it came to words, so Kemp changed tack.

'Has it ever occurred to you, Dale, that the second will might all this time be in the hands of some quite innocent person who has no idea of what it's all about?'

Van Gryson, whose everyday existence depended on the careful handling of important documents and who held wills to be as sacred as the pages of the Bible, was aghast at such a frivolous notion.

He repudiated Kemp's suggestion vigorously, ending '...and if there ever was such a stupid idiot, then they've not been in New York City—the press here have already had a field day over the Probert will case. It's the kind of publicity our office can well do without...'

Kemp sympathized, recalling the circumstances in which the second will was drawn up and executed. Poor Miss Janvier, she would be making her debut in the courtroom on his side. He wished her luck.

'Coming back to the reason you called, Dale... You want me to say whether I personally would agree to this further delay, or not? Well, quite honestly, I don't think I care one way or the other. I leave myself in Mr Benton's hands. I presume he does not want to give the other side more time?'

'I think he's reluctant to involve you in further costs, Lennox. He knows he can produce no evidence in rebuttal of revocation, and a protracted hearing will only run up a bigger bill.'

'He sounds honest,' said Kemp. 'So we go ahead on the sixteenth?'

'I think so. Even if Madison and Horth's lawyers press on with the motion for an adjournment, if the rest of us agree to resist, then in my opinion the court will deny it anyway. I'm glad to have had this talk with you, Lennox, you and I are always on the same wavelength, eh?'

Well, not altogether, thought Kemp as he rang off... And we never have been even right at the beginning when you came over the Atlantic to find out what sort of man it was who had been named in that inconvenient second will.

Would Kemp be the grasping kind, eager for a fortune and prepared to fight for it? Or might he turn out to be a spiritless country solicitor whose brain had gone to sleep, one who could be overawed by fast talk and any court proceedings more complex than defending traffic misdemeanours, easily persuaded to drop the case, thereby saving the good name of Eikenberg & Lazard?

Kemp grinned to himself. He remembered Dale being mightily impressed by Kemp's quixotic gesture on Muriel's behalf all those years ago... It had not seemed quixotic at the time, simply the life or death of someone he loved.

Would I do the same thing again, thought Kemp, running his fingers through his thinning hair, knowing what the cost would be? I was about Bernie Shulman's age when that particular catastrophe put paid to my career, I'm older now and perhaps have more sense...

Thinking of Bernie made him realize how eagerly he was awaiting that further letter, realize too that he was far more interested in following the trail of the wayward Madeleine Smith than in the outcome of his case before the Surrogate's Court.

If the result of his youthful indiscretion had taught him to have a certain fellow-feeling for the underdogs of the world the effect had still endured into his middle-age. He found he didn't really give a damn about who eventually got that fortune in Vegas, he just hoped the hounds would never catch up on their prey; she almost deserved to get away with it.

# SEVENTEEN

THAT NO LETTER from America arrived by the first post was a considerable disappointment to Kemp, and also an inconvenience. It would mean he should go back to his flat at lunch-time and that, in the circumstances, was impossible; he had to attend a long day's hearing of a civil case in the High Court. He tried to shake off this obsession that there were people about who would tamper with his mail but it persisted, so before he left for London he had a word with Tony Lambert.

'Do me a favour,' he said, 'just call in at my flat and pick up any letters that come by the second post. I'll be stuck in town till late afternoon at the least, and after that break-in I'm a bit concerned about personal papers.'

'I think I'd feel the same,' Tony said. 'Don't worry, I'll go in between twelve and one, and if anything comes I'll bring it round later this evening.'

Someone once called London the fairest of cities, but that was a long time ago. The Law Courts in the Strand had kept their architectural dignity but not much else on this grey November day. Emerging at last into five o'clock gloom with a grateful client who had won his case—or rather had it won for him by Counsel who stood now, smiling, to receive congratulation—Kemp found himself making excuses and hurrying off in the direction of Liverpool Street Station. There was no actual reason for such haste; after over an hour's train journey to Newtown there wouldn't be time anyway to call in at the office before it closed. He could well have accepted his client's cordial offer of a quiet drink before heading into the rush-hour traffic, and normally at the end of a tedious day in court he would have been glad of the chance to unwind.

Yet here he was as impatient and eager to be home as the rest of his commuter companions jampacked into the compartment engrossed in their evening papers and the prospect of supper. Kemp stared out at the Hackney marshes and wondered why on earth he was feeling as he did, nervy and apprehensive, full of a sense of foreboding, as if somewhere just out of reach of his knowledge a terrible event was about to happen, had already happened . . .

He had experienced such moments of grave disquiet before but then there had been cause enough; towards the end, the climax, of some of his cases when investigation had muddied still waters and elements of violence came to the surface. The moment when the murderer jumps . . . The hour of retribution which brings its own dangers . . . These had in the past brought similar sensations to those he now felt so acutely, the rising panic, the fear beyond reason. He knew he could never explain them away—they were more of the body than the mind. 'For we are flesh and blood, and apprehensive,' he would mutter on these occasions when instinct was a stronger force than logic.

If instinct's at work here, he thought, drawing back his feet to avoid being trampled by a herd of the species known as Essex man making for the door, then it's on its own. My mind at the moment should be happily dormant for I've no case to solve, I'm not an agent of justice presently on the trail of the perpetrators of crime, neither am I, so far as I know, closely involved with the iniquities of others.

Yet like one who, without cause, anticipates the arrival of dreadful news, the dark mood remained with him even as he fetched his car from the car park at Newtown, and drove home.

TONY RANG HIS BELL about eight o'clock that evening.

'These came for you by the second post,' he said, handing over some letters. Kemp noted the airmail envelope but
curbed his impatience to open it.

'I was just making coffee. Come and have a cup and I'll
tell you about our glorious exploits in Court. By the way,
thanks for recommending Richard Noble. He's a good bar-
rister, and I'd use him again any time.'

They discussed business for over an hour so that it was ten
o'clock before Kemp could settle himself down to read Bernie Shulman's report.

It began without preamble:

I'm catching on fast to what this woman's about. She don't
waste time. I figure that's her trade mark. And luck's what
she's had. If Mr V.G. been less of a slouch when it came to
getting that list out they'd have nailed her by now.

Because I figure for sure that this Madeleine Smith took
the rubies I goes for another walk with Leonie. She's got
that waitress job Eikenbergs set up for her—I'll say that for
them, they did all right by the girl—so she tells me she's
happy. It's done her communicative skills no harm either
and she opens up when I ask her about the nurse.

'You sayin' she stole them, Bernie? And her with a nice
job and all...'

'People in nice jobs got ambitions, Leonie, same's other
folk... You were the one that cleaned her room?'

'Yeah, every morning after I took up her breakfast.
Weren't that much to do, she kept it real neat.'

'What about her own stuff?'

Leonie looks down her nose. 'Well, she ain't got no
dresses nor make-up. Even her toilet soap's got no smell...
As for her underclothes, you'd think she's a nun... What
you want to know for?' she asks.

'I'm looking for clues, Leonie, and mebbe you can help.
Didn't she have no personal possessions lying about?' I'm

trying to get her back into that room and she screws up her eyes thinking.

'She'd magazines, and two-three books—even them, they weren't hers . . .'

'How'd you make that out, Leonie?'

''Cos I looked, see . . . When I'm dustin' around. They'd got a stamp on them like you get in libraries only they weren't from no ordinary library. Some hospital place.'

'Can you remember the name? It's important.'

It takes time. She's not been around much reading in her life this girl, but some things stick better in the memory when there's not a lot in it already.

'Chicago,' she says, 'Lakeside Home. I remember that 'cos it sounded nice and kinda peaceful.'

Well, I thanks Leonie, and tells her she's been real helpful, and next day I'm in Chicago.

She's right about Lakeside Home, though I'd call it dead rather than peaceful. It's for elderly incurables. Madeleine Smith worked there over three years ago. Nobody can tell me much about her 'cept she's a good nurse and they were sorry when she went. I guess they would be—it's not a place that's high in the market for professional staff. Most nurses only stick it a few months. Reason for this one's departure—a sick mother. I figure Madeleine Smith's had more sick mothers in her life than I've had jobs.

But that visit to Chicago pays off. I got a man in the Police Department there owes me a favour, so I has a word with him about records on stolen jewellery. There's a report just in. Shopkeeper, a Mr Gratz, got some pieces back in July from a woman, the usual tale, this time a widow down on her luck. That list got to the shop a week after she was in but Mr Gratz he's gone on vacation, and says his manager just sat on it. My guess is they mebbe got a market for the stuff but Mr Gratz he got scared so he finally goes to the police. I got a funny feeling about Mr Gratz. When I gets to talking with him he's cagey, a lot more than he needs now he's put it right with the cops and the stuff's in their hands. I figure he's been got at. He let out I wasn't the first so-called investigator who'd called.

That tip-off takes me to other jewellers in the Windy City, and sure enough they'd all had visits from a coupla men through July and August asking about rubies. What I figure is, Mr Kemp, those books of Madeleine Smith's, they'd be in her Brooklyn apartment and someone got there before us. They'd a lead on Chicago, that she might have gone back to that place she worked, mebbe her last stop before she took off.

Now I comes clean with the Chicago Police Department and I tell them all about Madeleine Smith so that they can go checking travel agents and the airlines out of there round about the beginning of July. She was at Gratz the jeweller's on the third, the day before the holiday. Hey, how about that for a twist? What if she took off on the Fourth of July, making a break for independence? She's got rid of all the rubies, she's carrying a fortune in her bag... That's another thing, I've got the Chicago PD checking the banks, and the passport places. From what I know of this lady she's never had a passport, she's never been outa the States, she's been too poor to travel, she needed all she ever made to support that crummy family of hers back in Vineland.

I figure that trip to Chicago was the end of the line for her... But it's a dead end for us too, Mr Kemp. The woman could be anywheres in the world by now, the money she's got.

Thing is, have those guys from Vegas got further'n me? They got a head start. I never did get past that big Swede at her apartment to get a look at the stuff she left. I been back there but he said it was thrown out when he repossessed the place. The neighbours say there were other men around at the time but nobody wants to talk about them. Mebbe they got more'n those books, mebbe they got an address, or her real name... I got a horrible feeling they're way ahead on the trail, and it's not rubies they're after, it's the woman herself.

Even if she took off from Chicago she'd stay in the States if she's got no passport—and I reckon she'd not take the risk of getting one while she's on the run. What I think is, she's gone South for the sun and the rich living, that's what most thieves do when they're in the money.

Well, God help her, is what I say if she's got the mob on her track, they'll catch up with her sooner or later. Sounds like I'm even sorry for the poor broad! Anyways, I kinda admire her speed . . .

With me handing over all my info to the Department in Chicago it'll go right back to Eikenbergs with the last lot of rubies. I think I did right, though. If the cops get to her first at least she'll live, mebbe in the penitentiary for a few years, but leastways she'll be alive . . .

Looks like I'm off the case, Mr Kemp, and I'll be sending along my bill. There's things I shoulda done at the start like mebbe taking a closer look at that room of hers in Flatbush, and I'm still sorry about the Hermanos woman, but it's always the way with cases like this, you can go only so far till you come to a dead end, and I reckon that's where I'm at right now.

KEMP GOT HIMSELF a drink and read the letter through again. Funny that Bernie once again seemed to echo his own feeling, half wishing that Madeleine Smith should get away with it... They certainly were on the same wavelength there.

She'd been clever, this woman, travelling fast through the States, places she knew, places where she'd worked and where she was familiar with the districts; she'd done nothing to attract attention to herself, she'd worked swiftly and to a plan. Like Bernie, Kemp found himself admiring her, criminal though she undoubtedly was.

What, he wondered, would such a person do with that will? If indeed she had it. If it was there in that suitcase which she'd stolen for the rubies, surely she would have recognized its importance. Even if at the time she took the case—and Kemp could now see how Muriel might well have brought it out from wherever she'd hidden it from Florence Hermanos just to show off the jewels to her nurse—she hadn't known the will was in it, she must have found it afterwards. But of course she could not divulge it, she could not afford to give the police any lead as to her whereabouts... Had she simply torn it up and thrown away the pieces because it would be evidence against her if she was ever caught?

That seemed the simplest explanation, and in a way Kemp was relieved, it seemed to lift a burden from his mind. But if Madeleine Smith had read it first, that would be enough for Madison and Horth—she too must be destroyed...

It was well after midnight when Kemp's telephone rang. He guessed who it would be, and picked up the receiver somewhat wearily.

Dale Van Gryson was not a man to allow resentment to colour his tone—he was too good a lawyer for that. If there was a hint of pique it was no more than an undercurrent.

'...and Julius agrees with me that you might well have had your reasons for instigating separate inquiries, Lennox,' he continued his carefully prepared opening. 'For myself, I guess I'm just a bit hurt that you did not share them with me.'

'We were on opposite sides of the fence by then, Dale,' Kemp pointed out, 'and I had no wish to embarrass either yourself or Mr Eikenberg as trustees of the first will.'

'Wa-al...I have to admit we should have cottoned on to the Smith woman but the Hermanos lead looked a lot more promising to the Police Department and we were constrained by their advice... We're not in the detective business, Lennox. I guess you can appreciate that... Now all these new developments are sure to play hell with the court case. Best we can do is get together with Madison's Coun-

sel tomorrow along with your Mr Benton, and we thrash the
thing out. It'll probably mean we all go before the Surrogate Judge and request more time...'

'Have the police got any lead on Nurse Smith other than
what Mr Shulman's given them?' asked Kemp, voicing what
was uppermost in his mind.

'New York's working with Chicago on this one. They've
already checked out travel agents and airlines in that city. No
one by the name of Madeleine Smith bought tickets or
booked in through the whole of July and so far as we've got
with the passport section she'd not got one—at least not
under that name. What they did get was that a woman who
could have been her changed a lot of dollars round the
banks in Chicago on the third of July.' Van Gryson gave a
high whinnying laugh of disbelief. 'Can you imagine anyone carrying that amount around in cash?' Money was a
serious subject with him and he believed it should be kept
where it belonged, in neat columns on sacred paper, not
carted around in handbags.

'That sounds like our lady,' said Kemp, 'and I don't suppose any of it has been paid into that account of hers in
Brooklyn?'

'The bank confirms there was about two hundred dollars
in her account in May, nothing's been taken out or paid in
since, and the Nurses' Agency says they still hold wages due
to her. But you know all this, Lennox...'

'So do a lot of other people by now... And whatever information your friends Madison and Horth have got on this
woman they'll keep to themselves.'

'They're no friends of ours,' Van Gryson said stiffly.
'Although we have to hold the entire estate in trust for them
under the first will, it's by no means an amicable relationship. They have their own legal advisers...'

'To whom they're not going to spill any beans on Madeleine Smith till their boys have found her and dumped her
body in some river like they did Florence Hermanos.'

At the other end of the line Van Gryson was silent for a moment as he digested this perfectly reasonable assumption. He was obviously not comfortable with it. 'Their lawyers deny any knowledge of Miss Smith's whereabouts. They're saying her involvement comes as just as much of a surprise to them as it does to us. Of course I take your point, Lennox, in view of Mr Shulman's suspicions that the people from Vegas have been on to her for some time.'

'But they've not caught up with her yet or she'd be dead, sir, long ago, like the bailiff's daughter of Islington...' Kemp was given to frivolous quotation when he was tired and by now he'd wearied of this twice-told tale that seemed to have one end, death. 'Sorry, Dale,' he said, 'but it's early morning over here...'

Van Gryson was sympathetic but could not resist a last effort to bring reason to bear on a matter he thought was getting out of hand. 'Of course none of us wish the death of this woman—' he was at his most Bostonian, his tone rotund with rectitude—'but one must remember she's a common thief. Those who steal property belonging to others must face the consequences of their action.'

It's as well Boston's a hole and the herring-pond is wide, the words crept unbidden into Kemp's mind. Had he and the American been face to face at this moment Van Gryson's eyes would have wavered when he recalled that Kemp too had once been a thief.

Perhaps he had indeed remembered for his voice was warmer as he bade Kemp good night, and apologized for keeping him from his rest.

As KEMP PULLED the coverlet over his head he resolved to put both Bernie Shulman and Van Gryson out of it and concentrate, as he often briefly did before sleep, on the next day's business but he still found just one more niggling cause for dissatisfaction with the day already gone... What was it, now? Something Tony Lambert had said before he left.

'Oh, by the way, your new secretary wasn't at her desk today. Is she off sick?'

'I don't know. I was away to catch my train long before the staff got in this morning. As a matter of fact I took Miss Blane home last night about seven. She'd stayed late at the office. She's probably got a cold as a result. It was freezing when I left her.'

'Well, I hope it's nothing serious. She's a nice woman, Lennox, and I don't just mean as an office asset . . .'

They had both laughed, Kemp not knowing quite why.

Now he knew what was nagging him. He had been looking forward to seeing her, especially after their talk the night before. He would miss her homely presence. Perhaps her cold would be nothing, and she would be there in her usual place.

He fell asleep thinking of her, of how pleasant she was.

But his dreams were not pleasant.

### EIGHTEEN

'MISS BLANE NOT IN?' was the first thing Kemp said to Elvira the next morning.

'She wasn't here yesterday, Mr Kemp. Someone phoned. Said she'd be off a few days. I didn't take the message...'

Kemp was already out of the door, and into reception. 'There was a message yesterday from Miss Blane. Did you take it, Lisa?'

'Yes, I did, Mr Kemp. A Mrs Beresford. She phoned in to say Miss Blane wouldn't be in for maybe a couple of days.'

'She say why?'

Lisa turned up her notes. 'Miss Blane had a family matter to attend to. That's all Mrs Beresford said. She's an old client of yours, isn't she? Mrs Beresford I mean...'

Yes, that's right. Miss Blane has a flat in her house... There's been no other message?'

Lisa shook her head.

Kemp went back to his office and dealt with the morning's mail which was never without problems. It was nearly one o'clock before he even stopped to think.

A family matter... But Mary Blane had no family. At least that's what she'd told him. There must be some misunderstanding here...

I'll go round there after lunch, he thought, and see what's going on. I can always make the excuse I'm visiting Lydia Beresford... Why the hell am I thinking of excuses? Miss Blane's an employee of mine, why shouldn't I be concerned for her?

But it isn't always easy to find time for a personal concern when you are running a solicitor's practice. Peter Carruthers called a session for all partners to consider new interest rates and their effect on clients' accounts. In the present economic climate such financial matters took precedence over all else. It was after two o'clock before the conference was concluded, and the remains of sandwiches and pastries finally consumed.

The afternoon was a busy one and it was nearly five o'clock when Kemp managed to get a call through to Mrs Beresford's number. There was no reply.

As he was signing the mail, Alec Cooper put his head round the door. Kemp looked up. 'What brings you here, Alec?'

Cooper was surprisingly diffident.

'I've just finished a completion with your conveyancer, but I wanted a word with you if you've the time.'

'Sure. Sit down, Alec. I'll just take these letters out to Elvira. She shouldn't be here in the afternoons any more but my new secretary's off, and Elvira's coping, as usual.'

On his return Alec said: 'I don't really know how to put this but could you possibly see Dennis Brinscombe some time tomorrow?'

'Brinscombe here? Surely that wouldn't be right, Alec? He's your client... Besides, I don't want a punch on the nose.'

Alex held up a hand. 'It's nothing like that, Lennox. He simply insists on seeing you. Says it's something urgent. And it's got no connection with his family affairs, I can assure you of that. Except that I think he wants to apologize to you.'

'Apologize? That doesn't sound like Dennis Brinscombe.'

'He's a changed man, Lennox. Anyway, he's grateful to you for the way you dealt with this little matter of Belinda's... But that's not the real reason he wants to see you.'

'What is it then?'

'I simply don't know.' Alex Cooper looked ruffled and ill-at-ease, as well as he might. 'He won't tell me.'

'You're his solicitor. I can't see why he should want to consult me. Anyway, its quite unethical.'

'I've told him all that. The fact is, I think he's got trouble with his men...'

'Given his temperament and their record, I'm not surprised. But surely it's something you can handle?'

'This isn't a case of switching solicitors. Brinscombe's adamant about that. He just says he must see you and could I arrange a meeting. That, incidentally, was my idea, I knew you wouldn't see him otherwise. I had to stop him going round to your flat...'

'Trouble with that crew of his? What sort of trouble?'

'He won't tell me,' Cooper said again. 'All I know is that he's sacked a couple of them and he came to me about dismissal procedures. I advised him on the law but he wouldn't give me the details I asked for... He's a very disturbed man, Lennox... All the bluster's gone out of him. I think he's scared about something. All he'd tell me was that he has to see you as soon as possible.'

The two men looked at one another for a moment without speaking.

'It's awkward,' said Kemp.

'I know. But I really think we have to take him at his word that it's nothing whatever to do with the family, it's not Vivienne or the kid.'

'If I do see him it's only right that you should sit in on it, Alec.'

Cooper shook his head. 'He won't have that. Wants to come himself. He's in a highly nervous state. Something's biting him and he wants it off his chest, and it concerns you. If I hadn't warned him off he'd be round here now.'

'If you and I agree that it's all right from a professional point of view,' said Kemp slowly, 'then I'll see him.' He pulled his appointments diary towards him. 'I've got a clear spot between three and four tomorrow afternoon. But I'll make it clear to Brinscombe that if he tells me anything you should know about then I'll pass it on.'

'I don't think there's anything more I care to know about him,' said Cooper, getting to his feet. 'Thanks, Lennox.'

When Kemp left the office at six o'clock he drove straight to the house in Station Road. There was a light in the porch; at least someone was at home.

Lydia Beresford was pleased to see him.

'How nice of you to come, Lennox. It's been ages,' she said as she let him in. 'Did you phone earlier? It's my after-noon at the library and I heard it ringing as I came up the steps.'

She made tea, and they chatted over it for some time in Lydia's large, old-fashioned sitting-room which looked out over the garden at the rear.

'It was a good idea of yours to split this place,' said Kemp. 'It was much too big for you.' He had already sensed that they were alone in the house.

'And lonely... It's so nice having another woman up-stairs, and Miss Blane is just right. We don't live in each other's pockets, you understand, but I find her a very com-panionable sort of person.'

'You know she works for me?'

'Of course I do, Lennox.' Mrs Beresford looked at him rather archly. 'Naturally she doesn't talk about her work, and I think she is reticent by nature, but from what she tells me she seems very pleased to be with you.'

'What do you really make of her?' He asked the question abruptly.

'She's not easy to get to know. A woman of her age, and unmarried... One does wonder... But then, of course, she's Irish and perhaps there have not been the opportunities.' Lydia gave a little laugh. 'I don't know what you want me to say, Lennox. From what I've seen of Mary Blane, I like her. She's unusual. So quiet. But she's got a good head on her shoulders. She never seems to get upset... Well, not until the day before yesterday...'

'She asked you to phone the office for her. Couldn't she do it for herself? What exactly happened?'

It helped that Lydia Beresford was an intelligent woman who liked to get her facts right and could give a straight narrative without too many side-stepping frills.

'As it was my morning for helping at the Women's Institute market in the town I had to go out early immediately after breakfast. I already had my hat and coat on when Mary came into the kitchen just before half past eight. She doesn't normally leave till quarter to nine, and then she'll knock on my door and call out that she's going. But that particular morning she wasn't even properly dressed, her blouse and skirt were just thrown on and her hair wasn't combed. She looked flustered.

'All she said was that her two brothers from Ireland were outside—she'd seen their car from her window which looks out on the road in front—and that it probably meant there was bad news from home. Would I please phone the office for her and say she might be away for a few days.

'I began to say something about how sorry I was but she cut me short. A relative was ill, she said. Of course I promised to do as she asked. Then she gave me some letters to post along with money for the stamps—Mary was always very particular about little things like that. In fact she slipped the letters into my shopping-bag herself. She was obviously in a terrific hurry.

'Then the front doorbell went and she said she'd get it. I heard their voices in the hall, and footsteps going upstairs to her flat.'

'You didn't see her brothers, then?'

'She'd shut the kitchen door. I got the impression she didn't want me to meet them, Lennox...' Lydia looked uncomfortable. 'At the time I though they were perhaps—how can I put it?'

'Rough Irish?'

'I was going to say of a lower class,' said Lydia primly. She was in the habit of curbing her snobbish tendency but education and upbringing were against her.

'Did you hear any of the talk going on upstairs?'

'Lennox,' she admonished him. 'You ought to know me better than that. Miss Blane and I may share this house but we do not intrude upon each other's lives. If they had some sad family matter to discuss the least I could do was to afford them privacy. I did not even go out into the hall or the front of the house again that morning.'

'Well, did you see them leave?'

'How could I? I had to leave myself almost immediately to get down to the market by nine. And I go out by the back door to the garage which is at the end of the garden and I drive along the next street so I didn't even see their car. I presume they were all still in the house when I left.'

'And Mary hasn't returned?'

'No. I do miss her. I had got used to her being there . . . You're looking very serious, Lennox. Do you think there's something wrong?'

Kemp was pacing up and down the room.

'Mary Blane gave me to understand she had no relatives either over here or in Ireland . . . Why didn't she phone herself and explain why she would be away?'

Lydia Beresford was hardly listening, she had been sidetracked by a recollection of her own.

'It was funny about those letters,' she said, 'putting them into my bag like that, almost as if she wanted to hide them. And then scattering coins on the table, pound coins . . . She left far too much money . . . Two of the envelopes were already stamped, her electricity account and one to a mail order place I think she bought clothes from. I just popped those in the box. I suppose she must have been thinking of the American airmail one because you have to hand these over the counter and they tell you how much . . . She probably had no idea so she left the money to cover it. Actually, though it was quite heavy it didn't come to over a pound.'

Kemp had stopped walking about, and was staring down at her.

'One of her letters was to America?'

'It was a long manilla envelope like you have in your office, Lennox. It was typed, and "by airmail" was typed in one corner, so I got one of those *par avion* stickers they have at the post office and put it on... I thought that's what she would have wanted but she'd been in too much of a rush to do it herself.'

Kemp came and sat beside Lydia Beresford. He took her hand.

'I know this must seem to you like prying, but I assure you it's not. You handed this letter over at the counter. You have good eyes, Lydia, you put that sticker on it... You must have seen the address?'

'I couldn't help seeing it, Lennox. And I remember the name. A Mr Van Gryson, then the name of a firm, Eiken—something—and an address in New York. I know you, Lennox, you will have a good reason for asking...'

Kemp said nothing, his mind in a turmoil. Mary Blane could have forgotten to post a letter in the office, taken it home with her, felt she was in dereliction of her duty not to get it off. But he'd not written to Eikenberg & Lazard for weeks... He'd no reason to believe such a letter had anything to do with the office. He was clutching at straws, trying to find a trivial answer to questions which were looming up now, dark, dangerous questions...

He got up with a quick movement which almost toppled the armchair.

'I have to see her flat.'

'But I can't let you do that! Not when she isn't here. It wouldn't be proper... Anyway, I haven't a key.'

'Then we'll just have to break down the door,' said Kemp calmly. 'I'm sorry, Lydia, but it has to be done.'

She saw the look in his eyes, and followed him meekly. She hesitated behind him at the door of the upstairs flat while he examined the lock, and when he asked for a hammer she went to the toolshed and fetched it for him.

As the flat was part of a house already furnished with security locks on the front and back doors not much attention had been given to this one. One swift blow and the door swung open.

On the threshold Lydia cried out, but Kemp who had seen it all too often before walked straight in over the debris of splintered wood and overturned furniture. Nothing had been left intact. Even the kitchen cupboards had been ripped from the walls, the stove had been taken out, every cannister and jar in pieces on the floor. The bathroom had had similar, systematic treatment, including the plumbing fixtures. In the bedroom the divan was upended, the mattress gaped open, the contents of drawers and wardrobes torn to shreds. No hiding-place had been left unmarked.

In the front room the chairs and the settee had been savagely knifed through to the wood. There had been a pine table now lying smashed. Underneath it lay broken china, and the remains of a breakfast.

'She saw them from here,' said Kemp, at the window. 'But why did she let them in? She must have known they meant her harm...'

Lydia Beresford had recovered though she was still shaking. 'I'll call the police,' she said quietly. 'After all, it's my house. You will know what to do about Mary...' She went downstairs, closing the door behind her.

Kemp felt frozen in body and mind. He had to move one of them if the other was to function. He steeled himself to go back into the kitchen. He had not let Lydia see it, that splash of blood in the sink. Now he examined it again, and the bloodstained rag beside it.

He stalked into the bedroom, looked down at the torn clothing, modest dresses, plain skirts and jumpers, all in a heap like the rubbish at the end of a jumble sale, even the shoes had their tongues cut out ... She had only one good suit, a woollen in a rose colour which must have suited her though he'd never seen her wear it. He picked up the jacket which fell away from its ripped-out sleeves and something caught his fingers, a brooch pinned to the lapel.

His legs gave way under him, and he sat down suddenly on the pile of clothes and looked at the little red berries nestling in the gold. Cheap gold but she'd liked it, knowing how pleased he had been when he bought it.

'They're so small, Lennox,' she'd laughed at him when he gave it to her that Christmas, the Christmas before the catastrophe, 'but at least they're real rubies ...'

# NINETEEN

SHE'D KNOWN AS SOON as she saw them from the window, the two burly men, the long black car. At the back of her mind always there had been the expectation that sooner or later they would come for her. They had international police networks now, she had thought in sudden desperation, they work together. I should have known.

She had stayed calm. There would not be much time. She had taken the envelope from the drawer. She had typed it anyway one day in the office, and put it away safely not knowing what to expect, at what moment she would send it. Now she didn't hesitate. She had other letters, it would all seem part of them.

Mrs Beresford was ready to go out. Her shopping-bag hung there on the hook in the kitchen. She'd slipped them in and asked her to post them. Mrs Beresford would be gone before the police began to search. She could stall them that long, she would cooperate with them... There was no other evidence left, she had thought grimly as she opened the door to them, led them upstairs, waited to hear Mrs Beresford's car leave from the back.

'I'll be away a few days,' she'd said, knowing it would be much longer. She had made up her story on the spur of the moment as she'd always done. They would all find out about her in time but she didn't want them to know right away, she couldn't face that...

They had been so good to her since she came, she had known more kindness here than ever in her life: Mr Cafferty, Mrs Beresford, the girls in the office, Mr Kemp... She didn't want to think about him, the things he had said about

Muriel. Funny to think that he'd been married to her... She still thought of the dead woman as Mrs Probert, she'd hardly known her, only through those brief six nights of talk... That was an episode long gone into the past.

The more recent past was more important now, the two days and one night since she'd been taken from Mrs Beresford's house, for she had learned the truth, and knew the peril she was in. She looked back to the moment when she'd guessed.

They'd been polite enough going up the stairs, they had not wanted to draw attention to themselves. They're not like American cops, she'd thought, breaking down doors and going in with guns... They had been very civilized—at first.

'If you'll just hand over that document you found along with the jewellery you stole, it'll go better for you.'

'I haven't got any such thing. I don't know what you mean. Am I being arrested?' It had been all she could think of to say while she waited for the sound of Mrs Beresford's car.

After that she hadn't cared. She'd watched them take the place apart, and knew what they were looking for. They'd both grinned when they found her Irish passport, that precious and only gift from her poor mother, and the deposit slip from the Dublin bank, but by then such things had ceased to matter; the game was up anyway. They weren't going to find the other document which was suddenly so important to them. She comforted herself with the thought of Mrs Beresford driving down to the car park by the market as she always did, crossing to the post office... The letter would be in the mail, there was nothing anyone could do now to stop it. Mr Kemp's case would go his way in that courtroom; whatever ill he might think of her, she had made amends.

It was only gradually that it dawned upon her that these two men weren't acting like policemen at all.

The one who had said: 'Come on, lady, where is it?' had struck her across the mouth when she'd stared dumbly back at him. They hadn't cautioned her like the English police were supposed to do, the way they read you your rights in the States—she'd heard enough Mirandas in her time, standing beside yet another of the Smith tribe in trouble with the authorities.

When they'd begun slashing the furniture she'd protested, saying it wasn't hers, and the other one had knocked her to the floor. She knew then. They weren't from the police, she wasn't going to be arrested and shipped back to America. Something much worse was going to happen to her.

She stretched out her legs on the straw mattress and wondered what time it was. She knew her captors were waiting for someone to come.

'All our job was to get the woman and the stuff. Well, it wasn't there, was it? But we've got her...' She'd heard that in the car. They'd gagged her like they do in films but they'd forgotten to clamp her ears.

'Our instructions are to wait for the American. He's flying in. He'll know what to do with her. Your place safe?'

'As a vault.' He'd laughed, the bigger of the two, the one with the moon face. 'They'll never find her...'

They'd put a sack over her head as they hustled her out after the long drive. Perhaps it wasn't that far, they'd turned a lot of corners, maybe going in circles to fool her into thinking she'd been taken some distance. There had been a stair with ragged carpet on it, then this room which looked out on nothing she could see, for the window was boarded up. There was an iron bedstead, a chair and table, and in a corner a stained washbasin and a lavatory that smelled of disuse and dead animals.

They'd taken off the gag. 'Scream as much as you like, lady, there's no one in miles to hear you. Hope you're satisfied with your new quarters...'

She hadn't bothered to look at him, the younger of the two. If they thought to frighten her by the squalor of her surroundings they'd got the wrong party. She'd grown up in a shack in Vineland.

For want of anything better to do she began thinking back to those days. It had never been in her nature to look back, there'd not been time, and anyway introspection, as she'd heard it called, was for neurotics. It was all very well for the elderly and the senile she'd nursed to keep harping about their youth and she had never withheld compassion from them, but for people who blamed all their ills on deprived childhoods she had no respect.

But thinking was preferable to just sitting here on this hard bed staring at nothing. That was how she remembered her mother, sitting for hours, staring at nothing, waiting for the better times that never came.

She didn't want to think about her mother, in the past it had brought tears to her eyes, and she couldn't abide tears. Yet now she might be able to bear it, now that Mr Cafferty had spoken so nicely of her.

'So you're Maddie Blane's daughter,' he'd said when she met him that day in Enniskerry. He'd advertised for a typist to work in his Dublin office and when she'd phoned he'd arranged to meet her in the local hotel.

'. . . and you're an American?' he'd gone on.

'I'm Irish,' she'd told him, smiling because she was at ease with him. 'I was born right here in Enniskerry. . .' And thank God for it and the journey her mother had taken those thirty-five years ago just for that.

'And are you well set up, Mary?' Mr Cafferty had put it to her kindly.

'I've enough, but I'm looking for a job.'

'And what sort of work have you been doing over there in the States?'

She had been careful, there must be no mention of nursing. 'I've been in offices.' Which was the truth, though she

had not added that it was through her calm efficiency as a
hospital clerk that she had been persuaded to take up another career. 'I took classes at the shorthand and typing...'
She had slipped easily into his idiom, it was the way her
mother had talked.

'Well, now, Mary, I'm in want of a secretary. Mine's away
to get married. You'll not be thinking of that yourself?'

'I've never given a thought to it, Mr Cafferty. It's maybe
a bit late in the day. I'm just glad to be back where I feel I
belong.'

Mr Cafferty had shaken his head. 'There's none of the
Blanes left now in Enniskerry. They all of them emigrated
about the time your mother did, for there was but a poor
living hereabouts... I see it's your mother's name you use.
I'd heard she was married to a Yankee, wasn't it Smith,
now?'

'He was a deadbeat, Mr Cafferty, and a bad memory to
me even if he was my father. So I prefer the name my
mother gave me, her one Irish-born child...Mary Madeleine Blane.' It was a relief to be able to speak it cleanly now
after all the other names she'd gone under. It was hers at
last.

'So that's the way of it...' Mr Cafferty had asked no more
questions. He had tut-tutted when she told him of the manner of her mother's death.

'I'm sorry to hear of it. She was the best of them, Maddie Blane, as bright a girl as ever left Ireland...'

She would never have told him anyway about the rest of
it, about the dirt and degradation in that old frame house in
Vineland where her mother and she had struggled to bring
up the brood of Smith children—she'd not considered herself one of them. They'd all taken after their father, and,
like him, gone to the bad in their several ways: Gerry in the
juvenile court before he was out of grade school, Sharon
pregnant at fourteen by an itinerant farm labourer and now
on the streets, baby Clara, the pretty, spoilt one, caught

shoplifting too many times... As each new crisis had arisen
it was always Mary that was sent for, her presence in the
court to bolster up their lies, her earnings to save the family
from slipping even further down the poverty slope... All to
no avail. Smith—she never called him anything else—only
drank the more, grew harsher in his beatings, while her
mother crept about like a shadow till the cancer caught and
killed her. No, she would never tell anyone about those
years, the years that had made her what she was.

So far gone was she into the past that this time she never
heard the steps at the door she usually listened for. When the
door burst open and she turned to face it there were tears on
her cheeks. She struck them away with the back of her hand.

'Crying'll do you no good.' It was the younger man, carrying a tin tray. Bread, some cheese and a cup of milky tea.
'Got to keep you alive for the big chief.' He put the tray
down on the table beside the bed.

'What's the time?' she asked him.

'What's it to you? You're not going any place.'

'I have to know when to take my pills. I'm a diabetic.'

It was something she'd thought up before they'd pushed
her out of the flat and down the stairs. She'd gone to the
kitchen to get some water to bathe her mouth which was
bleeding. She'd picked up a torn teacloth to wipe up the
blood and seen the scattered tablets all over the floor. They
were out of the few medicine bottles and packets she'd kept
on the glass shelf near the sink. She herself was rarely ill but
like any good nurse she always had a supply of the commoner remedies, things like aspirin and codeine, capsules
for colds, and some cough lozenges. They won't know the
difference, she'd thought grimly as she picked up as many
as she could and put them in her handbag. They'd not ob-
jected to her taking her bag with her; they'd been through
it anyway.

'Bloody hell!' The man was glaring at her in consterna-
tion. 'Where'd you keep your pills, then?'

'They're in my handbag. Your friend's got it.'

The man hesitated. She gathered he was the second-in-command and he'd have to get instructions.

'What happens if you don't take these things?'

'I go into a coma, and eventually I die. I've been here a day and a night, and now it's the second day and I need to know the time.'

'Bloody hell!' said the man again, making for the door.

'And I'll have to have better food than this,' she called after him, 'if you want to keep me alive...'

In his rush downstairs he banged the door shut behind him but she didn't hear him turn the lock. She leapt off the bed and opened it a fraction. She could hear the voices downstairs.

'Says she's a bloody diabetic... She's got pills for it in her handbag. Give it here, Mike.'

Mike must have taken a look. 'Yeah, there's some tablets at the bottom. She can have her bloody bag. I've taken out the pens and stuff. Didn't want her writing little notes and collarin' a passing pigeon...'

There was a clatter of pots and pans so they must have gone into the kitchen downstairs, and she heard no more, but when the younger man again appeared he was carrying not only her bag but a bowl of steaming soup.

Well, it worked, she thought, putting a cough sweet in her mouth and taking a sip of tea. When the young man had told her it was five o'clock she'd said: 'Then it's time I took one of my tablets. Thanks for the soup. I'll have it when it's cool.'

He'd stood watching her, goggle-eyed as if in the presence of imminent death, before going out and locking the door. I'll play this one for all it's worth, she said to herself, and if the going gets too rough I can always swallow the lot... Or at least I can fake a diabetic coma—I've seen so many of them.

These were sombre thoughts and she knew where they led. She would have been better off at the police station, but too late to think of that.

It had been hard for her to come to terms with the contents of the American file in the office, so much of it in legal jargon she could not understand, but that accident that nearly happened to Mr Kemp on the building site, those break-ins, they meant trouble for him so she had read the file through again, more carefully. She guessed what they were after, those men from Las Vegas, it was that second will, the document Mrs Probert had said wasn't important. But it was important to them and they would go to any lengths to get hold of it.

Many times she had thought of simply handing it over to Mr Kemp, or leaving it somewhere so he'd find it... But she quailed at the explanations that must follow, the consequences to herself. She didn't feel like running away any more... Where was there left to run to? She knew she should have posted it before now, but not with a Newtown postmark—that, too, would only give rise to investigations she dreaded. She'd meant to take it into London one day and mail it from there, but somehow there hadn't been time...

She wished now she had stayed in the peace of Ireland. She'd been so happy there, going up by bus to Dublin every day, working in that old dark office by the Liffey, everyone so pleasant to her as if she'd been a returned prodigal, and Mr Cafferty treating her with such courtesy.

It was ironic that it was curiosity alone which had finally brought her to Newtown. She wanted to see for herself what he was like, the man Muriel Probert had remembered at the end, the one standing against the trees in that photograph.

She had burnt all the photographs when she came first to Enniskerry—clearing her decks, she'd called it—and very nearly did the same with the will document. That was before she'd seen the advertisement in the Legal section of *The Times*.

'Did you ever hear of a place near London called New-town?' she'd asked Mr Cafferty one day.

'Sure and it's where one of the Blanes went as a maid. But that was years ago, Mary. She'll be dead by now. Why are you asking?'

'There's an advertisement in *The Times*. An agency there's looking for secretaries.'

'You thinking of moving on, Mary? I'd be sorry to hear it. You've been here nearly two months now, and you've worked well ... But I'll not stand in your way if you're set on going. I can't be offering you what they will, and you've your own life to live. You're alone in the world and you're right to think of the future and what you can earn ...'

She hated it when he talked to her like that; that enormous deposit in her Dublin bank mocked her for a hypocrite, a hypocrite and a thief. She was embarrassed by her gratitude to him, his unquestioning acceptance—but gratitude had never been an easy emotion for her, so she stumbled over her explanation.

'Just for a while,' she'd pleaded. 'It might not suit me, the life over in England ... It was just seeing the name of that place in the paper, I must have heard talk of it from my mother ... Maybe that's what made me fancy it ...'

None of this was true, of course. She'd only seen it in the will, but the coincidence had struck her as if it was intended she should go where a Blane had been before. Even that was too vague for a reason; the real truth lay in her own curiosity. This Lennox Kemp who was mentioned in the will, he worked in Newtown, he was a solicitor there ... She wanted to see what kind of man he was. Only then would she make up her mind about the will, destroy it or send it on to those lawyers in New York.

She hadn't actually planned on taking up a job with Gillorns but once she'd registered at the agency as a legal secretary it seemed inevitable now that she should have been sent there. She'd only wanted a glimpse of this man, Kemp... But once she'd seen the American file her eyes were opened, and she began to have an inkling of what was going on. Although she had never given much sign of it in her work she knew she was not a fast thinker unless spurred to it...

She'd been spurred all right by the rubies, by the prospect of the money. Now this was something else, her very life was in danger. About that she had no illusions.

She finished the soup and put the bowl back on the tray. Whatever daylight had filtered through the slats nailed across the window was fading and the room was dark. Another night... When would the American come? Would it be the one they called Horth, or was she important enough to bring Prester John Madison himself across the Atlantic?

Though she knew vaguely what was at stake for these men she'd no fear of the Mafia. She'd probably nursed a few of them in her time. She knew she'd been at the bedside of some of the rich people they protected, and she'd found they died just like anybody else, of gasping heart attacks, of strokes that left them limp and speechless; their organs deteriorated like the rest of the human species, for all their kidney transplants and expensive operations. In the end, the way she saw them, they were only bodies and subject to the same failings of the flesh as the derelicts taken off the streets into the downtown hospitals.

Such thoughts went this way and that through her head as she lay back now in her thin blouse and crumpled skirt. It was cold but she'd been cold often before, it never interfered with her blessed gift for sleep.

# TWENTY

KEMP SPENT THE MORNING at Newtown Police Station. He felt some sympathy for John Upshire, a conscientious officer and a good friend now thrown into a crime committed on his territory but which had international repercussions and could affect the outcome of a court case about to be heard in New York.

'For God's sake, Lennox,' he'd exclaimed half way through Kemp's story, 'not the Mafia! My super will do his nut... He's head of an English police force and does what he can with the resources at his disposal, but men from Las Vegas... Give us a break!'

'It's this connection I'm after,' said Kemp earnestly, 'for they're here, I've not a shadow of a doubt about that. They're here in Newtown and it's them—I know it's them— who're holding Mary Blane. If indeed she's still alive...'

Inspector Upshire was no fool. All the proper things had been done; contacts made with the New York Police Department to correlate the facts they had on Madeleine Smith, checks carried out with the passport offices in Liverpool and Dublin, and phone calls made to banks in the latter city. All confirmed what they suspected; Madeleine Smith and Mary Blane were one and the same person.

It was Kemp himself who had spoken to Mr Cafferty.

'And what is it she's wanted for back there in the States, Mr Kemp?' The soft voice was disarming. It occurred to Kemp that this was a man to whom nothing would come as a surprise where it concerned his countrymen—or women.

'I see...I see... She'd be forced into something of the sort, no doubt. That's a hard world over there, Mr Kemp.'

'She stole a fortune in rubies, Mr Cafferty, from a patient she'd nursed.' Kemp put it bluntly.

'Well, that's as may be,' came the slow response, and there was a sigh. 'I'll tell you all I know of her...'

It hadn't helped Kemp's state of mind to learn that so much of what Mary Blane had told him was true. She was Irish, she'd been born in Enniskerry, she'd gone back and worked there last summer when she'd fled the States, she no longer had any relatives there...

Inspector Upshire had instituted the necessary inquiries and ordered a search for a missing person, but he had been wary of publicity.

'This woman's a thief, she's wanted in the States, how do we know they're not all in this together? You've no evidence they're holding her against her will. Maybe it's a case of thieves falling out over the loot, maybe there was meant to be a share-out of that money in Dublin.'

'There was that blood in the kitchen sink,' said Kemp stubbornly.

'Could have come from any of them if a fight broke out. They were pretty free with knives in that place. Without this story of yours, Lennox, all we've got here is breaking and entering, and criminal damage to Mrs Beresford's furniture.' He held up a warning hand at Kemp's protest. 'For the moment I'll go along with your version that this Mary Blane is in danger but I don't want a great hue-and-cry going on that might show us up as fools in the end. You think she's still in the district?'

'I've no idea. Up to a point they want her alive just so they can tie up any loose ends. Who she's told about the second will, for instance. They can't afford the risk that she might have told someone...'

'Well, you're the obvious one. Why the hell didn't she give it to you?'

Kemp ran his fingers through his thinning hair in a gesture of exasperation.

'Because it would immediately label her a thief. If she stole the rubies, she's got the will. If she's got the will, she stole the rubies... What I can't understand is why she ever came to Newtown in the first place. She was safe in Ireland, the New York Police would never have traced that Irish passport... I think it was when she got into my office she was linked up with me, and that's how the other lot hooked on to her.'

'Perhaps she suffers from your trouble,' said Upshire blandly. 'Too much curiosity... You think that's how they got to her, these mystical men from the mob?'

'They're no myth,' said Kemp shortly. 'Yes, I think they reached the same dead end in the States as my man did. But when my office was raided they looked at the records of new staff and the fact one was from Ireland alerted them. Perhaps they got some lead back there in her home town that we missed... Could have been her name...'

Mary Madeleine Blane. Kemp could understand the Inspector's scepticism about the bogeymen from Las Vegas and the possibility of kidnap. It would have been very different had she been an innocent victim, but in John Upshire's view she had shown herself to be a scheming female of infinite resource, and any trouble she was in she'd brought upon herself.

Kemp broached the subject of Dennis Brinscombe, but the Inspector would have none of it. 'If his name comes up in the course of our inquiries I shall deal with it,' Upshire said stolidly, 'but he's a respectable citizen of this town, and if you're trying to connect him with the Mafia then that's a very serious accusation.'

'He had Clive Horth's business card in his wallet.'

'And it might just be what it says, business,' snapped Upshire. 'You keep clear of Brinscombe, Lennox. There's been enough harsh words between the pair of you from what I hear.'

Kemp heeded the warning in as much that he forbore to
tell the Inspector that he would be seeing Dennis Brinscombe that afternoon. He would need to curb his temper by
then.

For it was already raging within him as he left the station, though for the moment his anger was mainly directed
at himself.

She had worked there quietly in his office, under his very
eyes, since September. At first he hadn't noticed her at all,
just one of the temporary typists—and a plain one at that.
Afterwards he had seen her as a pleasant enough person of
no great distinction set against a background of misty
green ... He'd remembered a maid his mother had employed during one of his father's prosperous periods, Irish
Mary they'd called her—and not just carefully behind her
back. Somehow Mary Blane had reminded him of that girl.
Wrong. Wrong. Wrong. How could he have been so hood-
winked?

For Kemp this was a devastating blow to his ego. He had
always prided himself on his perspicacity, his ability to read
character and sort out the good from the bad. His most
successful cases had been built on it, what he thought of as
his greatest skill.

Yet he had been taken in, suborned, not by a pretty face
or fine figure but by this nondescript woman whom he had
considered not even very clever.

He sat in a corner of his local inn, hardly tasting his
lunch, and hoping no one would speak to him. Anger was
something he could cope with but not the other underlying
fear, the return of that apprehension and panic he had experienced on the train the other night. Now he knew that
even then Mary Blane was already in their hands.

But she had made sure the will was posted to New York
before she was taken so she must have known what they
were after. Had she thought that move would save her? By

now she must have learned the truth—nothing she could say or do was going to save her.

When he reached his office Dennis Brinscombe was already in reception.

'I told him his appointment was for later,' Lisa whispered, 'but he took no notice.'

'That's all right. I'll see him now. Come in, Mr Brinscombe.'

Kemp hardly recognized the man. It was as if someone had pricked his skin and let out all the air. Even the protuberant eyes had sunk into hiding, and his ruddy complexion faded to an unhealthy yellow. He slumped into a chair and leaned his elbows on the desk.

'I couldn't wait another hour,' he said, 'I've got to tell you all this, Kemp... It's going to come out anyway sooner or later. But I can't take it any more...'

'A drink, Mr Brinscombe?' It was not often it was offered by Kemp but he felt it might help to oil whatever cogwheels were turning in Brinscombe's mind.

'Thanks. I could do with one.'

The small digression seemed to calm him though he took up the glass with a hand that shook.

'Perhaps you should start at the beginning, Mr Brinscombe.'

'All right. Some years ago when I was in the States I made some acquaintances. That's all they were, acquaintances. You know how it is at these conferences, half business, half social... This one was in Nevada...'

'Come to the point. One of your acquaintances was a Mr Clive Horth?'

'Horth? I never knew *him*—it was Cutler, my foreman, who latched on to Horth.'

Kemp raised his eyebrows. 'His business card was in your wallet, Mr Brinscombe.'

'Well... these things get handed about. You've got to believe me, Kemp, I never had anything to do with Horth.

It's Cutler who's been taking orders from him... And I only found that out when I sacked him.'

'You sacked Cutler? Why?'

'He'd gone too far... He's worked for me for years, he kept the men in order. OK, I know what you're going to say... I should've known his methods and maybe I did, but he's kept me in the dark about a lot of things...'

'How does this affect me? Why d'you suddenly want to see me?'

'That's just it. That's what started off this last bit of trouble. These friends—acquaintances—in the construction business over in the States, they'd got overseas interests... there was a lot of money involved...'

'They helped finance your company?'

Brinscombe nodded. 'Helped me to expand. The future, world-wide, looked rosy. At first there weren't any strings... But the climate's changed this last year, and I got a bit, well, extended financially.'

'And they wanted their pound of flesh?'

The other man didn't think much of the expression. 'They needed a few favours done. Wasn't much. Well, Cutler was handling that side of things...'

'Including having a go at me?'

'It wasn't anything personal, you understand...'

'The hell it wasn't. They wanted me scared, and you couldn't resist putting your own boot in.'

'It seemed like it was all a bit of a joke at first. Cutler said you'd got some case on in the States which rubbed Horth up the wrong way and they just wanted you frightened off.'

'Like breaking in to my flat and office?'

'I swear I didn't know, not till after... It was Cutler and his mate, McGivern, and some of the men. When I heard... well, I knew it was them so I gave them a ticking-off...' It was a feeble description coming from a man like Dennis Brinscombe and Kemp didn't for a moment believe that part of it, so there was a hint of sarcasm in his voice when he asked:

'And how did they take this mild reprimand?'

Brinscombe wiped his brow. 'They just laughed at me...said I was in it up to here. They said I'd dance to their tune from now on. You've got to understand, Kemp. These people back there in Nevada, they're owed a lot of money. I was in too deep...'

'So why are you here in my office now?'

'I got to tell you. There's some woman involved—someone Horth wants. He's coming over. I told Cutler I'd have no part in it. I sacked him and his men. They laughed in my face. They did more than that, they started to threaten. Cutler told me Horth was Mafia... My God, Kemp, I didn't know what I was mixed up in...I swear I didn't know.'

'But you never questioned the high finance, did you, Brinscombe? I bet you never even asked where the money came from.'

'That was business. It was only afterwards I realized the whole thing was shady.'

'This woman that Horth wants: what are Cutler and his little gang saying about her?'

'I hear they've got her somewhere safe... They're being paid, and after it's over Cutler and McGivern are off to the States. I got to thinking it's maybe murder they're planning...I don't know enough to go to the police, I don't know the half of what Cutler's been up to, but the whole thing began with you and that case of yours...'

'Where's the woman being held?' asked Kemp, reaching for the phone.

'Christ! If I knew d'you think I wouldn't tell you?'

Kemp dialled. 'Inspector Upshire, please.'

While he waited he looked across at Brinscombe. The man was sweating. He was obviously scared, but having gone so far in confession it didn't seem as if he knew any more about the most urgent issue.

'John? I've got Mr Dennis Brinscombe with me, and I think he'll be coming to see you shortly. You know we spoke of the connection in Newtown? Well, it's Mark Cutler the foreman at Brinscombes, and a Mr McGivern. No, I don't know if there are others involved... Another thing, would you check the airlines to see if a Mr Clive Horth has landed from America in the last few days? Yes, I'll be down in about fifteen minutes.'

Kemp put the phone down.

'Mr Brinscombe, this is a case of kidnap and possibly murder. I think you should see Inspector Upshire right away. Shall we go in my car?'

During the short drive Kemp asked how Brinscombe had learned that a woman was involved. Since they left the office the man had been struck dumb. He was probably contemplating the future rather than the past, like a captain watching his ship go down.

'Huh? I was up at the site the end of last week—things hadn't been going well there lately. I think the men had got wind of... that Cutler was in charge, not me... Anyway, I was outside the hut and I heard them talking, Mark and McGivern. Then Cutler came out and said I knew more than was good for me, and that I'd be hearing from the man who was really the boss.'

No wonder the stuffing had been knocked out of Brinscombe, the power platform being snatched from under his feet. His voice was thick as he went on:

'Then yesterday morning I got an early call at home. I don't know who was speaking but it wasn't Mark. It sounded trans-Atlantic... I'd regret it if I interfered, they'd see my company ruined...they'd smash me... And I don't think they meant only financially, Kemp.' He gave a gulp. 'They knew I'd a daughter...' His face reddened, and there was a flash of the old Brinscombe when he said: 'I wasn't going to take that kind of talk from anyone. Damn the business, I thought... So I went to Mr Cooper, told him I had to see you. It had all started with them wanting to play rough with you, Kemp, so I thought you'd be the one to straighten things out—keep them off my back...'

Brinscombe's motive in coming forward was a mixture of bravado and self-interest that came as no surprise to Kemp, but he had to give the man credit for the fact that it was Belinda's safety that had triggered him in the end.

At the police station Inspector John Upshire was at his magisterial best, playing strictly by the rules.

'I'm not interested in your business activities, Mr Brinscombe, only in so far as they might concern this case of a missing woman. Since Mr Kemp spoke to me I've put out a call for these two men, Cutler and McGivern, to be brought in. Now I want details of both of them from you—descriptions, home addresses and any other information that will help us pick them up. They are not, I may say, on your building sites but you wouldn't expect that, would you? I understand you have terminated their employment?'

The studied suavity, the even tone of officialdom acted like a tonic on Dennis Brinscombe. He pulled himself together, perhaps saw himself for the moment as the honest citizen helping police with their inquiries. He positively spilled over with information.

Upshire used the phone a lot, his officers came and went with computer print-outs, the outer room buzzed with activity.

Kemp went to have a word with Sergeant Cribbins. 'It's all coming through,' he was told, 'but no real lead yet as to where they've gone. Cutler and McGivern, they never seem to have had homes to go to like simple folk. They've lived in hotels all over the land wherever there was big construction work going on, organizing labour was supposed to be their job... They been in Newtown on and off for over three years. Cutler's more than just foreman at Brinscombes, that's just a front by my reckoning. Place he and McGivern were in they packed up and left a week ago. We're bringing in some of the rabble off the site now but they're a tough lot—shan't get much out of them.'

'Dennis Brinscombe must know some of the men,' said Kemp. 'Maybe he can get them to talk.'

'He's on a greasy rope, Mr Brinscombe, and they know it...'

'It's worth a try. Any of them local?'

'One or two. I'll let Mr Upshire know when they come in.'

Kemp went back into the Inspector's office. Brinscombe was being given a cup of tea but there was no indication that he was being allowed to leave. Kemp took John Upshire aside. 'Let Brinscombe have a word with any of his workmen who're local. One of them might have some idea of a place Mark Cutler uses as a hideout.'

'Will do. Oh, by the way, your Mr Clive Horth arrived at Heathrow eight this morning. He was on the passenger list of a Pan Am in from New York. Don't glare at me like that, Lennox, all we could do was check the airlines. We can't hold him even if we knew where he was—you should know that...'

The police station office was crowded at four o'clock when the men from Brinscombes were herded in, asking with various degrees of profanity what the hell they were doing there. Kemp, loitering as a spectator by the Sergeant's desk, spotted the one who had grinned down at him that day from the scaffolding. He was only a lad, and he looked sullen but sheepish when Kemp walked over to him.

'You live in Newtown?'

'What d'you want to know for?' But he caught Sergeant Cribbins's eye on him and changed his tune. 'Yeah, Leadale Council Estate. I ain't done nothin' wrong. That were an accident.'

'Which Mark Cutler put you up to?'

The young man smirked. 'Mr Cutler, he's the boss...'

Kemp glanced down at the entry in the Sergeant's book. 'Mr Lang, I think Mr Brinscombe would like a word with you, if you'll come this way.'

Kevin Lang was not so much subdued by seeing Dennis Brinscombe as he was by the presence of Inspector Upshire, who was a large man and famous for putting the fear of God into errant juveniles.

'Kevin Lang,' said Kemp briskly. 'Lives on the Leadale Estate with his mother. I got her rehoused last year when she had a bust-up with her husband. She's a hard-working woman and a very decent sort... I think young Kevin here is going to cooperate with us.'

Kevin gave him a startled look. This wasn't the way things were supposed to go in police stations. They knocked you about and all you had to do was say nothing, like the IRA men. That's what Mr Cutler said.

It took half an hour of mingled cajolery, persuasion and lightly-veiled threats to bring young Lang to the talking point. Kemp had to hand it to Dennis Brinscombe, the man took the right line from the outset, it was no wonder that he had built up a loyal workforce before succumbing to the likes of Cutler. He treated Lang like an adult, an equal in their shared trade, for all that the lad was a mere apprentice carpenter; he never once came over the heavy boss, and he left the glimpse of mailed fist to the Inspector who came in on the dot with hints of conspiracy to crime, and the implications of aiding and abetting.

Their combined efforts worked.

'He's got a place, Mr Cutler has... Took us all out there once for a party. You'll know where it is, Mr Brinscombe... That land that was goin' to be developed, like, only there weren't no planning permission. Where there's all them trees...'

'Broxton Wood?' Dennis Brinscombe sat forward in his chair. 'Where those old houses were demolished?'

'Not all of them, Mr Brinscombe. There be two left all boarded up. Mr Cutler uses them. He's got them all fitted up, kept the water and power on an' all . . .'

The Inspector was already out of the door, shouting instructions. Kemp followed him. Upshire gave him a look.

'You can't stop me,' said Kemp. 'I have to be there.'

### TWENTY-ONE

SHE HAD WAKENED up early, stiff with cold. The only blanket was greasy and she'd thrown it off. She exercised her body to bring some warmth into it, splashed water on her face, and used the lavatory. The sound of her pulling at the rusty chain must have roused them, for soon there were footsteps at the door.

They came in together, the two men. For the first time she realized they'd never been masked. That was a thought that led to an ominous conclusion so she didn't dwell on it.

'I have to eat,' she said. She made a fuss fishing about in her handbag and bringing out a yellow capsule. It was only a remedy to back a cold but it would do. The younger man watched her with avid eyes.

'Get her some breakfast.' She knew the speaker's name was Mark, and he was the one in charge.

The younger man clattered downstairs. The other came over to her. In the faint light his face was like the moon.

'You're no better-looking than you were yesterday—and that's not saying much,' he said with a grin.

He smacked her hard across the face so that she fell back on the bed. He's bored, she thought, he needs the action, I've met his like before.

'The Chief says to rough you up just a little, lady, so's you'll be in the right frame of mind when he gets here...'

He walked out and locked the door. Some minutes later she heard the sound of a car starting up. She ran over to the window and tried to peer out through the boards, but she could see nothing except pale light in the sky. She listened. There was only the faint rustle of trees in the wind.

Breakfast was a long time in coming and when it did arrive sunshine was trying to get in at the window so it must be about ten o'clock, and the room facing east.

This younger man, he'd a different accent from the other one, something like the Irish but with a harder edge, she thought he might be a Scot. Perhaps there was a chance of getting somewhere with him. He was already fascinated by the idea that she might slip into a coma at any moment. She guessed he'd be the sort to watch medical soaps on the television, getting his second-hand kicks from fading blips of heartbeats on the monitor or the surgeon's bloodied fingers probing in the abdomen.

'You ever watch someone die?' she said, biting into leathery bacon and a slice of fried bread.

He stared at her as if wondering what she was up to, but he was by nature boastful.

'I've seen enough dead bodies.' It wasn't what she'd asked. 'Did a spell in the Army, Northern Ireland...' He proceeded to tell her some of his exploits.

'I can see you're a hard man,' she said. 'Why'd you leave?'

'Can't stand taking orders from a bunch of nobodies.'

'You take them from them...' She gestured downstairs.

He shrugged. 'The money's good, and I got a cast-iron getaway.' He pulled himself up, realizing he was talking too much. 'I know what you're up to, you clever bitch. Striking up a relationship, isn't that what it's called? Well, you're no Brigitte Bardot, and even if you were, you're a no-go area as far's I'm concerned.'

'If they take away my pills, I'll die. It won't be a pleasant death and it'll take time... And it'll be murder.'

'Shut your mouth.' He grabbed up the tray and went out, slamming the door behind him. A minute later she heard him come back and lock it.

I've put him in a temper, she thought, and perhaps sown a seed of doubt. He's seen people shot, maybe even blown up, but illness scares him.

Nevertheless she carefully transferred half the pills to the pocket of her skirt.

Now there was nothing to do but wait.

The winter sun had abandoned the window by the time they came. She reckoned it must be about one o'clock when she heard the car, and voices outside. Some ten minutes passed before her door was opened.

The stranger who came into the room, followed closely by the one she knew as Mark, had nothing of the thuggish look of the others. He was middle-aged with smooth black hair, greyed at the temples, and he wore big glasses on a sharply-pointed nose. He could have been an accountant, a lawyer or a businessman—whichever it was there was no mistaking the air of success, of authority.

'So you're Madeleine Smith? You sure had us foxed. Treated you well, have they?'

'If you mean have they knocked me about, the answer is yes.'

'Don't try and smart-ass us, Madeleine. You're no lady nor ever have been, so don't come on like an English dame. You've been a bad girl, and you've caused us a lot of trouble...'

She sat silent, weighing him up. He was like so many of the men with whom she'd been acquainted in the big houses where she'd nursed. Of course she'd never really known them for they hardly spoke to her save for the odd 'Good morning' or 'How's the patient?' Most of the time they were at their offices, or closeted with their cronies behind study doors, or sitting up late after dinner which annoyed the kitchen staff. They were all in the money, they bought the priceless objects the maids had to dust, they paid for the services she was employed to give to their dying wives, their aged relatives. Oh yes, she knew his kind, had heard their

perfunctory murmurings of regret, watched them depart for
the funerals in their expensive topcoats, then scurry back to
divide the spoils...

'Is it Mr Horth, then?' she asked, making a guess. She'd
imagined Prester John Madison as a bigger man.

He turned on his heel. 'Bring her downstairs,' he said
curtly.

'Yes, Mr Horth...' The man called Mark was stopped by
a look.

He made up for his slip by yanking at her arm with unnecessary force. She'd been coming anyway.

The downstairs of the house was quite different from the
room she'd been in. There were carpets here and the place
was fully furnished, heavy curtains closed tightly across the
window even though it was daytime.

It looked as if two rooms, or even two houses had been
made into one, and there was a surprising amount of luxury, deep armchairs, sofas, side tables, a cocktail cabinet,
and lamps burning everywhere. There was even a marble
fireplace in which imitation logs glowed. There must have
been other heating too for the air was hot and stuffy.

Horth had seated himself on one side of the fireplace beside a table on which were set out a plate of sandwiches,
several bottles and glasses.

'I got you some lunch. Thought you could do with it after your trip.' The younger man, the one she now thought of
as the Scot, had been hovering in the background, and now
came forward as he spoke, ingratiating, almost servile.

Horth took no notice, poured himself what looked like a
large brandy, and began to eat a sandwich. He nodded to
Mark. 'Put her in that chair.'

She was thrown down on the armchair on the other side
of the fireplace. She sank into its depths, letting herself go.

'If you're sensible this won't take long.' As he was speaking he continued to munch crusts of the roughly-cut bread,
and there were bits of ham stuck to his lip. Betraying his or-

igins, she thought, he's not always been at the top. 'Where's the goddamned will?'

She'd anticipated the question for so long and had so many answers ready—depending on who asked—that for the moment she couldn't think of one.

'What will?'

'Aw, come on... We gotta plane to catch. You fool around with me, sister, you'll be sorry. The will you got when you lifted the rubies.'

'What rubies?'

Horth gave a sigh of utter world-weariness. He finished his sandwich, picked up another, took a sip of brandy and said to the moon-faced one:

'Give her a cigarette, man...'

Cutler took the glowing cigarette out of his mouth and pressed it hard into her wrist.

She couldn't help giving a yelp. 'I've got to take my pill,' she stammered, groping in her pocket. Her handbag was still upstairs, the man called Mark had thrown it on the bed before he pushed her out of the room. She managed to cram a couple of tablets into her mouth; she hoped they were codeine or aspirin, though even those would be slow-acting as painkillers.

'What the hell...' Horth had started forward out of his chair.

'She's a diabetic. She'll go into a coma if she don't take her pills—' the Scot had come up to the table—'and she'll mebbe die.'

'Godammit!' Horth sat back. Then he gave a slow smile. 'A diabetic. Well, well, now there's a thought... How many of these pills she got?'

'I'll get her bag.' Mark was away and out of the door, like a dog on his master's errand.

She swallowed hard. It was difficult getting the tablets down dry.

'Here, have a shot of this.' Horth poured a large measure out of the same bottle he'd had himself, and handed her the glass.

She drank, feeling the pills dissolve in the alcohol. Her wrist throbbed with pain. She wasn't sure how much of that she could stand.

'All I want to know is where the will is.' Horth was coaxing now. 'We know you had it. Just tell me where it is now.'

They'll go to any lengths, she thought, and they won't give up.

'I destroyed it,' she said. 'I tore it up. Wasn't my business, anyhow.'

She'd always been an accomplished liar—when she'd heard the words as a child she'd thought they added something to her stature. Then it had seemed the only way to survive; lying at school about the bruises, then about the others' truancy, lying in the juvenile courts, lying to the folks in authority, and always lying to Smith himself to avoid getting beaten, she'd learnt to lie from the moment she was born.

'Where?' Horth barked. 'Where and when did you destroy it? *If* you did.'

'I swear it. It was evidence against me if I was caught. I tore it up along with the rest of the stuff in the suitcase, the one with the rubies in.' She was desperate to make it sound convincing. 'There were a lot of old photographs, sentimental things like that. I tore everything up. They were nothing to me.'

Horth was watching her closely. His long, pointed nose, thin lips, the dead eyes magnified by the glasses, he looked like someone who'd outfaced plenty of liars in his time, bested them, busted them wide open...

'Where?' His expensively-capped teeth were white and even but they could well be shark's teeth for all the mercy they would show.

'St Louis... Minnesota... Chicago... I don't remember...'

'Who'd you tell, sister? Who'd you tell about the will?'

'No one. How could I? They'd know I stole the rubies.'

'You musta told someone, for somebody sure knows about that will. You think we're stupid?' Horth's mouth curled with disgust, and he motioned once more to the moonfaced man. 'Just remind her we don't do business with liars.'

This time the burn was on the back of her hand, and left her gasping.

Horth took her bag and opened it on the table. He poked a finger at the various tablets that fell out. 'All these for diabetes, eh? I think you're a lying bitch. I got a friend, see, who's a diabetic... and he injects himself with insulin. He don't take pills for it.'

Somehow she managed to get her good hand into the pocket of her skirt. Half a dozen assorted shapes. She got them all to her mouth at the same time, swallowed hard and drank down the brandy that was in the glass before Horth grabbed it from her. Why had she never taken to drugs, she wondered, hazily. I could have had a nice supply of uppers and downers on that kitchen shelf that could've knocked me right out... But she'd seen enough stomach pumps used, washed enough of the results down the sluices... Anyway, she'd always needed to keep her wits about her.

'Not them,' she spluttered, pointing at the table. 'The ones I've just taken. They're hypoglycaemics, they control the disease...'

At any rate, it had slowed Horth down. He was eyeing her now with a mixture of exasperation and speculation. 'That right about her being a diabetic?' It was the first time he'd talked to the Scot.

'It's like she says. If she don't take them she goes into what she calls a coma.' The younger man was all too eager to share his medical knowledge. 'I've seen that on the telly.

They pass out, and if they don't get the treatment they don't come round...'

Horth got up and walked about, stroking his chin; he might have been considering a suddenly lucrative business deal. So far things had not gone as easily as he had expected, but this ... this might be a bonus.

'Search her,' he said.

The Scot was not as rough as the moonfaced man—perhaps, she thought, he's afraid I'll fall to pieces in his hands—but he was thorough.

'That was the lot,' he said, straightening up. 'She's got no more.'

With a sweeping gesture Horth gathered up the tablets from the table.

'Put them down the john.'

Mark took them from him and hurried out. She heard the plug being pulled and he came back grinning and rubbing his hands. 'What now?' he asked, looking towards his chief.

'Reckon she'll live a while,' said Horth. 'Long enough to tell us what we want.'

The burns were stinging now so that she flinched from the thought of more. She sensed that Horth was not like other people, he knew when you were lying ... Should she come up with the truth? How long did it take an airmail letter to reach New York? In that file there had been hints that Madison and Horth were powerful enough to get spies planted where they wanted ... Could they intercept it before it reached Mr Van Gryson? Was there a telephone in this place? She'd never heard any of them talking on a phone...

Horth was leaning forward. 'You just gotta tell us the truth: where the will is, and who you told about it ... Otherwise my friend here might break a few fingers.'

She tried to think what time it was ... how long since the American had arrived. He'd come at one...was that an hour ago, two hours? There was no daylight getting into the room so she couldn't tell...

'It's gone to New York.' As she said the words she could feel her body droop, her eyes going swimmy. That mixture of codeine, aspirin and cough sweets, washed down with brandy...

'How? When?' Horth was beside her, gripping her wrists, rubbing at the sore places.

'When they came to the flat—those two. I posted it...'

'She never did!' The moonfaced one was angry. 'That's a lie! She never had no chance. We brought her here straight, didn't we, Jock?'

The younger man was calmer. 'She never posted it, Mr Horth, there was no way she could've. And it wasn't anywhere in that flat. We turned it over like you said.'

Horth got to his feet. 'You bungled it,' he said coldly, 'and you'll pay for that... The organization don't tolerate mistakes on a job.'

Even in her now dreamy state, half in, half out of awareness, she could feel the tension between the three of them.

It was Mark who spoke first, his voice tight.

'Don't threaten us, Horth. We made a bargain and don't you forget it. We delivered the woman, and there was no will. That's your problem. And there's not much time left. We're booked out on that plane from Heathrow at eight, and it's already—' he looked at his watch—'getting on for five o'clock.'

Horth was bending over her, his glasses glinting in the lamplight, his eyes like black stones. 'But you read it, didn't you? So you're as good as dead, you lying bitch. You can die out there in the wood in the freezing cold... How long you reckon it'll take, eh? Coupla days without the pills? And it'll be a natural death, that'll suit my people back home just fine... This ain't anything personal, but I hate liars.'

Quite casually he smacked her hard across the face. Then he stood up. 'That won't show. Lady lost her way, lost her handbag, hit her head on a tree mebbe... Jesus, your English climate, it'll finish her off in no time. Here, Cutler, you throw that bag in the woods some place... Then you and McGivern can dump her somewheres else. You know the area. Somewheres she'll lie for weeks...'

She wasn't quite unconscious as she listened to them moving around her, she guessed they were clearing the room up. Dimly she heard an argument, the Scottish voice:

'But it's bloody murder, Mark. I never agreed to be part of that...'

'Shut your whining. You've been well paid, haven't you? And we've got the plane tickets. We'll be long gone when they find her, and she's got no connection with us anyway.'

Horth was in command, smooth now. 'Get this last job done real neat, and I reckon I can forget you bungled part of it. So just get moving with the broad...'

She kept her eyes closed, her body slumped in the chair, she breathed through her mouth in rhythmic snorts—as near as she could get to faking coma—but all the while her ears were alert.

There must have been some delay. Horth's patience was running out, and with it, like melting wax, the veneer of respectability. Now he sounded like the gangster he was.

'What the hell's wrong with youse English guys? Do I have to spell it out? You're supposed to be tough... Jesus, what did they give me, a bunch of softies?'

She felt herself being lifted. She knew it was the moon-faced man by the roughness of his hands. She tried to keep her body limp. Through closed eyelids she caught a glimpse of daylight as the younger one opened the door.

'Christ!' She was dropped heavily on the carpet, her head hit something hard. She heard the Scot shout: 'Bloody hell... it's the police!'

The door was banged shut. Horth was quick across the room, he knelt, peering out between the curtains... She saw his running feet, then she saw nothing more.

# TWENTY-TWO

KEMP WAS with John Upshire and two other officers in the first car. There were more vehicles behind them but no sirens as they swept through the streets of Newtown and out into the countryside. He glanced at his watch, and made a rough calculation. They would have met Clive Horth at Heathrow around eight that morning. Even allowing for heavy traffic they could be in Newtown by midday. But if Horth only contacted them on his arrival that would mean a double journey for the driver...

Young Lang had said there was no phone at Cutler's place—even he hadn't been able to bribe British Telecom to leave it connected—but there was a call-box at the end of the abandoned road leading to the site. As they passed the spot Kemp saw one of the cars stop, and drop off a constable to check the kiosk.

When the road swerved round the edge of the wood the convoy came to a halt at the piles of debris which marked the demolition area. This end had been systematically cleared save for the ruined walls which had once separated the dwellings. These would provide good cover for Upshire's men as they went cautiously forward according to Brinscombe's directions. He had produced decent plans, and pointed out the position of the two remaining houses at the end of what had been a long row. These houses Cutler seemed to have retained rather cleverly for his own use, but they were round the corner and, as yet, out of sight. Upshire waited till his force was so deployed that the whole place was surrounded, only then did he order his driver to proceed up the road.

It had been a bright day, and there was still enough low red sun striking through the trees to light up the gaunt outline of the two semi-detached houses, the last of a pre-war development now gone under the hammer. Cutler had been smart; local people thought the site deserted—as indeed it should have been.

'Your men armed?' asked Kemp tentatively.

'What do you think? My super has taken this as a house siege. It might just be the woman, but there could be other hostages. First, we try the softly-softly approach...'

The Inspector got out of the car as the other vehicles closed up behind them, and a small knot of police officers gathered at the broken gate between a straggle of hawthorns.

'Well, they should know by now we're here,' Upshire said laconically, 'let's see if they'll open up.'

There had been only tiny front gardens to the properties so there was no great distance between the road and the steps going up to the doors. It looked as if only the first one was in use, the other was boarded up. At that moment the door swung open, a man was glimpsed on the threshold but within the space of a second he'd jumped back inside, and the door was slammed shut.

Kemp was sure he'd seen a movement of the curtain which completely covered the lower window, the only one not boarded up. He ran up the short path and leaned on the outside sill, trying to see through the dusty panes from where there was a glimmer of light.

John Upshire pulled him back. 'I thought you said these were men from Las Vegas,' he said. 'That means they're dangerous. Leave this to us.'

One of his sergeants from the covering units came up. 'It's like young Lang said, Mr Upshire, back entrances and windows all have steel bars on 'em ... Place is as good as a fortress, save for the front door...'

The Inspector and a constable went and stood on the bottom step of the ruined flight leading up to the door.

'We're police officers . . . Open up . . .'

The constable went forward and banged on the stout panels.

'That door's been newly put in,' he told the Inspector, 'and it's a fair lock, but we can smash it.'

'Not yet,' said John Upshire. 'Let's do things the right way.' He raised his voice: 'Mark Cutler, Jock McGivern . . . you are required to come out quietly.'

He waited a moment, then shouted again:

'I have reason to believe you are holding a woman by the name of Mary Blane. Bring her out unharmed, or face the consequences . . .'

Now they could hear noises from inside the house, the sound of falling furniture, the crash of glassware.

Still Upshire waited.

Two things happened almost simultaneously. There was a shot from inside the house, and the door was flung open. A man threw himself out and down the steps, landing at the Inspector's feet. The door closed and they heard bolts being drawn across the inside, and something heavy being dragged over the floor.

'That's McGivern!' Dennis Brinscombe shouted from the road.

The constable already had the man by the arm, hauling him to his feet.

'Jock McGivern?' said Upshire.

McGivern nodded. He was panting and looked as if he'd been in a fight. He'd a bruise over one eye, and a cut lip. He made no effort to shake off the policeman's hold.

'Ach, what the hell,' he gasped. 'OK, OK, I'll come quietly . . . Yon's a bloody maniac in there, that American . . . Name's Horth. Mark Cutler got the guns for him . . . I wanted out soon's I saw what they got . . . One of the buggers took a shot at me . . .'

'Is the woman Mary Blane in there?'

McGivern gulped. 'Yes, but she's unconscious. She's...'

'Anyone else?' Upshire barked.

'Only Cutler and the man Horth, but they've got a bloody armoury in there.'

'What kind of guns, how many?'

One thing Jock McGivern knew about was guns, and as an ex-soldier he had more respect for them than the average civilian whose knowledge might be less. As the details were being relayed to the covering force, Upshire turned to Kemp.

'Well, you were right. This is real gangster stuff...' He began walking back to the cars. 'We'll make a tactical withdrawal while we consider the new situation. I'm not putting any of my men in danger of being shot by some lunatic from across the Atlantic. We'll play this slow. Nobody in that house is going anywhere.'

The officers went into a huddled conference, and John Upshire waved to the men surrounding the site to come in closer.

Kemp took the opportunity to listen in to the questioning of McGivern in the car while he was giving his statement. The Scot was only too eager, once he'd been issued with the usual caution, to cooperate.

'Diabetic coma?' Kemp exclaimed. 'She's never a diabetic, Mary Blane. I've seen her eating Mars bars in the office... But Madeleine Smith now, she was a nurse, and a damned good liar... Did you get a close look at these pills?'

McGivern shook his head.

'I thought not. They might have been anything.'

McGivern wasn't anxious to talk about Mary Blane. By now his statement was becoming more an effort at self-exoneration than informative.

'What do you mean, they roughed her up?' Kemp interrupted sharply.

'It was Cutler did that, I swear it. It was him burned her...'

'What?' Kemp had him by the collar, and was only re-
strained by one of the constables. 'Now, now, sir, let him be.
You'll not get anywhere by throttling the man.'

'There was no way I could stop them,' muttered Mc-
Givern. 'Horth was calling the shots... I wouldn't have
touched her—not after I knew she was, well, some kind of
invalid...'

But Kemp was already out of the car and tackling Inspector Upshire.

'Look, I know you have your methods, but that man
Horth in there, he wants Mary Blane dead—she might even
be dead already. Maybe she pulled that ruse about being a
diabetic just to gain time. But I have to know whether she's
alive...'

'So do we. We're about to enter the second stage, Lennox. You come along with me.'

Now that it was growing dark it was easy to see the light
behind the curtained window on the ground floor as they
approached the house.

John Upshire had a loud-hailer in his hand and as he
raised it his voice boomed out, echoing back from the wood.

'Mark Cutler, you get one more chance. Throw away
those guns and come out with your hands above your head.'

All they could hear was the wind rising in the trees. From
the house, nothing.

By now the line of police had closed in along the broken
walls on either side, the car headlamps flooding the whole
of the front.

'This place is completely surrounded,' the Inspector
roared. 'you've no way out...'

The curtain was twitched back, the pane of glass shattered by a blow, and there was a glint of light on a gun barrel. The man that answered Upshire was shockingly cold.

'If you are in charge, I'll tell you what I want... No, not
a step nearer or I'll put a bullet through your head.'

'That's Horth,' whispered Kemp.

'I gathered as much,' said Upshire, putting down the hailer. He didn't have to even raise his voice now, though he made no move towards the window. 'You heard me, Mr Horth. You too... you put down that gun and come out along with Cutler... And bring the woman, Mary Blane.'

From behind the broken pane Clive Horth laughed.

'Come in and get her, you goddamned English cop! But first, get a load of this...'

The shots that rang out made more noise than their number might account for—in fact Kemp thought there were only two—but the effect as the bullets ricocheted off the walls and rough stones on the path was deafening.

'My God!' Upshire breathed. 'The bastard means it... and as if I didn't have trouble enough, here comes the Super.'

Superintendent Bracknell stepped out of his long official car and made a brief survey of the scene. He came up to where the Inspector was standing.

'Looks a bad business, John. I heard on the car phone. Any idea what this man wants?'

'I was just going to get on to that when the bullets started flying...'

'H'm. From what the men say, he's been firing in the air—at least so far. Let's see if I can get some sense out of him.'

This time it was the Superintendent who took up the hailer.

'Mr Clive Horth? I understand you are an American citizen. You are disturbing the peace of my County, you are threatening my men, and you are holding a woman hostage...' He stopped to listen, but no sound came from the house. The curtain at the broken window flapped, the gun barrel still rested on the ledge, and there would be a finger on the trigger. Nevertheless, Bracknell continued: 'No one wishes for bloodshed... Before that happens, I want to know what it is you want.'

There was a long silence before Horth spoke again, his voice like a cutting saw: 'OK... Let's cut a deal, whoever you are. I want a car to Heathrow and no interference with my flight to the States. No charges brought, and no questions asked. That way no one gets hurt. What d'you say to that?'

'I'll consider it. But first, you must release, unharmed, the woman you are holding.'

'No deal. The woman goes with us. She's alive, if that's what you want to know. But she's a citizen of the United States, and she goes back there with me.'

'Only if she goes of her own free will.' The Superintendent's voice was firm. 'Mr Horth, this woman is a resident in this country. It is my duty to see she comes to no harm...'

'She's a criminal,' Horth snarled. 'She's wanted in the States.'

'Then she will be taken there under due process of law if the facts of the case warrant it. Let my officers into the house, Mr Horth.'

As the gun went off with a spurt of flame in the darkness, even the Superintendent ducked though the shot had, once again, been fired in the air and only spent bullets rattled the stones.

Both senior officers retreated to the cars, and it was there that Lennox Kemp spoke to them. He had spent some time writing rapidly in his notebook by the light in Upshire's car, the words so often already drafted in his mind now flowing easily over the short page.

'Superintendent Bracknell, I know what this man Horth wants, and I've a way to make him release Mary Blane...now that he's admitted she's still alive. I think I can get him to let me into that house.'

'It's too dangerous, Lennox,' John Upshire protested. 'You don't even know how to fire a gun...'

'It's because of the guns I'm going, John. You know enough of the story by now to guess what this paper I have in my hand means to Horth. To me it's not worth the life of any one of your men ... If you rush the house there'll be a shooting match, and some people are going to get killed. It'll be the woman first, and then any policeman who makes a move.'

Kemp turned to the Superintendent.

'When I get in there I still may have to bargain for Mary Blane's life. Have I your authority, sir, to promise Horth safe passage back to the States?'

After having had a shotgun fired at close range to himself, Bracknell was not as amenable to reason as he had been before.

'Look at it this way ...' Kemp was at his most persuasive. 'I think I know what this man Horth is like. He's a top name in the organization, he didn't get there by being stupid and shooting up coppers. That's why he's been shooting in the air so far ... The last thing he wants is to murder on British soil. Give him a way out and he'll jump at it ... And, believe me, he'll jump at this bit of paper when I tell him what it is ... As far as the police are concerned, no one gets hurt and the incident is closed.'

Reluctantly, Bracknell agreed. 'But not the fellow Cutler.'

'No,' said Kemp, 'not Cutler. But I think when I give Horth this paper he'll dump Cutler like a piece of old wreckage ... Now I would like yourself and John Upshire here to witness my signature.'

The short document was signed on the bonnet of the Superintendent's car.

'I suggest you get your men back behind the wall, sir, and dowse the lights,' said Kemp. 'If I do a deal with Horth we've still got to watch out for Cutler ...'

# TWENTY-THREE

STANDING on the bottom step at the front door, Kemp had no need of the loud-hailer. 'I'm Lennox Kemp, Mr Horth. I think you are well acquainted with my name...'

'Move up to the window so's I can see you right.'

When Kemp walked over he found himself looking into the round black hole at the end of the barrel; it was just about level with his head.

'It's no good you taking a shot at me, Horth... You might hit me and you know by now I'm more use to you alive than dead. Muriel Probert's second will must be at the offices of Eikenberg & Lazard within a few hours and from there it'll go straight to the Surrogate's Court unless you and I can do a deal.'

The position of the gun didn't shift but there was a change in the American's voice.

'You mean you want to talk business, Kemp?'

'I'm willing to discuss the matter. But not out here. I'm coming in. But first, I need to be assured that Cutler won't jump me the minute I come through the door. And if any harm should happen to me while I'm in there that Superintendent of police you spoke to earlier will see you're charged for it here in Britain. There'll be no safe-conduct to the States.'

There was the sound of movement inside the house, and the mutter of voices. Some kind of hurried discussion was taking place. To Kemp it seemed as if time stood still, but then bolts were drawn and the door swung back sufficiently for him to see and recognize Mark Cutler—and another shotgun.

Cutler waved him into a passage which opened out into a large room, the door behind him was slammed shut, locked and bolted. Kemp wondered why Daniel had ever gone into the lions' den . . .

He took a quick look round.

The man he knew to be Clive Horth was comfortably seated by the broken window, cradling the stock of the gun trained on the cars outside.

Auld Nick himself, thought Kemp, the family man, nursing a dangerous offspring . . .

He was recalled to his senses by the abrupt voice: 'If this is some police trick . . . Frisk him, Cutler.'

'No trick,' said Kemp, raising his arms. 'Isn't it time you called off your dogs, Horth? One's gone already.'

'Cover this window.' Horth gave the command, and rose slowly to allow Mark Cutler to take his place. 'And if anyone shows nearer than that wall, let them have a blast.'

That's my top-of-the-mob man, thought Kemp, keep your fingernails clean and don't give a damn what your minions do . . . Moonfaced Mark didn't look any too happy and Kemp saw no reason to cheer him up.

'You shoot a copper, Cutler, and you go down for life—and it won't be a pleasant one,' he told the big ex-foreman.

'And I'll blow this woman's head off.' Horth didn't even raise his voice. 'Cut the crap. Say what you've got to say, Kemp, and stop wasting my time.'

Kemp walked to the centre of the room, and saw her. She was lying outstretched, half-hidden by a sofa, on the floor at Horth's feet. He for his part was now lolling in an armchair but he had Cutler's gun across his knees, and he used it to twitch the collar of her blouse.

Kemp looked down at Mary Blane. Her face under the tangled hair was yellow-white, she was breathing heavily, but she was alive.

'No point in that,' he answered Horth's threat. 'You don't want a murder on your hands, not here in England . . .'

Horth sighed. 'That's not the way I see it, Kemp. I follow this woman over here because she stole something don't belong to her, right? She's a wanted criminal back in the States, mebbe she steals guns as well. Mebbe she don't wanna come back. Mebbe a gun goes off...'

'Nice scenario, Horth,' said Kemp, 'but I don't buy it.'

Behind the big glasses, the American's eyes were black as coals.

'Look at it from our point of view—you're a lawyer. We can mebbe get round that second will in the court—could be a forgery, eh? But this bitch, she's read it, see? She's a witness to where it came from... Our organization, they can't afford she stay alive.'

Kemp sat down in the chair opposite Clive Horth and drew it up close so that they were almost touching—and so that their conversation could not be overheard by Cutler at the window.

'Then I will give you this in exchange for her life.' Kemp took the paper from his pocket. 'First, I'll read it to you:

'*I Lennox Kemp, Solicitor of Newtown, hereby waive all rights and renounce all claims I may have under the will made the fifth day of April 1989 by Muriel Probert, widow, of New York City. I also declare it to be my wish that the first will made by the said Muriel Probert dated the twentieth of March 1987 shall stand, and the persons named therein being Preston John Madison and Clive Horth shall remain the beneficiaries of the whole estate of the said Muriel Probert. Signed by me this twenty-fifth day of November 1989.*'

'My signature on this document, Mr Horth, has been witnessed by Percival Bracknell, Superintendent of Police, and John Upshire, Inspector. What more do you want?'

While Kemp read, which he did slowly and clearly, Clive Horth's sallow features had undergone a series of expressions ranging from blank incomprehension to utter bewilderment. But he was not ignorant of legal language—indeed some of his most successful contracts had been couched in its convoluted terms.

Now he took off his glasses even though it meant letting the gun slide into his lap, and wiped his brow. It was some moments before he spoke.

'You gotta be joking...'

'No joke, Horth, and if you lot hadn't started playing silly buggers with me you'd have got it sooner. I never wanted any part in Leo Probert's enterprises.'

Horth was again silent. Then he said: 'You doing this for her, Mr Kemp?'

'Not entirely... More for those men outside.' Kemp folded the paper and held it up. 'Now you tell Cutler to drop his gun. You give me yours, and you shall have this document. Remember, you put a finger on me, and I'll see you're both charged with assault. But if you do this thing quietly I am empowered by Superintendent Bracknell to assure you a safe-conduct to the airport and no charges will be brought...'

'You sure are one strange guy,' said Horth slowly, 'but I reckon you're levelling with me... You really mean it.'

He got to his feet and handed the shotgun to Kemp, taking no notice of Cutler's muttered imprecation. Kemp broke the gun, emptied it and put the cartridges in his pocket.

'Put that gun on the floor, Cutler,' Horth rapped out sharply.

'What the hell...?'

'Do it, now.'

Before Mark Cutler could move, Horth was at the window and had wrestled the gun from Cutler's hands, but he made no effort to unload it.

'What the hell's going on?' Cutler's moonface was a picture of bafflement.

Still carrying the shotgun at his side, Horth came back to Kemp and said, smiling like a tiger, 'You and me, Mr Kemp, we got a bargain. That don't necessarily include him.'

Kemp hesitated only a moment, then he put the paper into Horth's outstretched hand. The man looked it over and was satisfied. He put it carefully in his pocket. 'I'll get copies made at the airport, and mail 'em...' Clive Horth was used to covering every eventuality.

Then he remarked casually to Kemp: 'Did ya ever see that film *The Maltese Falcon*? That bit where Bogart says to Sidney Greenstreet, "Let's give them the punk" and the fat man laughs?'

Kemp guessed what was coming; he was a bit of a film-buff himself.

'You mean Cutler's expendable?'

'You cotton on fast...'

Cutler, much reduced by the loss of his gun and suspicious of what was going on, came at them with fists swinging.

Horth brought the gun up. 'You ... Out!' he said curtly.

'What?'

'Just out. By the door.'

Mark Cutler gaped at him in horror, but the sight of the levelled gun stopped any idea he had had of rushing them. He began to back away into the passage. Horth followed him, the gun still aimed.

'Open that door, Cutler, and get the hell out, or I'll bust your kneecaps.' The threat was the more menacing for being spoken quietly.

Kemp watched from behind Horth's shoulder. My God, he thought, how cosy it is to be on the right side of gangsters ... He felt almost sorry for Cutler.

'I think he's making you an offer you can't refuse, Mark,' he told the man pleasantly. 'Either way you're going to jail, it's up to you whether you go on two legs or get carried in.' Later, he wasn't proud of the remark, but he'd seen the burns on Mary's hands as she lay on the carpet ...

Cutler was already struggling with the bolts, Horth standing over him. Somehow the door got opened, and Cutler disappeared into the darkness outside.

Horth came back into the room, emptied the gun and threw it on the floor. He walked calmly across to where his camelhair coat hung on a hook. It seemed to have missed the scuffle that had taken place earlier but he shook it just the same. He smoothed the velvet collar, and put the coat on. There was even a white silk scarf in the pocket. As he went past Kemp who was kneeling beside Mary Blane, Horth touched her leg with a pointed, patent-leather shoe. 'That's one helluva dame. She oughta been in our organization... You got me that car to Heathrow?'

Kemp went out on the step in the glare of the headlamps and called for the Superintendent. He saw that Mark Cutler was in the grip of two constables. He'd left the front door wide open; the car lights had been switched on because the siege was over.

If Percy Bracknell was surprised to see a smart, well-dressed businessman in what he had anticipated to be a scene of possible mayhem, he gave no sign of it.

'Mr Clive Horth?' he said, stiffly.

'That's me.' Horth smiled benignly.

Bracknell turned to Kemp. 'Is the woman all right?'

Kemp nodded.

'Then, Mr Horth, if you'll follow me, I will see you are escorted to the airport.'

It was John Upshire who told Kemp afterwards of the little exchange that took place when Clive Horth was getting into the car. There were two officers, and Bracknell's driver.

'See that this man gets to Heathrow fast, and don't leave him till he's on a plane for New York. He's polluted this country long enough... And if you're wise, Mr Horth, you'll never come back for I'll be watching out for you...'

The Superintendent slammed the car door.

Clive Horth rolled down the window. 'I gotta hand it to you,' he said. 'I think you British policemen are wonderful...'

### TWENTY-FOUR

THERE SHOULD BE triumphal music, joy and elation, thought Kemp gloomily, as he sat the next day in the Inspector's office—all the ingredients of a happy ending. Instead, there were ruffled tempers and a mass of paperwork.

'All right for the Super,' grumbled Upshire, 'he can take himself off to higher things, we're the ones left to clear up the mess...' He put his pen down, and addressed Kemp in a tone far from amiable.

'We'd a devil of a job keeping the press out... Shotguns fired at the police, rumours of a siege, right up their street, that is... A nutter we said, and no further statement. It'll be a while before it dies down... And all this bloody accounting. I'm telling you, this little exercise cost a packet.'

'It cost me quite a bit, too,' said Kemp mildly. 'Put that stuff away, John, and listen: you've got Cutler on the firearms charge, and both him and McGivern for kidnap and assault...'

'Aye, and your Mary Blane wanted across the Atlantic.'

'You can forget that.'

'What about all the data from the New York Police Department?'

'There'll be no charges,' Kemp told him firmly. 'The whole thing will be dropped.'

Upshire glowered at him. 'How can you say that? What if they ask for extradition? Damn it, that'll be more paperwork...' Even the thought of it plunged the Inspector into further despondency. 'And I'll have to hold her in case she scarpers.'

'You won't—and she won't. She's got no place to go. But you can't hold her unless you charge her, and there'll be no charges either here or in the States.'

'How can you know that? What about that bloody great deposit in her Dublin bank?'

'I'll give you three reasons. One, if she stole what may have belonged to the executors, my friend Mr Van Gryson won't prosecute—he's only too anxious to get shot of the whole affair. Two, if she stole what rightly belonged to Madison and Horth, they won't prosecute either—they've got the whole estate and the last thing they want is her testifying what they got up to in order to get it. Which leaves only me...'

'How'd you come into it?'

'Well, if a will speaks from the death as it's supposed to, it was my property she stole... I inherited under the good will, the second one. It was my collection of rubies she stole. Interesting proposition, don't you think?'

But Upshire was lost in the legal complexities, which weren't all that clear to Kemp either, though he wouldn't admit it. He had spent a long hour on the telephone with Dale Van Gryson in the early hours, and shaken that phlegmatic Bostonian right out of his pinstriped body. When he had recovered they settled the civil side of the case between them but Van Gryson wasn't sure he could swing the criminal authority to Kemp's way of thinking...

'She's a common thief,' he said, not for the first time, 'and the police here are hopping mad...'

'Let them hop,' said Kemp tersely, 'I'll handle them...' When he explained that now the first will would be allowed to stand the rubies should have gone to Florence Hermanos, and as she was dead they might be claimed by her absconding spouse, Dale was stunned into silence. He was happier computing the insurance figures, and possible payments out to deceived jewel merchants all over the States.

When it got to this point, Kemp put the phone down and went to sleep.

Now as he made his way to Newtown Hospital he was in a state of considerable confusion, and embarrassment. How do you talk to someone who has in a short space of time undergone a complete metamorphosis in your mind? Two days ago she had been plain Mary Blane, his Irish secretary, with whom he had established a pleasant rapport—and perhaps something more, for he was aware that a certain romantic streak in him had been touched. The cadence of her voice, that quirk of humour, the eyes that matched his own, the background he had seen her in, quiet, misty, soft like the darkness of her hair... There was a lot he wanted to say to that Mary Blane... He pulled himself up. It had all been illusion, she had never existed except in his imagination.

The reality was different, facts were real and could not be shrugged off. What could he say to Madeleine Smith, this clever female sneak-thief from God knows what sordid substratum of society, who had pilfered a dead woman's house, ripped off a dozen shopkeepers, lied and swindled her way across the States? What was he supposed to do? Congratulate her?

Entering the hospital, he still didn't know what to say, what to expect. She hadn't wanted to go there the night before...

'There's an ambulance outside,' he'd told her.

'No need for that,' she'd said. 'I might be sick after all those pills but I'm far from dying.'

'Those burns, they should be dressed... Anyway, you've no place else to go. Your flat's in a mess, you can't go there.'

'So it's the hospital, is it, or the police station?' She'd looked at him then out of those light grey eyes which he saw now had the same veiled opacity as his own, eyes that could never easily be read by others...

'You need sleep,' he had said roughly. 'I'll talk to you to-morrow.'

And this was tomorrow. What was he to talk about?

She was up and dressed, standing by the window in a clean jumper and skirt.

'One of the nurses gave me these. I guess when you're one of them there's a bond.'

She sat down in the cane armchair, spreading her hands carefully. The burns looked hideous under the yellow stains.

'They're not that bad,' she said, 'it's just the stuff they put on. They'll heal.'

Kemp drew up another chair.

'How long have you been a nurse, Madeleine?'

'Years. Seemed I had the gift for it. I'd not much else. I was never very good at school when I was a kid so I ran away, but I used to go and sit with old folks round about, poor as we were. They'd be on their own, no one was going to come and see them.'

She began to talk to him about Vineland, about her life, as if he had the right to know. Her short, matter-of-fact sentences, the flat tone she spoke in, the American accent now more pronounced than the Irish, gave a stark picture of what it had been like.

He commented on her varied accents but she only shrugged. 'They're easy to pick up when you get around to listening. I wasn't one for talking, so I listened. I was a lot with my mother... I'd take her back what the old people gave me. It wasn't much, some black-eyed peas, a bit of salt pork. When Smith was on a drinking binge there was never the money to buy anything... But sometimes I'd get the odd brooch or a string of beads and Mother and me we'd pretend we were rich, that they were diamonds and pearls. They were mostly trash but I liked their glitter, and there'd mebbe be a piece of jet or a gold chain we could sell... If Smith saw the things he'd beat me and knock my mother to the floor. He said I'd stolen them. But I never did. I couldn't help it if they gave me things, they said I was kind to them, fetching their water in for them, or getting their groceries... I liked old people, they were quiet somehow, and all they wanted was someone to talk to... Even later, when I got to nursing the rich I found they were the same as those back in the shanties, nobody really cared for them, their own folks were just hanging about waiting for them to die. They'd give me things, too, nothing valuable you understand, but they helped with the money I sent back home.'

'You went on assisting the Smiths?'

'I had to. I couldn't bear the way my mother was getting the rough end of it. She loved that family though they were a rotten lot. She'd ask me for the money when there was trouble, and there was plenty of that, and for me to speak up for them with the welfare and the courts because, she said, I could always find the words. So I learned when to speak, and when to keep silent...and when to lie...I heard so many lies, Mr Kemp, in those courts I reckon I could've graduated in the subject.'

Kemp found himself smiling; the games people play when faced with any kind of authority were not new to him. 'And then you came to New York?'

'When Mother was gone, and then Smith, I thought at last I'd get a life for myself, but there were still the little ones. I paid out of my wages to have them looked after...and I went on paying when they got into trouble. I'd promised my Mother I'd look after them...but I couldn't stand Smith's brood, the dirt and the squalor. Perhaps I felt guilty leaving them, I don't know...I just kept sending money but it didn't do any good. Private nursing paid well but my money was drained away on them. I suppose I did it out of a kind of duty. Mother had been very strong on duty. I don't think I was unhappy, but I was alone and I don't make friends easy. Sometimes I felt there must be more in life... I guess I was hoping something really great would happen to me. I wasn't attractive enough to marry even if

I'd wanted it, so it wasn't that I was waiting for... Just a chance, an opportunity...'

'And it came?'

A nurse brought in a tray of tea. 'You all right, Mary?' she said brightly.

'I'm unburdening my soul here to Mr Kemp...' The Irishness of Mary Blane was back.

'He's a lawyer. You look out now or he'll be charging you for it.'

The laughter that followed still lingered in the room when the nurse had closed the door behind her. 'I'll do that,' said Kemp, pouring out the cups. He hoped the thread of Madeleine Smith's story hadn't been broken by the interruption. It seemed that it had, for she was silent for some moments as she took the teacup from him and put it on the table beside the window.

'You know,' she said at last, 'it's years since I thought back to Vineland, but sitting there in that bare room they kept me in I'd nothing else to do but think... And I realized how they'd got on to me. When I went off to train in the City—I did night school first to learn typing and all that but they thought I'd be better at the nursing—well, when I left home my mother packed her old trunk for me. It was the one she'd taken across the Atlantic when I was born. I still had it in my apartment in Flatbush. When I got to thinking back I could see it standing in a corner, a battered old thing covered in torn labels. But inside the lid—I never thought of it till the other night—she had her name: Madeleine Blane.'

Kemp nodded. 'Those men hired by Madison and Horth to investigate you, they saw it. They would have made a note of it. And later, when they broke into my office they saw the staff files, the Irish name, the same name.'

'I guess that's what happened. Why do you keep calling me Madeleine? My name's Mary.'

'I'm confused,' said Kemp truthfully.

'You didn't sound confused yesterday when you made that bargain with Horth for my life.'

'You know about that?'

'Of course I do. I heard everything, lying there on the carpet. I'd only bumped my head on the sofa leg when they dropped me and passed out for a while, but I'd my senses back and my ears as well by the time you came in. I'd have tripped up that moonfaced Cutler if it had been needed ... Why did you give up your claim, Mr Kemp? Was it really on my account?'

'Partly ... But there were good men outside who might have been killed.'

She nodded as if the remark confirmed what she thought—though it was in itself no compliment. 'You didn't want to see blood shed.' She paused. 'You never wanted that inheritance in the first place, all those casinos and things in Vegas. You said as much to me the other night when we talked in the car about Muriel ...'

Kemp made no direct comment; his thoughts about the fortune that might have been his were still ambivalent. Instead he brought her back to the crux of the matter.

'Muriel, yes. Tell me about Mrs Probert, and how you came to take the rubies from that apartment. It may be unpleasant for you, but I have to know if I'm to square things with the New York police.'

She took her time. She finished her tea, placed the cup carefully back on the tray. She had never been one for reliving experiences, and words did not come as readily to her as they could when she dealt with present circumstance.

'It all happened so fast. People talk about the spur of the moment—they don't know the half of it. When I saw them, the rubies in their dear little boxes, I didn't stop to think. It was like all my life had led to that chance ...'

'Go on.'

'It didn't seem like stealing—not at first. Later, as I sold them, I realized what I'd done but by then it was all a great game, the excitement was in it . . . But it hadn't started that way, not when she gave me the suitcase.'

'She gave it to you?'

'She told me where it was at the end of the wardrobe, and I was to get it out for her. You surely never thought I'd rooted around and found it myself? She'd already had me bring out dresses from that wardrobe when she wanted to touch them. And this was on the last night . . .'

Kemp did not prompt her, his legal training made sure of that. He let her tell it in her own words. There was nothing wrong with her memory and she was good on facts; where the bed was in the room, the size of the wardrobe, the timing of the patient's waking, the brief conversations . . .

'What did she say, exactly?' he interrupted at one point.

'She said, "I want you to have it and everything that's in it"—I said that it wasn't possible, that it was wrong, I know I thought at the time the idea was ridiculous . . . I'm sure of her words because she had such a sweet voice, like a young girl's. She said the papers in the suitcase weren't important any more. She said the case wasn't to be opened in that house, I was to take it with me when I went. I did wrong there, Mr Kemp. I opened it in my room when she'd gone to sleep, just before I called Dr Seifel. I suppose it must have been then I decided not to tell—I'd seen the rubies by then.'

'Did she say anything else before she slept?'

'When she saw me standing with the case in my hands she seemed, well, pleased—as if a load was off her mind.'

Kemp had been holding his breath. 'She knew she was going to die?' he asked.

'Oh yes. I've seen it often before. There's a kind of peace comes over them. An acceptance that the end has come.'

'And she knew what she'd done when she told you to take the case?'

'She was clear in her head, Mr Kemp, your Muriel, right up to going off into her last sleep. Some get confused, they say wild things, but not Mrs Probert. And she meant everything she said. I wouldn't tell you otherwise. You loved her once, and she'd kept your photographs. I'm sorry I tore them up. But I wouldn't lie about someone gone to her death—not to anyone who had loved her.'

Kemp was silent, listening to each word as if its placing in the context of every sentence was the gauge by which to measure its meaning. He noticed Mary Blane said: 'You loved her once, and she'd kept your photographs... Not the other way round, not: 'She loved you...' That alone held the ring of truth, that was his Muriel; she had talked to this nurse just hours before she died, spoken to her of their lives together, and the nurse had quite unwittingly picked out the truth of it. Well, it might have hurt once, but not after twenty years...

He must keep his mind clear; there was a pressing need for it.

'Tell me once again, Mary,' he said. 'Just go over it again, slowly.'

When she had finished, he murmured more to himself than to her: 'I wonder... is it possible? Yes, it could be... *Donatio mortis causa* ...'

'Why, Mr Kemp, that's what she said. Just before she went off to sleep. I knew it was in some foreign language, but then she said: "He told me once." And that was all. Was it in Italian?'

'No, it's Latin. *Donatio mortis causa*, a gift made in expectation of death. And I remember I did tell Muriel about a case a long time ago...'

'Is that what it means? I don't know.'

Kemp sprang to his feet. He wanted to take hold of this woman and dance her round the room. He wanted to shout it from the rooftops... Instead he struck a clenched fist into the palm of his other hand, and yelled at her:

'Oh, Mary Blane, Mary Blane, why the hell did you have to run?'

She stared at him, blankly. 'Because I'd taken the rubies, of course. Because the suitcase was at the bottom of my holdall by then, and I had to move fast.'

'You silly little fool! They were yours!'

He sat down. 'I'm sorry. I shouldn't have called you that...and I shouldn't have shouted at you. Let me explain. Those rubies were yours from the moment Mrs Probert died. She knew she was going to die, she told you to get out the case, she wanted you to have it, to take it away with you when you left, she knew exactly what it contained... Mary, she was making you a gift of the rubies. She even told you the keys were in her purse.'

'Who'd believe that?' Her voice was scornful. 'The lawyers? The police? That may be the way in your world, Mr Kemp, but not in mine. Even when I was given paste diamonds or imitation pearls they'd ask, how'd she get round the old lady? And if ever I left a house with as much as a wee keepsake there'd be murmurs about thieving... Oh no, I knew what I was doing when I ran, it was my only hope. Fat chance they'd believe she gave them to me—I'd only known her a few days...'

'But she did. It might have been only a whim but that makes no difference. Anyway, it would be just the kind of thing Muriel would do. She'd fallen out with Mrs Hermanos, and even though you'd been there only a few days she'd become attached to you, she liked you... Those rubies were a good and proper gift, Mary, there was no need for you to run. And you can stop your running right now. You never stole anything. You're not a thief.'

She was slow at taking things in when they were personal to herself, things that were outside her own experience.

'It's true I never felt like one,' she said, at last, 'but then I'm not much good at imagining what it's like to be other people, so I don't know what thieves feel like... I've only ever been me, and that was hard enough at times.'

'You don't have much opinion of yourself.'

'Opinions are what other people have, Mr Kemp, and often as not they're a bit too free with them. I guess you've heard some pretty damning ones about me in the last twenty-four hours.'

But Kemp didn't want to think about that, in fact he had come to the end of his thinking. He wanted to go over and touch her soft brown hair, he'd wanted to touch it from the first moment he'd seen her...

'They said you were fairish...' he murmured.

'You shouldn't believe everything you hear,' she said, 'I've got light grey eyes and eyelashes of no colour at all—just like yours. Makes us look insignificant, not worth a second glance... Of course it's all very well for you, Mr Kemp, you're somebody people take notice of for other reasons, but me, well, I simply fit into any background they make up...'

But Kemp was laughing in a way he had not done for years.

'Mary Blane, Mary Blane,' he said, when he could find the words, and even these were inadequate, 'what on earth am I going to do with you?'

Author of *Larkspur*

## Sheila Simonson

# SKYLARK

### A Lark Dodge Mystery

*First Time in Paperback*

**CULTURE SHOCK**

When San Francisco bookstore owner Lark Dodge and her friend Ann rent a flat in London, they anticipate a bit of bookseller's business and a lot of touristy fun. They get murder.

A new acquaintance, a Czech poet, is stabbed on the tube, and Lark makes a quick copy of a valuable manuscript he'd handed her before turning the original over to the police. Perhaps that explains the ransacking of her flat. But what about the brutal murder of her stuffy landlady and her beloved pooch?

"Self-aware and intelligent, the clearly drawn Lark is a promising new presence on the mystery scene."
—*Publishers Weekly*

**Available in June at your favorite retail stores.**

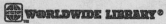 **WORLDWIDE LIBRARY®**

SKYLARK

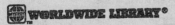

A
JOHN
COFFIN
MYSTERY

## Gwendoline Butler

### DANGEROUS TWISTS AND TURNS

The crimes begin in a bizarre fashion. First, a busload of tipsy sightseers braving London's terror tour disappears on notorious "Murder Street." Next, a child's stuffed toy is kidnapped, brutalized and buried.

For Scotland Yard Inspector John Coffin, things go from odd to alarming when the tour bus is found, its passengers alive except for one—an armchair crime enthusiast who has been murdered. Worse, the young son of a visiting American actress disappears in the wake of a series of child abductions.

But nothing is as it seems—not the people, not the events on Murder Street, which Coffin fears may continue to live up to its bloody history.

"Butler...keeps the reader moving quickly...."

—*Publishers Weekly*

### Available in July at your favorite retail stores.

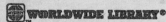 WORLDWIDE LIBRARY®

MURDER

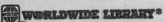